From Megan

Dear Diary,

I always knew Michael's bride would be special, but the offer to Jenny of a Green Card marriage so Michael could father the future Earl of Epingdale leaves me amazed, as well as delighted.

Not even I could have dreamed of a little English baby as a way to reach my beloved godson's heart. And for Jenny to make Michael see that his own mother may have given her babies up for more than selfish reasons has been a miracle. God bless my beloved godchildren, and may their continuing search for their birth mother be as heartwarming as Michael and Jenny's own splendid love story.

Dear Reader,

There's never a dull moment at Maitland Maternity! This unique and now world-renowned clinic was founded twenty-five years ago by Megan Maitland, widow of William Maitland, of the prominent Austin, Texas, Maitlands. Megan is also matriarch of an impressive family of seven children, many of whom are active participants in the everyday miracles that bring children into the world.

When our series began, the family was stunned by the unexpected arrival of an unidentified baby at the clinic—unidentified except for the claim that the child is a Maitland. Who are the parents of this child? Is the claim legitimate? Will the media's tenacious grip on this news damage the clinic's reputation? Suddenly rumors and counterclaims abound. Women claiming to be the child's mother are materializing out of the woodwork! How will Megan get at the truth? And how will the media circus affect the lives and loves of the Maitland children—Abby, the head of gynecology, Ellie, the hospital administrator, her twin sister, Beth, who runs the day-care center, Mitchell, the fertility specialist, R.J., the vice president of operations, even Anna, who has nothing to do with the clinic, and Jake, the black sheep of the family?

We're thrilled to bring you another dramatic and heartwarming addition to the Maitland Maternity saga, *Adopt-a-Dad,* by popular author Marion Lennox.

Marsha Zinberg,
Senior Editor and Editorial Coordinator, Special Projects

MARION LENNOX

Adopt-a-Dad

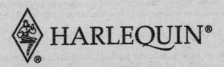

HARLEQUIN®

TORONTO • NEW YORK • LONDON
AMSTERDAM • PARIS • SYDNEY • HAMBURG
STOCKHOLM • ATHENS • TOKYO • MILAN • MADRID
PRAGUE • WARSAW • BUDAPEST • AUCKLAND

If you purchased this book without a cover you should be aware
that this book is stolen property. It was reported as "unsold and
destroyed" to the publisher, and neither the author nor the
publisher has received any payment for this "stripped book."

HARLEQUIN BOOKS
225 Duncan Mill Road, Don Mills,
Ontario, Canada M3B 3K9

ISBN 0-373-65075-2

ADOPT-A-DAD

Copyright © 2000 by Harlequin Books S.A.

Linda Brumley is acknowledged as the author of this work.

All rights reserved. Except for use in any review, the reproduction or
utilization of this work in whole or in part in any form by any electronic,
mechanical or other means, now known or hereafter invented, including
xerography, photocopying and recording, or in any information storage
or retrieval system, is forbidden without the written permission of the
publisher, Harlequin Enterprises Limited, 225 Duncan Mill Road,
Don Mills, Ontario, Canada M3B 3K9.

All characters in this book have no existence outside the imagination of
the author and have no relation whatsoever to anyone bearing the same
name or names. They are not even distantly inspired by any individual
known or unknown to the author, and all incidents are pure invention.

This edition published by arrangement with Harlequin Books S.A.

® and TM are trademarks of the publisher. Trademarks indicated with
® are registered in the United States Patent and Trademark Office, the
Canadian Trade Marks Office and in other countries.

Visit us at www.eHarlequin.com

Printed in U.S.A.

Marion Lennox, who's previously written for Harlequin as Trisha David as well, is an Australian author with forty Harlequin novels to her credit.

Adopt-a-Dad is a new venture for her. Marion hails from a southeast Australian dairy farm, and she's written this novel based in Austin, Texas, surrounded by glossy brochures and lots and lots of advice from Texas author friends. Happily, it's meant she's completely fallen for Texas.

This time next year she's hoping to swap gum boots for big hats, and head our way to visit. She needs to see the bats swooping under the Austin's Town Lake bridge for herself—and to see firsthand what she's been writing about!

With thanks to all my new Texan friends
who walked me through Austin.

PROLOGUE

MARRIED! The first of her babies was now a married woman.

LeeAnn stared at the pages of the Maitland Maternity Clinic newsletter, and the laughing face of her firstborn daughter glowed at her. It was Lana, LeeAnn's precious child.

Lana was one of her four children, but she was standing now not as a sister, but as part of a couple. What did the caption say? *With This Ring, I Thee Wed.* The insert photo was of a truly breathtaking diamond.

Lana Lord, married to Dylan Van Zandt.

Who was this Dylan? LeeAnn ached to know. His face was proud yet gentle—tender yet firm. He looked as if he'd be a loving husband to her daughter, but how could she tell from a picture?

She stirred in bed, wincing from the pain. Why didn't she have the courage to face them? she asked herself bleakly. Why couldn't she take this last step and meet her children in person?

There was another shot next to the wedding picture— one of the guests. Almost every person there had some connection to the clinic. And right in front of her on the page was the rest of her brood.

The caption stated they were Megan Maitland's godchildren and identified Megan as the founder of Maitland Maternity, but LeeAnn knew that already. She'd found out so much in these past few weeks. She'd managed to get

herself onto the mailing list for the clinic's newsletter, and
she'd hoarded every piece of information she could find
from the last twenty-five years.

So now she almost knew them. Here was her lovely Garrett, looking strong and stern and proud. Garrett was her
firstborn. He'd been the one to take charge even from in-
fancy. Shelby was next to him, her auburn hair just what
her mother's had been so many years ago, and that lovely
smile... And Michael, standing slightly apart.

LeeAnn's heart stilled. There was trouble with Michael.

She looked at the picture for a long, long time, searching
these faces she really didn't know at all and yet knew so
well. They were part of her. Michael was her son. Even
though she'd abandoned her children as babies, she knew
his face like she knew her own.

There was trouble in Michael's face, she thought. His
expression was shuttered, and with a pang of distress she
saw a suffering there that she recognized as her own all
those years ago when she'd left her four small children to
be cared for by strangers.

"Michael," she whispered. "My little one. What's
wrong?"

There was no answer. How could there be? LeeAnn was
in a hospice in the final stages of incurable cancer, and her
children didn't even know her name. They were no longer
her little ones. They were adults, and unaware of her existence.

Or maybe not. Had Megan Maitland given them her
gifts? Given them her message? She'd sent the three little
sweaters she'd made herself all those years ago, each embroidered with a triplet's name, and she'd tucked in Garrett's teddy, the one she'd used as her only comfort over
the years.

It didn't matter, she told herself bleakly. She'd sent them.
That was enough. They were tokens to tell them that they
were loved—nothing more. These lovely young adults,

smiling at her from the newsprint, were no longer part of her life. She'd forfeited her right to know them when she'd abandoned them as babies all those years ago.

But she couldn't stop gazing at the pictures, question after question forming in her heart. Did they know she'd had no choice? Did they realize that once Gary had died, there'd been so many debts, so little money—no support at all—that to keep them would have been cruel? Did they judge her harshly?

Or could they sense that the cruelest cut had been to her—to walk away from their lives and leave the loving to strangers?

She loved them still. How could she not? But she was their mother by birth only. They had no need of her.

But... Dear Lord, she needed them.

And Michael. What was wrong with Michael?

CHAPTER ONE

GRAY SUITS were Gray Suits, no matter which side of the world they were on. Jenny saw them coming from a mile off and panicked in style.

As secretary to Michael Lord, head of security at Austin's Maitland Maternity Clinic, she was used to people arriving at her desk. Staff, patients, cops and media—she knew them all and welcomed them with cheerful efficiency.

But not Gray Suits. Not when they were coming for her.

They hadn't seen her yet. They'd stopped at reception and were asking directions. Peggy was smiling and pointing toward her door, and they were turning to look. The security offices had one-way windows, however, so staff could see the reception area without patients and visitors knowing they were being observed.

Which gave Jenny time. She had a whole ten seconds to consider her choices. Fainting? Falling to the floor in hysterics? On second thought—six seconds of second thought—maybe those choices weren't all that useful.

There was only one option left, she figured. Escape through her boss's office.

Michael would hate it! Bolting through his office was hardly something a professional secretary was supposed to do.

But she had no choice. She stood up, staggering a little with the weight of advanced pregnancy, and took a leap like a scared and very pregnant rabbit right through Michael's door.

"GARRETT, this is a waste of time." Michael Lord swiveled in his leather chair and sighed into the phone. What Garrett was arguing was water under the bridge—twenty-five years of water, in fact, since they'd been abandoned on the hospital steps as babies.

Those years hadn't been bad, Michael decided. He, his triplet siblings and their big brother, Garrett, had been granted great adoptive parents. They had good lives in their chosen professions, with friends and family all around. The woman who'd deserted her babies so long ago obviously hadn't wanted anything more to do with them, so why wouldn't Garrett leave it alone?

She didn't want them, and they didn't want her. Simple as that.

"It wouldn't hurt to search," Garrett said.

"We've had great parents," Michael said stubbornly. "We don't need any more family."

"Sometimes I don't think you need the family you have," Garrett snapped. "You sit there in your cold-as-ice apartment without even a dog to—"

"Are we talking about finding our birth mother or are we talking of my private life?" Michael's voice was as harsh as his brother's, and it was Garrett's turn to sigh.

"So you won't help?"

"I've already told you I'm not interested. And anyway, I don't see how I can."

"With your resources... Mike, you've been a cop. You have Maitland Maternity's network behind you, and you know Megan will support us. You have contacts everywhere, and money's hardly a problem. Look, come to dinner on Saturday night and we'll talk about it."

"There's already Camille and Jake's wedding celebration on Sunday. I don't need any more family events this weekend."

"Yeah, and I'll bet you intend to stick around for the party after the wedding. Just like you did after Lana's.

Look, Mike, this is just us. Shelby's cooking, and Lana and Dylan will bring the baby.''

Domesticity was closing in. Michael's resolve firmed. "No way!"

"If you're not there, you'll be the only one of the Lord kids who's not.''

"Tell Dylan to take my place, then. The family's changing. Now Lana's married—well, things aren't the same. We don't need each other as much."

Funny how his gut kicked at the thought of it, Michael reflected wryly. There'd always been the four of them—Michael and Lana and Shelby, the triplets, with Garrett watching over them like a hawk. Michael hadn't thought he minded that Lana was married. Who could, when she was so happy? But...

His gut definitely kicked.

"We're still family," Garrett said stubbornly. "We need to talk through our plans to find our birth mother.''

"Your plans. I told you. I'm not doing any—''

Michael stopped in astonishment.

His secretary—calm, unflappable and cheerful Jenny—crashed through the door as if the hounds of hell were after her. She shoved the door closed behind her and leaned against it, as wide-eyed and pale as Michael had ever seen her. She looked terrified.

He wasn't head of security for nothing. Their birth mother could wait.

"Emergency," he snapped, and dropped the phone into its cradle before Garrett had time to say another word.

ONLY IT WASN'T an emergency, or not one he could see.

Michael crossed swiftly to the window and stared out. As in Jenny's office, his interior windows were only transparent one way. He could see Jenny's reception area, which was empty, and the main foyer beyond.

There were a few visitors milling around reception.

Nothing noteworthy there. The receptionists looked calm and unconcerned. Two innocuous men in gray suits were walking toward Jenny's door.

The way she was acting, you'd think the men were carrying machine guns. Which was crazy.

But Michael was trained to act first and ask questions later. What he saw on Jenny's face was terror. He'd be a fool to ignore terror, and Michael Lord was no fool.

In one fast motion he tugged Jenny away from the door, pulling her easily against his chest. Then he flicked the switch she'd been leaning against. Smoothly, the security panels slid into place, locking the doors and windows and making the smoky glass an impervious, bulletproof screen.

They'd needed these precautions just once since the hospital was built, and he'd hoped he would never have to use them again, but by the look on Jenny's face, he needed them now.

"Okay, Jenny."

"Out the back." She pulled away, tugging out of his arms. She was breathing way too fast for someone as pregnant as she was. "Michael, I need to go. I must. They're after me. The back door."

Yeah, he had a back door, a handy little escape route that led into the rear parking lot, but you didn't bolt from the enemy before you knew who your enemy was. They were secure enough here.

"If they're searching for you, then maybe they'll have someone waiting out the back. Jenny, who are they?"

She shook her head, her face bloodless with shock. Michael's hold on her tightened, his big hands gripping her shoulders. Heck, she was thin. He'd never really noticed that before. In a detached sort of way—the way he saw most people—he'd noticed her pregnancy but not the frailness of her body beneath it.

With her green eyes huge in her pale face, and her mass of dark brown curls shoved from her face in terror...

She was really quite beautiful, he thought suddenly, holding her against him. Funny how he'd never noticed that until now.

Her terror wasn't subsiding, though. Once again, Michael turned to stare at the gray-suited visitors. They'd entered Jenny's office and were inspecting her desk. One reached over and opened her drawer, rifling through her belongings.

Michael's jaw set in anger. They had no right to be searching the place. He was half inclined to throw open the door and demand to know what they thought they were doing, but Jenny's terror stopped him. He hit the one-way intercom on his desk so he could hear what they were saying, then turned to Jenny.

"The door's locked," he said quietly, trying to allay her shuddering fear. "They can't hear us, they can't see us and they can't get in. There's no way someone can get in here short of using dynamite."

"They'll wait. Gloria must have put them onto me. Now they know. I have to leave—now!"

What on earth was going on? Who the heck was Gloria?

Michael didn't have a clue. He could only wait until she was calm enough to tell him. He put his arms around her shoulders and drew her against him, restraining her urge to dash for the back door. She was so darned small, five four or so compared with his six foot. He'd hardly noticed her in the past few months, apart from being grateful he'd finally found someone efficient to run his office. How could he not have noticed how pregnant—and how lovely—she was?

There was a thumping on his door as the men turned their attention from Jenny's desk to his inner sanctum. From outside the room, the walls looked like mirrored glass. They'd see nothing and they'd hear nothing.

"Is anyone in there? Mr. Lord, could you come out please? We need to speak to you." The voice of the older of the men seemed accustomed to command. The two of them looked annoyed, but nothing more. This wasn't a pair of menacing thugs. There wasn't a gun in sight.

More knocking, exasperated this time. They were bureaucrats, Michael thought. So what on earth was Jenny scared of?

And then there was a female voice, and Michael sighed with relief as he saw Ellie enter Jenny's office. Ellie Maitland was the hospital administrator and the only person who'd know the security screens and bolts had come down in his office. A small red light would have flashed on her desk as the screens dropped. She'd figure that for some unknown reason Michael was in trouble or else there'd been a mistake, but Ellie wasn't the sort to assume he'd made a mistake without checking.

She should have telephoned, Michael thought grimly, instead of coming, but the gray-suited visitors didn't look physically threatening. Ellie certainly didn't think they did.

"Can I help you, gentlemen?"

She cast a flickering glance at Jenny's desk, and Michael knew she'd noticed the opened drawer and the shifted jumble of papers on the desktop. She'd be puzzled, trying to figure out what was going on, but nothing of that was sounding in her voice.

"We're here to see Mrs. Morrow," the older suit said.

"Mrs...." There was a trace of uncertainty in Ellie's voice, as if she was trying to place the name—which she wouldn't be. Ellie knew the names of every one of her staff members and every detail of their lives, right down to what they'd had for breakfast that morning. Her uncertainty was assumed, buying time. Finally her voice cleared. "Oh, you mean Mr. Lord's secretary, Jenny."

"That's right." The voice was in no mood for hesitation. "Where is she?"

Silence. Michael couldn't suppress a grin as Ellie gazed around the outer office with helpful and entirely assumed stupidity.

"She doesn't seem to be here."

"Can you open the inner office, please?"

"It's the office of our security chief," she apologized. "I'm afraid I can't do that. I don't have authorization. Isn't Mr. Lord inside?"

"He's not answering, and we need to check. We're from the Department of Immigration." There was a pause as two ID cards were produced. In Michael's arms, Jenny quivered once and was still. "Open, please."

"I still can't do that," Ellie said apologetically. "Unless you people have a warrant."

"We don't have a warrant."

"Has Mr. Lord done something illegal?"

"No. It's Mrs. Morrow we're interested in."

"But she's not here." Once more, her tone conveyed helpful stupidity.

"She may be in with Mr. Lord."

"If Michael was in his office then he'd answer the door."

"Not if he was hiding someone."

"Why on earth would he be hiding someone?" Ellie asked, exasperated. "Hiding Jenny, do you mean? Why would he be doing that? She's been sitting out here for all the world to see for the past few months. She's probably just gone to the ladies' room. If you people would care to wait, there's a coffee shop down the hall."

"Contact Lord," the older suit ordered.

Ellie visibly stiffened. "I beg your pardon."

"If he's your security chief, then you can contact him," the man said brusquely. "Surely."

"Of course I can contact him."

"Do it."

Ellie practically bristled, and once more Michael had to suppress a grin. Jenny was still struggling in an attempt to reach the back door, as if the men could burst in any minute, but there was no chance of that. Ellie might have a key to his office on the bunch at her waist, but by their rudeness, Jenny had just gained herself a powerful ally. Once annoyed, Ellie was one mean opponent.

But Ellie didn't refuse to contact him. She gazed at the two men for a long, considering moment, then raised the cell phone at her belt. She dialed, and the phone on Michael's hip vibrated.

"Shh. It's okay. They can't hear us. But stay right here! That's an order." He put a hand on Jenny's hair in reassurance and gently moved her away from him, then pressed her into the chair by his desk. He fixed her with a look, waited until he was sure she wouldn't argue, and then he pushed the response button on his phone.

"Yes?"

"Michael?"

"I'm right here, Ellie." There was nothing in his voice to suggest he could see her, and there was nothing in hers to suggest she knew he probably could. "What can I do for you?"

"There are two gentlemen in your office from..." She paused, and Michael saw her lift one of the men's cards from his hand, then the other. "From the Department of Immigration. A Mr. Harness and his associate, Mr. Gibbs. They're looking for Mrs. Morrow."

"For Jenny?" He deliberately spoke loudly, so they'd hear what he said through Ellie's handpiece. It was lucky he'd checked these screens for soundproofing, he thought. "What do they want with Jenny?"

"I have no idea. Will you tell me where she is?"

Will you tell me where she is... Great, Michael thought wryly. He had no idea what was going on, and until he found out, he had no intention of handing Jenny over, but he still didn't like lying. If Jenny was involved in something illegal, he didn't want to get any more involved than he already was. *Will you tell me where she is* let him off the hook nicely.

He deflected things. "I've given Jenny the rest of the day off," he said. "I'll be out of the office myself this afternoon."

"The officers want to interview her."

"What for?" he asked mildly, and watched through the glass as Ellie turned and put her question to the officers.

"Why do you need to speak to Jenny?"

He half expected no reply, but they answered, maybe seeing no risk in letting Ellie know their business, and with the intercom on he could hear every word. "Her entry visa expires on Monday," the older man said. "She's due to leave the country."

"But it's only Thursday." Ellie frowned. "If I remember correctly, she's due to finish up here on Friday—tomorrow. She's British, isn't she? I assumed she'd be flying home then."

"According to our information she's eight months pregnant," the officer snapped. "The airlines won't carry women on international flights when pregnancy is so advanced."

"That's hardly my business," Ellie said mildly. "But I don't employ illegal immigrants. Nor does Jenny expect me to. I remember Jenny made it very clear when she applied for the job that she'd only be working here for a few months."

"So she'll be back tomorrow?"

"I imagine so." Ellie glanced at her watch, signifying her time was short and not to be wasted. "I believe the secretarial staff is having farewell drinks for her in the cafeteria tomorrow afternoon. Now, if you'll excuse me..."

"Do you have her home address?"

"I do." Ellie sighed. "It'll be in personnel records."

"We need to see it."

"Then come this way," Ellie said dourly. "But it may take me some time to find it. My computer has just crashed. I'll have to send someone to the basement for a hard copy."

Bless her heart, Michael thought. She was giving him time, and letting him know it.

"Did you get that, Michael?" she said into the phone. "If you see Jenny, let her know Immigration wishes to speak with her." She clicked the phone dead. "Come with me, gentlemen," she said, and ushered them firmly out of the office.

But as she closed the door behind them, she faced Michael's office through the one-way glass.

And raised her eyebrows in a very odd look.

THE DOOR was barely closed behind them when Jenny was out of her chair, heading for the back door. Michael caught her as she passed and held her wrist as one might a fugitive.

"Jenny."

"I must go."

"Not until I know what's going on."

"I..." She took a ragged breath and tried for control. Her eyes were huge in her pale face. She looked about sixteen, Michael thought, though he was sure her personnel records said mid-twenties. "I guess... I mean, they're right," she stammered. "I'm an illegal immigrant."

"According to them, not until Monday." He frowned. "It's unlike our Immigration Department to check on people before they've overstayed."

"I told you, Gloria will have sent them."

"Who's Gloria?"

"My... my mother-in-law."

"Your mother-in-law." He considered that a moment, but no, he couldn't figure this one out at all. Jenny was British, he knew, but he'd never heard any talk of a husband. Come to think of it, he'd never heard any talk at all. Jenny was bright and bubbly and talkative—about everyone but herself. But she did wear a wedding ring.

"Jenny, you're not going anywhere unless you tell me what's going on," Michael said mildly. "Ellie and I have just perjured ourselves—or almost perjured ourselves—to protect you. We have the right—''

"I'm not a criminal," she said, and a flash of anger behind her eyes showed Michael that she was recovering. The woman had spirit. Her spirit was the one thing he'd noticed right from the start. It was why she still had a job.

Michael had gone through about six secretaries before Jenny arrived. He was professionally demanding and he expected his staff to work as hard as he did. One by one, secretaries had left, and mostly they'd left with a litany of complaints.

Mr. Lord didn't appreciate them, they said. Mr. Lord expected them to work overtime without complaining and he didn't care about their social lives.

But Jenny had arrived, set herself efficiently to work and hadn't looked back. She'd come on a temporary basis when his need had been urgent—the last of his line of secretaries had left without warning in the middle of a work crisis— and she'd stayed for as long as he could keep her. Sure, Michael had snapped at her, and usually she took it without a murmur. Occasionally, though, she'd stood up to him, and when she had, she'd done it with spunk.

"No, Mr. Lord, I can't stay tonight. I have an appointment after work."

"I don't care about your appointment. I have work that needs doing *now*."

She'd smiled and gone on with her typing. "So what did your last slave die of? Sorry, Mr. Lord, I can't do it. I do have the civility to care about your work, even if you don't care about my appointment, but it doesn't make one bit of difference. I can't change my appointment. If you don't like it, then phone the agency and hope they'll send you someone more amenable. Or, alternatively, I'll come in early and see what I can do then."

"That's not good enough."

"That's the best I can do, Mr. Lord. Like it or lump it."

And she'd smile sweetly and take herself off to her appointment, with him staring after her, baffled.

Then he'd come in the next morning to find his work done, as promised, and Jenny acting just as if she hadn't refused him at all, but he knew she would again. Finally he'd learned to ask rather than demand, and the last few months had been tension free.

But she was leaving tomorrow, he thought. He frowned. Jenny's baby had to come sometime, and secretaries came and went. They weren't something he bothered about.

He was bothering about Jenny now.

"So tell me," he growled, and the spark of challenge flared in Jenny's eyes. She really was recovering.

"Or you'll sack me? Nice try, but I'm leaving tomorrow, anyway. In fact..." She sighed. "I guess now I'm leaving tonight. I'm sorry, Mr. Lord, but I'm being forced to quit early. Can you say goodbye to everyone for me?"

"Where are you going?"

"I don't think you want to know that," she said gently, looking longingly at the door. "You've helped me enough. I don't want you to lie on my behalf."

"I can act stupid," he assured her. "I don't need to lie."

"You, act stupid? Ha! And you don't need to know."

Silence. There was no answer to that.

This was the end, then, he thought. She was asking no more. Michael could open his door, let her leave and never see her again. That should suit him fine. He didn't get involved with anyone, much less a hugely pregnant, malnourished illegal immigrant of a secretary with the worries of the world on her shoulders.

So he could say goodbye and leave it at that—but for the life of him he couldn't.

"Are you going back to England?" he asked, and watched as the color washed from her face again.

"No, but..."

"Do you have somewhere to go?"

"Mexico," she said softly, only a tiny tremor in her voice spoiling the bravado of her words.

"You have friends in Mexico?"

"No, but…"

He sighed. "You know, you can't go back to your apartment. They'll expect you there."

"I know that."

"So you're heading for Mexico without baggage, without friends. And how do you expect to get over the border? They'll have immigration checks there, as well."

"I'll manage." Her words were an angry, defensive snap, but there was fear behind them. "The border's hardly heavily policed. I can do it."

"What, by hiking through the desert in the dead of night? Very clever."

Silence.

He shouldn't get involved. No way! But how could he not? Michael sighed, took a deep breath and jumped right in. He grabbed his jacket from the back of his chair and opened the door.

"Let's get out of here," he said.

"But…"

"But what?"

"You don't need to come." She glared. "I'm on my own."

"I can see you're on your own. That's what I don't like."

"It's none of your business."

"You know, if you said it was my business, then I'd fight you every inch of the way," he said sourly. "But damn it, woman, I have enough moral fiber to think I can't allow you to sneak over the border with nothing except the clothes you're wearing. And no friends to meet you."

She glowered again, trapped. She didn't want his help. She didn't want anyone's help. "I don't need your morals."

"Neither do I," he said dryly. "I don't need 'em at all. Unfortunately I have 'em, and so does Ellie. She'll want to know what the heck I've done with you, and if I tell her what you intend doing and that I've allowed it, she'll be after me with a horsewhip. So you can say I'm doing this because the Maitlands are head of this place and I work for the Maitlands. Good enough for you?"

She glowered again. "No."

"It'd better be." He took her arm. "Because that's the way it is. Like it or lump it, lady. Let's go."

CHAPTER TWO

HE TOOK HER to her apartment first.

"We have maybe twenty minutes," he told her. "Ellie will hold them that long. So we move fast."

"You don't have to—"

"Just shut up," he told her kindly. "Like it or not, I'm embroiled in this mess, so I might as well be embroiled all the way."

Which wasn't exactly true, he decided as he drove fast through Austin's afternoon traffic. He wasn't really embroiled in this mess—yet. At this stage he could put her out of the car and walk away.

But there was no way he could do that, and it wasn't the thought of Ellie's anger that was keeping him in here. It was the set look on Jenny's face, the look of despair combined with that stubborn look of pride. She'd go to the wall alone, he thought as he watched her. She had sheer, raw courage. Whatever mess she was in...

She wasn't facing it alone, he decided. Not while Michael Lord was around to help her. But why he felt that way, he didn't have a clue. He didn't get involved with women. Not ever.

A very pregnant secretary didn't really count as a woman, he told himself. Did she?

He couldn't answer that question. Instead, he concentrated on driving fast and outmaneuvering the Suits.

Some questions were just too hard to answer.

THE PLACE she lived in was the pits. Michael stopped in front of a run-down apartment block in the poorest part of town and grimaced, then steered his Corvette around the corner and out of sight. The neighborhood was no better around the corner. It wasn't the sort of place to leave a Corvette, much less a pregnant woman.

"You've been living here all the time you've worked for me?" he demanded.

"Why shouldn't I?" Jenny's voice was defensive. "What's wrong with it?"

"It's a dump."

"Can we spare the thoughts on my taste in housing for some other time?" she asked with asperity, worry replaced by indignation. "Anyway, I like it. It's friendly. You try being a poverty-stricken single mom in a rich neighborhood and see how many friends you make. So if you really are going to help me…"

"Yeah, right." He sighed. The place he'd put the car was deserted and well out of sight. Jenny would have to stay in the car. He didn't like leaving her, but there was hardly a choice. He had to move fast, and if there was one thing Jenny's bulk didn't let her do, it was that. "Tell me which is your apartment and give me the keys."

"I'm coming." She was still crabby.

"No, Jenny, you're not." He put his hands on her shoulders and propelled her onto her seat. "I'm going in fast. I'm staying out of sight, which is something I've been trained to be good at. I'm getting out of there even faster, and if there's a knock on the door while I'm in there, then I'll be out the back window like a rat down the drainpipe. Assuming there's a back window."

"There's a back window, but—"

"No buts. Can you shinny down a drainpipe?"

That brought a grin. She glanced at her pregnant bulge, and her eyes twinkled with sudden laughter. She looked better that way, Michael thought. "Maybe not, but—"

"Then leave the shinnying to me." He hesitated. "I can't bring everything. I'll just grab what I can. I may only have a few minutes."

"I don't have much. There's a bag under the bed. You'll hardly fill it."

Funny—why had he known she'd say something like that?

THE LADY WAS RIGHT. There sure wasn't much. Michael stared around her dreary apartment in stunned silence.

He had two sisters, and Lana and Shelby nested. In fact, when they'd lived together, his sisters had nested all over the house. He was used to masses of clothes, bathrooms cluttered with toiletries, bedrooms with bright fabrics and huge cushions—the sort of place where a girl could come home and relax with style.

There was no way Jenny could come home and relax in any comfort at all, he thought, much less with style. The one-room apartment had a narrow iron bed in one corner, which was made up with essential bedclothes. There was a shabby wardrobe. A card table had one chair beside it, another chair acted as a bedside table, and there was nothing more.

He had no time for investigation, though. A leather suitcase was under her bed. He grabbed it and discovered it was already half packed. With little furniture, she was obviously using it for storage. That made things easy. There were a couple of dresses in the wardrobe—shapeless things like the one she was wearing now. It took him two minutes to collect her meager toiletries from the bathroom. There was nothing else except for a small clock and a picture frame on her bedside chair.

They all went quickly into the case, though he paused a moment to glance at the photo. A young man stared at him, fair and good-looking, laughing at the camera as if he was laughing at life in general. He looked as if he didn't have a worry in the world.

Was this the son of the fearful mother-in-law who was haunting her? Michael wondered briefly. He didn't look as if he'd haunt anyone.

There was no time to think of that now. He shoved the lid closed, noticing with a mind trained to notice that the suitcase was good quality leather, with the initial M burned into it. At some time in the past, Jenny hadn't been as broke as she was at the present.

She shouldn't be broke now, he thought, frowning. He paid her good money. Nothing made sense, but now wasn't the time to sort it out. He grabbed the case and crossed to the door.

There were footsteps on the landing. Uh-oh. Ellie hadn't delayed them as long as he'd hoped.

"She's not here." It was a garrulous female voice, and the speaker sounded annoyed. The landlady? "So why do you want her? What's so urgent?"

"We're from Immigration." Silence followed, and Michael imagined them flashing their ID cards. "We need to ask her a few questions."

"No, you don't." Yep, the landlady was definitely annoyed. Authority wouldn't be all that welcome around here. "You leave her alone, poor kid. She's done nothing to no one, and she's the nicest kid."

"We just need to ask her—"

"She's not here." The voice rose belligerently, and Michael blessed the woman. "I see everyone as they go in and out. She went to work this morning and she hasn't been back since. No one has."

That was because Michael had taken great care not to be seen, he thought, moving fast. If they knew he was inside packing her baggage...

He crossed to the window. The apartment was three

floors up, but an outside ledge led to a fire escape. It was a piece of cake—as long as they didn't suspect anything.

He was out of there with lightning speed, and even if he wasn't forced to shinny down the drainpipe, he would have done it if he'd needed to.

HE THOUGHT he'd left trouble behind him, but Jenny had company—and trouble of her own.

When he'd left her she was sitting alone in his gorgeous car. Now she was surrounded by five or six youths, and one look told him they meant no good. Michael rounded the corner and froze, melting swiftly against the brickwork. As a cop, he was trained to stop and assess before moving, and he didn't like the scene before him one bit.

It had been stupid to bring the Corvette here. If he'd known...

"Get out of the car, lady." The youths had been drinking, he figured. They were loud and aggressive, egging each other on. Could he handle five of them if they turned nasty?

There wasn't much choice, he decided, thinking longing thoughts of his gun, which was safely and uselessly locked in his office at the hospital. He'd hardly been planning to turn it on immigration officials, so he'd left it behind.

He couldn't leave Jenny on her own while he went for backup. He had to move. But as he made to emerge from the shadows, Jenny's voice stopped him short.

"Why on earth would I want to get out of the car, Jason Hemming?"

"What?" It was the tallest of the youths—a kid of about nineteen—and his bravado sounded a bit shaky. "How do you know who I am?"

"We want your car, lady," another youth butted in, his voice threatening. "Get out or we'll take you—"

"Me?" There was laughter in Jenny's voice. She didn't sound one inch afraid. "Come on, Tommy. That's not your speed. Driving with pregnant women."

"I'm not—"

She didn't let him finish. "Tommy, I've seen you with ten different ladies since I moved in here, and every one is a heap more attractive than me. I don't want to ruin your reputation."

"You live here?" It was the same voice, raised in incredulity.

"I sure do. I know your mom, Jason—and yours, too, Tommy. In fact, I helped your kid sister with her homework last night. Adele's your sister, isn't she, Tommy? She's a real cutie. I live up in number thirty-seven."

"Hey, I think I've seen her around," one of the boys said, his voice nervous. "She's not lying."

"So why are you driving this?" Tommy was disbelieving.

"Me? Driving this? You have to be kidding! It belongs to my boss," Jenny said cheerfully. "He's loaded. Isn't it the best?"

"We want it."

"You and me both, but you want to get me sacked?" Her voice grew reproachful. "Or me to have my baby right here?" A tremor entered her voice, and Michael started forward. Maybe she was afraid. He stopped again as he heard what she was saying. "I'm off to the hospital." She sounded almost proud. "I've got labor pains. My boss offered to drive me. He's just gone up to get my toothbrush."

"You're kidding!"

"Nope." Michael peered around the corner and saw Jenny open the car door, get out and stand so they could see just how huge she was. She staggered a little and put her hand to her back. "You want to know what a baby on the way feels like? He's kicking so hard. Heck, it hurts, though."

"You—you're having the kid?" It was the first voice— Jason—and all the aggression was gone. "It's Jenny, isn't it? I recognize you now. Heck. You want me to get my mom?"

"Thanks, Jason, but I think I need a hospital more than your mom." Jenny was allowing the tremor in her voice to grow. "If Mr. Lord would only get back..."

That was a cue if ever he heard one. Michael emerged from the shadows, carrying her suitcase.

"Mr. Lord." Jenny practically fell on his neck. "You took so long."

"Is it getting worse?" Following her lead, he appeared not to notice the youths.

"Two minutes apart," she said, clutching her back and grimacing. "I'm having a bad one now. Please...let's go."

Michael threw the case in the back and climbed into the car. His face was grim. "Yeah, right."

"Good luck," one of the boys said, and Michael looked up as if he'd only just noticed him.

"Thanks."

"I meant the lady," the boy said, and as the car started, he added, "hey, don't spit the kid out onto his leather seats, Jenny. You'll be sacked for that, no sweat!"

There was good-humored laughter as they headed out of sight.

"THAT," MICHAEL SAID carefully as they nosed onto the street, "was amazing." He moved the car forward, not fast enough to draw attention—the Corvette got enough of that as it was—but fast enough to be out of there if anyone had followed him down the fire escape. "I thought there was going to be trouble. That was great acting."

"Who said I was acting?"

He almost crashed. The car veered toward the wrong side of the road, and Jenny grabbed the wheel and chuckled. "Hey, okay, I was joking. Watch the road."

His blood pressure lurched and settled, and he glared at the woman by his side. "Thanks for the advice."

She dimpled. "My pleasure. Honest, though, there was no problem. They're not bad kids."

"Yeah?"

"Yeah. They steal cars, but maybe I would, too, if I was as bored as they are. And they won't hurt anyone. Besides, it's stupid to drive a car like this."

"Yeah, right." He grimaced. "You sound like a schoolmarm."

"Well..." She managed another smile. Smiles seemed her specialty, and he realized suddenly why he'd liked having her around the office the past few months. Her smile lit up all sorts of dark places, and some of those dark places were right inside him.

But she hadn't noticed his reaction. "I guess if you're rich enough to afford it then you can drive it," she said, "but you should have an ordinary one so you can pretend to be an ordinary person sometimes."

"Pretend?"

"I'd never presume to call you an ordinary person," she said, eyes twinkling. "After all, you're my boss."

"Gee, thanks."

"I know which side my bread's buttered on." She dimpled nicely, as if butter wouldn't melt in her mouth, and then hesitated, her laughter fading. "But I guess you're not my boss now. If you could take me to the bus station..."

"The bus station?"

"It's where you go to catch a bus when you don't have a car like this to drive. Or any car to drive." Her smile suddenly didn't reach her eyes. "Michael—Mr. Lord—I'm really grateful—"

"You're not working for me anymore, so it's Michael," he said curtly. "And you're not going to any bus station. The immigration guys were arriving at your apartment as I left. Your landlady will let them in, they'll discover your gear is gone, and they'll think, 'She knows we're looking for her. She's on the run.' So where do you think they'll look?"

"The airport?" she asked doubtfully, but he shook his head.

"No. They'll never let you on board a plane looking this pregnant, and immigration knows that. So where?"

She was silent, sitting in the plush leather seat and trying to make her jumbled mind think. "I guess the bus station's not such a hot idea, then."

"No."

More silence. Michael turned off the main road and headed to the river.

"Where are we going?" she asked. She chewed her lip, stubbornness returning. "I guess if you could drop me at a hotel, somewhere cheap—"

"They'll think of that, too. It'll take them twenty minutes to phone every hotel in town, and you're not exactly easily disguised."

She closed her eyes.

"Do you have any money?" Michael asked her curiously, and he saw her anger flash again.

"Of course I have money. Why do you think I've been living so cheaply for the past six months? I've saved everything."

"So you're intending to live on what you've saved from six months' salary while you have the baby?" Michael asked incredulously. "No wonder the immigration people want you out. You're hardly independent."

"I'm independent."

"You're not." He sighed and steered his car to where the oaks lined the cliff tops overlooking the river. There was a place there he knew. Quiet. Private. It was hardly the sort of place detectives would look for a fugitive.

He pulled to a stop and turned to face the woman beside him, and discovered she had the look of someone who expected to be slapped. Hard. It was a dreadful look. He gazed at her for a long moment and discovered feelings shifting inside him that had never shifted in his life. Feelings he didn't understand one bit.

It put him off balance. Michael Lord was unemotional, detached, cool as ice, and now he suddenly found himself emotional, attached and hot as fire. Damn, who had done this to her? he thought savagely. He had to know.

"Tell me about this person you're so afraid of, this Gloria," he said, and waited.

For a while he didn't think she'd tell him. She sat staring straight ahead at the deep-running river below. The weather was perfect, Michael thought inconsequentially, autumn perfect. He'd put the top down on the Corvette, and the sun was warm on their faces.

She looked as if she needed its comfort, he thought, and suddenly had to resist the urge to put an arm around those frail shoulders. She was making him feel too proprietary for words.

But he still had to know about Gloria. "Tell me," he said softly. "You can trust me, Jenny." He teased her gently. "Have I not shinnied down drainpipes on your behalf?"

That brought an answering smile. "There was a perfectly good fire escape. If you chose the drainpipe..."

"Heroes always choose drainpipes," he told her, smiling. "It's far more heroic."

"But much bumpier." She managed a chuckle. "Not to say risky—especially if you're thinking about the future production of little superheroes. Think of what all those sharp edges on the way down could have done to your manhood."

That took him aback. He stared at her in shock. His quiet, demure secretary making remarks about his manhood! And then slowly, his deep green eyes creased into laughter.

HE CHUCKLED, a low, lazy rumble that Jenny hadn't heard before. Very few people had. Michael Lord wasn't much given to laughter.

It transformed him, she thought. Michael was big and solid, with a blaze of burnt-red hair, deep green eyes and strongly boned features that made him classically good-looking. His aloofness had repelled her, though, during the time she'd worked for him. She hadn't noticed what she was noticing now, that the laughter behind his eyes made him seem not just classically good-looking. Impossibly good-looking!

She had other things on her mind, though, apart from Michael's good looks. She tore herself away from the laughter in his eyes and forced herself to answer his question. After all, she did owe him the truth.

At least talking bought her time. She didn't have to get out of this lovely car quite yet and face whatever was before her alone.

"I told you. Gloria is my mother-in-law," she said in a low, husky voice that Michael had to lean forward to hear. "Or she was my mother-in-law."

"You're divorced?"

"No." She gave a half smile but it didn't reach her eyes. "My husband...Peter is dead."

"Oh." It was hopelessly inadequate. "I'm sorry."

"He died seven months ago," Jenny said tonelessly. "I'm used to it now."

"Seven months isn't long." Michael thought back to the death of his partner on the police force. Was it two years already since Dan had died?

Grief and shock stayed with you forever, he thought, and the emotional damage lasted a lifetime. No, seven months wasn't long at all.

Jenny was studying him curiously. "You look like you understand."

"I don't know how it feels to lose the person you love,"

Michael said. "But I'd guess it must be just about as bad as it can get."

"It is," she said forcibly, staring at the river. "One minute I was telling him I was pregnant and watching his face, and he..." She shook her head as if shaking off a nightmare. "No matter. The next thing, the hotel phone's ringing and they're telling me Peter's plane crashed and I'd best get to the hospital because he's dying." She flinched, and her eyes looked inward. "Peter died four days later, but in the hospital we talked about the baby... And his mother came from England and he told her...told Gloria..."

"Told Gloria what?"

"That I was pregnant."

He frowned, still not understanding. "So there's a problem with that? I'd imagine it might have been the only piece of good news in the whole tragedy."

"But you don't know Peter's mother. She's Gloria Hepworth-Morrow, eighth Duchess of Epingdale," Jenny said bitterly. "The title makes a difference."

"I imagine it might." Then he shook his head. Maybe he couldn't imagine. "No. I can't. Why does it make a difference?"

"Because Gloria wants my baby."

She looked desolate.

It took sheer, Herculean effort for Michael not to lean forward and take her in his arms.

Which was stupid. He didn't get involved. Not ever.

Did he?

"Why does she want your baby?" he asked, and if his voice ended up sounding half-strangled, she didn't seem to notice.

"You have no idea what she's like," Jenny said bitterly. "She's so...regal. She swans around chairing her charities and opening fairs and making pronouncements on the state of the world, and people think she's wonderful. What a matriarch, they say. But she controls everyone. She must. Her husband had no will of his own, and Peter…''

"Peter, your husband?"

"Yes. Peter, my husband, her son. She never let go, even though he could never live up to what was expected of him. She tried to control him every way she knew how, and I saw what it did to him. She used every means in her power to impose her will, and when he married me…''

"She didn't like the match?"

"My father was a coal miner from Wales," Jenny said bitterly. "What do you think?"

"I think Peter made a very good choice of wife," Michael said, and Jenny flushed.

"Do you? It's nice of you to say so, but I'm not so sure Peter did. In fact, I know he didn't. After a while…after a while I figured that he'd just married me as one more act of rebellion. He didn't stop, you see. It wasn't enough that he'd married someone she hated and was ashamed of. He kept taking risks, doing things she disapproved of—making headlines in his own right.

"He brought us to Texas because there were so many extreme sports over here that he hadn't tried before, and he was killed doing aerobatics in an aerolite that was sold to him by people only a fool would be crazy enough to trust. We fought about it all the time. I was so frightened. We'd…we'd been thinking of separating, and then I found I was pregnant."

"Which was a disaster?"

That brought her chin up and the spark into her eyes. "No! There's no way I regret my baby. He wasn't planned, but I want him so much."

"And so does Gloria?"

"Of course. And I have no money to fight her. My parents died a long time ago, I have no family, and Gloria's moving in for the kill. As far as she's concerned I'm only the breeder—a very poor-class breeder at that—and I deserve no say whatsoever in the way he's raised. My baby is the next Earl of Epingdale, and that's all she's interested in.''

He thought this over and found a flaw. ''Your baby might be a girl.''

''No such luck. I checked.'' She grimaced. ''It was a strange reason for gender testing, but there it is. I was desperate. So yes, I'm carrying the ninth earl. Gloria doesn't know it yet, but the minute he's born she will. She'll pay to find out, and her spies are everywhere. That's why the immigration officers arrived today. She'll have been watching, waiting, and she'll see her chance to move.

''I was lucky in a way that we were here when Peter was killed, but if she gets me back to England, there's no way I can immigrate here—or anywhere else—with a tiny baby. She'll have bribed whoever she had to bribe, or blackmailed them if they can't be bought.''

''But, Jenny, you're this baby's mother,'' Michael said gently, still puzzled. ''No court in the land will take your baby.''

''No, but...'' She shook her head. ''You don't understand. If I stay in England it'll be easy for Gloria to take control. I saw what she did to Peter. She ruined any chance he had for happiness, and she's not doing the same for my little one. She's already told the British press I'm pregnant, so there'll be no privacy. The minute my baby's born she'll be showering him with expensive gifts, pushing me into the lifestyle she dictates.''

''Maybe it's not such a bad lifestyle. Other people have learned to live with money.'' He tried a smile, but she didn't smile back.

''You don't know Gloria. She just takes. She's so strong. Peter tried to fight her, but she destroyed him. She'll destroy my baby with her corrupt values. The only things that matter to her are publicity, money and power. I won't let her give my son those values.''

"You don't have to accept."

"Ha!" She laughed mirthlessly. "Can you see a child refusing what she offers? Being given a trip to Disneyland with his wonderful grandmother, and his dragon of a mother refusing? Or me refusing to let him go to the most expensive schools? Gloria will make sure the press knows, and the press would have a field day. 'Mother makes ninth earl live in poverty.' I can't afford to do anything but send him to a government school and live in an apartment. Do you think Gloria will let her heir do that?

"She can be charming and she's absolutely ruthless. She wants this child, and if she has her way he'll be brought up in a goldfish bowl of publicity with the eyes of the world press on him. But there's no way. He's mine!"

And she put her arms around her swollen body and hugged it, as though she was protecting her baby while it was still in the womb.

Michael sat back, stunned.

Things were starting to be clear, but the clearer they became, the less he liked them. If so much money and power were involved...

What would he have done, he thought, if he'd been Gloria and he wanted this child home in England?

Exactly what Gloria had done, he decided. Keep tabs on Jenny while she was pregnant. Watch from afar because there was little he could do to pressure her before the baby was born. Then, as the birth neared and Jenny wasn't in England, he'd make sure she returned. Warn the immigration officials that she was planning to make a run for it. Even offer...

"How much money does Gloria have?" he asked, and Jenny shuddered.

"Millions. I don't know, exactly. I've never asked, but Peter said it was ridiculous for one person to control so much wealth."

"So if she wanted you back in England, she could offer immigration a private jet with a doctor on board?"

"I'd imagine so. Yes. Of course."

"They'd go for that, too," Michael guessed. "It'd get the problem out of their hair, and you could hardly plead the case that you needed refugee status. Fleeing from money doesn't meet any refugee criteria I've ever seen." He sighed. "Jenny, why didn't you leave the U.S. before this and go someplace where there was a chance of you staying permanently? Pregnant, with no family support, you meet no immigration criteria at all."

"No, but…" She sighed. "Have you any idea how hard it is to get immigrant status *anywhere* when you're pregnant? Unless you're rich. The U.S. isn't the only country with tight immigration laws." She flashed him a smile that contained a hint of her usual spunk. "Anywhere's impossible, really. I wanted to stay away from England—as far as I could. That was all I could think of to start with. I was shocked, bereaved, confused—and Gloria scared me to death with her assumption that the baby would be hers. I'd be paid off and I'd have no say at all. She has so much power… It scared me to death. So I stayed here."

"And hoped."

"And hoped. Stupid, really, but desperation makes for stupidity. I guess I hoped I'd be inconspicuous and Gloria would lose track of me. I found the job with you, you were happy with me, I was enjoying working for you, and the Maitlands were great. Then, when I tried to apply for permanent residency, I discovered it was impossible. As my pregnancy advanced, everywhere else seemed to close their doors, too. So I had a choice—stay here illegally or go home to Gloria. There are so many illegal immigrants, and I was desperate. The choice seemed obvious, given what was at stake, but now… I might have known Gloria wouldn't give up."

She shrugged. "But hey, I guess there's still Mexico and

a whole bunch of immigration officials who mightn't be as efficient. And I'm a great secretary. As soon as the baby's born I'll be able to work." She was smiling, reassuring him that she'd be okay, but he was grim. She was trying to make light of it, but...

"Even if you make it into Mexico, she'll find you," he said.

"No."

"Yes. Or you'll starve. For heaven's sake, Jenny, you'll have no health insurance, and as an illegal immigrant you'll have no status. What if something goes wrong during the birth?"

"It won't."

"What if it does?"

"Then I'll cope," she said flatly. "Stop scaring me, Michael Lord. I can manage."

"I don't think you can."

"Watch me. Or rather, don't watch me."

"I'm not letting you go to Mexico on your own," he told her. His mind was racing, and it didn't like a single thing it was coming up with.

"There's no alternative." She tilted her chin, and a trace of fear shadowed the courage in her eyes. "Unless you're planning to put me on Gloria's plane. Hand me over to the authorities."

She wasn't quite sure that he wouldn't, he realized. She didn't quite trust him.

She must. There was no other way out of this mess.

"I won't hand you over to the authorities." He gave a self-mocking smile. "After all, you're not illegal until Monday."

"Yeah, heaps of time."

"Not enough—but there is an alternative," he said softly, his voice steady. An idea had flashed into his head. It was a crazy, lunatic idea, but the more he thought about it, the more it seemed like the only way out of this mess. "It's the only one."

"Which is?"

"You're sure you won't go home?"

She swallowed, but the look in her eye was one of iron determination. "No way. I'll lose my baby."

"For this to work, you'd have to trust me."

"I don't trust anyone," she said flatly. "Not where my baby's concerned."

"You need help, Jenny."

"You're proposing to hide me in the basement until Gloria goes away? She won't. Now she knows where I am, she'll be around forever."

He smiled. "I don't think hiding in a basement is a sensible solution."

"No, but..." She shook her head. "Believe me, there's nothing you can do. There's no possibility I can stay here legally, and now the immigration officials are aware of me, I have to move on."

"There is one thing you can do."

"Which is?"

"You can marry me."

CHAPTER THREE

As a conversation stopper it took some beating. Jenny sat with her mouth open for all of two minutes. There was not a single word she could think of to say.

It was Michael who finally broke the silence. Jenny looked as if she'd still be goggling in half an hour. "Aren't you going to say something?" he asked, half amused.

"I don't think I can," she said breathlessly. She sounded as if it took a real effort to make her voice work. "I feel like I've been slapped in the face by a wet fish."

"Gee." He chuckled again, the second time in one day. Amazing! He smiled at her stunned expression. "As a romantic, maidenly reply to a proposal of marriage, that takes some beating. Slapped in the face by a wet fish. Good grief!"

She smiled, but her face was worried—humoring-a-lunatic worried.

"Michael, this is just plain crazy. You don't want to marry me."

"No," he agreed. "I don't."

"Well…"

"But that's just it," he continued smoothly. "I don't want to marry anyone. So it might as well be you."

"I beg your pardon?"

He sighed, and his face tightened. He didn't discuss his private life with anyone, but there was no getting out of this. Not if she was to take his proposal seriously.

"Jenny, let me tell you something. Like you, I've done the love thing."

"I don't..."

"Just shut up and hear me out." He closed his eyes, and when he opened them he was no longer seeing her. He was seeing events of two years ago, and he was seeing them as though they'd been yesterday. "You know I've been a cop?"

"Yes." Her frown deepened. What on earth was he talking about?

"And I left the force when my partner was killed?"

"I've heard that, too," she admitted. Gossip among the staff at Maitland Maternity had told her that much about him, though Michael's private life was very much a closed book. He kept himself to himself—absolutely.

"What people don't know," he said heavily, "was that my mind wasn't on my job the night my partner died." He hesitated, then went on, but he sounded as if it hurt to say every word. The pain was real and terrible. "I'd gotten myself into a relationship," he confessed. "My first. I'd never had much time for women. But Barbara... Well, she seemed different—special—and I thought I could get involved." He shrugged. "Okay, so I got involved, and I was stupid."

"But what happened?" This wasn't making any sense.

"Dan and I were on night duty, but we'd just attended a call near Barbara's place. It was quiet, we were due for a meal break, so Dan went for a hamburger while I dropped in to see Barbara."

"And?" She didn't want to ask, but she knew he had to tell. The words were being torn out of him.

"She was with another guy. In bed. Stupid, sordid, the sort of thing that happens every day—but to others, not to me. I was so damned angry, so hurt that I slammed out of the house without a word—and then Dan got killed."

He still wasn't making any sense. "Would you mind

telling me," Jenny said carefully, "how you getting two-timed by some woman with no taste in men could get your partner killed? I don't see it."

Part of his mind registered the compliment, and a weary smile curved the corners of his mouth, but the story was too black for humor. The smile died.

"It was easy," he said bleakly. "My mind wasn't where it should have been, and I needed every scrap of attention that night." His words were savage, and she could tell the night was still nightmare fresh. "We had a call to say there'd been an armed robbery. What they didn't say was that the owner had shot one of the intruders. So we got to the store and the owner was out on the pavement yelling about a carload of kids that had got away. As I said, I wasn't on the ball. I radioed in details of the car, and while I did that, Dan went into the store to check damage."

"Oh, Michael..."

"The kid was lying on the floor, wounded, out of sight of the doorway, and he shot Dan from almost point-blank range," Michael said bleakly. "And then he died himself. It was a stupid, stupid waste." He shook his head. "So when backup arrived, I was blubbering like a baby, and I left the force soon after. To this job." He compressed his lips and squared his shoulders.

"That was the first time in my life I've ever tried having a relationship," he went on bleakly. "My sisters and brother—they're the emotional hotheads. I've always had a sense that I should stand apart. Be alone. Maybe it's because our birth mother dumped us—who knows? I only know the feeling's deep-seated and real. And then, the one time I cracked and let Barbara close, the world exploded around me. Stupid, stupid, stupid. So you see, I'm not in the market for any sort of relationship. Ever."

Jenny shook her head. What on earth...? His birth mother dumped him? There was so much she didn't understand about this man, but maybe it needed to be put aside for now. He was holding himself responsible for another man's death, and who could believe that of Michael?

"Michael, Dan's death couldn't have been your fault," she whispered. "Even if your mind was a hundred percent focused, it might have happened anyway. Dan must have assessed the risks, too. You won't always feel like this."

"Yes, I will," he said flatly. "I've never felt emotional. I told you—my brother and sisters have enough emotion for the four of us combined. I've never seen the sense of this love bit, and when Barbara betrayed me and Dan was killed—well, that was the first and last time I'll ever feel like that. Giving yourself to someone…"

He shrugged again and gave a self-conscious grin. "Enough. We're not talking about me. All I'm saying is that I intend to stay a bachelor, which means there's no reason I shouldn't marry you to get you immigrant status."

"A green card marriage." Her mind switched to her problems, but a part of her stayed with his.

"It's been done before."

"It's not legal."

"Legal enough." He gave a bitter smile. "We'll be married. I have a huge town house."

She gasped and almost visibly withdrew. "You're saying you want me to live with you?"

"No, but we'll need to for a bit." He gave one of his characteristic self-mocking grins. "Call it self-preservation. This way I'll get myself a decent secretary again."

"You'd want me to keep working for you?" Her voice was rising to squeak level.

"Not right away," he said, considering. He'd gone into the efficient mode she knew so well—the Michael Lord she worked with every day of the week. "I mean, I guess the baby will keep you busy for a while, and if you need me to, then I'm happy to support you while you do that." He gave a slight shrug. "My adoptive parents were wealthy, and I have a good income. And apart from that…"

"Apart from that?" She couldn't believe she was having this conversation.

But Michael was totally believable—honest through and through. He gave another wry smile. "Yeah, well, I'm not all that proud of it, but after Dan was killed I took to gambling for a bit. Stupid. The only problem was, I won, and it started getting addictive. Luckily, reality hit home somewhere along the line, or maybe it was my sisters and brother worrying themselves into a white-hot melt, but I was smart enough to get out while I was ahead. It well and truly bankrolled me, so there's no rush for you to head back to work. When you want to, well, that's okay, too, and if there's one thing Maitland Maternity is good at, it's child care. So there's your permanent status fixed up."

"But, Michael…" She was staring at him as if he'd arrived from another planet.

"Yes?"

"There's no way you're supporting me," she said flatly. "No way in the wide world. Thank you for the offer, but no, thanks. I've saved. I can support me and my baby until I can go back to work."

"Okay, then." He spread his hands as if surrendering. "Fine by me. I'm offering marriage, though, Jenny. If it'll help."

She gazed at him for a long, long moment. "Do you have any idea what you're letting yourself in for?" she asked. "Marrying a pregnant woman, offering to support her, even offering to share your apartment—*with a baby?*"

"The guest room is on the other side of my living quarters and downstairs from my room," he told her, still in efficient mode. "I don't expect I'd hear it. I only use the place to crash at night."

This was like a business proposition. Calm. Considered. Crazy!

"You think we could run separate lives?"

"I do. Otherwise I wouldn't offer. I mean…you loved your husband, right?"

"Right."

"Then you don't want another relationship yet, either. It could suit us both." He grinned. "Hey, and it'd get my family off my back. My sisters are always trying to set me up with some woman."

"But I can't…" She closed her eyes, and her fingers touched the band of gold on her left hand. "I don't…" For the life of her she couldn't stop her fingers trembling.

He reached out and closed his fingers over hers, stopping her shaking. For the first time a hint of tenderness came through the efficiency. "You can. It would work."

"You don't want to marry me."

"I don't mind. Honest." He tilted her chin so she was forced to look at him, and the smile in his eyes was infinitely gentle. It gave her a massive jolt.

On one level this Michael was just as calm and in control as the man she worked for—but on another level he was about a zillion miles from the aloof Michael Lord she knew at Maitland Maternity.

"It could work, Jenny," he told her. "And don't look too worried. It's not forever, so let's not push this too far. In time you'll be over Peter and want to be free, and maybe…well, maybe I'm wrong and maybe I'll want a life, too. So then we divorce. But as long as we can stick it for a couple of years and your baby's born into our marriage, then you'll have a little U.S. citizen as a baby and you'll be safe. Meanwhile, tell me what your options are. Run? I don't think so."

"I can."

"You can't." He lowered his broad hand to the rising bulge of her pregnancy and placed it there almost unconsciously. It was a gesture of comfort and warmth, nothing more, but it set every fiber in Jenny's body tingling in response. "You have a baby to think about. I have a stupidly gained fortune I don't mind supporting you with. It'd take the edge off my guilt a bit. And once you're married to me, your dreaded Gloria can't touch you.''

His smile faded, and the look in his eyes was suddenly dangerous. "The worst she could do is give us a bit of unwanted publicity, but it'll fade. There's no way she can touch you if you're my wife," he repeated. "I'd like to see her try.''

"But…" Jenny's eyes searched his, troubled. "Michael, I don't want to be beholden.''

"Can you cook?''

"I…yes.''

"Then there's our deal," he said triumphantly. "Let's leave the beholden bit out of it. I hate eating out, but I do it all the time because I've been known to burn baked beans. You cook for me, and we'll live happily ever after.''

"I'm not living with you." There was an edge of panic in her voice.

"No?''

"No! No way. Not in a million years.''

"Jenny, this is not for a million years," he said as he watched the confusion in her eyes mount to panic. "It's just until we have your immigration legalized, this baby safely born and Gloria off your back. It's just until you have a breathing space to figure out what you want to do with your life. If you raise this baby in the U.S. there's not a lot Gloria can do to control you. You can raise him the way you want, and then when he's old enough, he can make his own decisions about his inheritance. But you'll be the one who's influenced him.''

She took a deep breath. She couldn't think. She was so confused….

The temptation to let this man take charge was irresistible, but to be so indebted… The thought was unbearable.

"Michael, are you sure? I mean…''

"I'm sure." He wasn't. He was as confused as she was, but he wasn't letting on. Somehow he made his voice firm, and he looked down and saw the bulge beneath her dress move all on its own. His eyes widened, and he grinned.

"I'm guessing your son's in agreement, too," he said. "Will you look at that?"

Jenny wasn't looking at her bulge. She was looking straight at Michael. "You realize if we're married—if people found out that you've married me, and they will—then people might assume you're his father. I mean, why else would you marry me? And the immigration people... I don't know what we'd tell them. But you'll have a pregnant wife. Even the person who marries us will assume it's a shotgun affair. That this is your baby. That's why he'd be a U.S. citizen. I don't want you to face that. It isn't fair."

Michael's eyes widened.

Hey, things were happening too quickly here, he realized, doubts surfacing thick and fast. He hadn't thought this through.

But an image, insidious in its strength, slid into his mind and stayed—an image that had been with him all his life. A woman walking toward Maitland Maternity and leaving four babies on the steps.

And then walking away.

Jenny was fighting every way she knew to keep this baby. She wasn't walking away, and by marrying her, he'd give her the only chance she had.

"I can handle that," he said, and if his voice didn't sound so sure to himself, it was convincing enough to cause a flood of gratitude and absolute relief to wash across Jenny's face.

"You really mean it?"

"I mean it." He grinned, lessening the tension. "Hey, there's a few things we should clear up before we make a final pact." He thought hard. "Like, I hate custard."

"We're not living together!"

"Maybe we have to, for a while at least. Tell me you won't make me eat custard."

She choked. "Hey, it's good for you."

"You make custard, and the deal's off."

She managed a wavering smile. "You drive a hard bargain. But okay. As long as I don't have to eat pumpkin."

"No pumpkin pies for Thanksgiving?" He sounded shocked, and she chuckled.

"I'll make you Spotted Dick instead," she promised, and his brows rose.

"Spotted Dick?"

"My very favorite dessert. England's soul food."

"You eat something called Spotted Dick?"

"Sure do." She chuckled. "And so will you."

"What am I letting myself in for? Aagh!" He clutched his stomach in mock horror and then managed a shaken grin. "Okay. I guess I can live with that. What else should we work out? You don't snore too loud?"

"Nope."

"Or watch WWF wrestling on TV?"

"Nope again." She smiled. "You?"

"Nope. Promise."

"And you don't decorate your apartment with *Playboy* centerfolds?"

"I'll move 'em all into my bedroom," he said magnanimously, and she laughed again. Then her smile died.

"Michael, you won't expect... I mean..."

He knew what she was asking, even though she couldn't bring herself to say it. "No, Jenny," he said. "No way. This marriage is in name only. I promise you that."

She believed him. Maybe she was being a fool, but she looked into his deep green eyes and she trusted him. Absolutely.

But she'd been down that road before. Trusting a man whose reasons for marrying her weren't what they seemed.

"You don't fly aerolites?" she asked, and there was a faint tremor in her voice.

"No, Jenny, I don't fly aerolites. Do you?"

"What do you think?" She grinned, her good humor flooding back. Okay, this was crazy, but it was better than the alternative—getting on a bus and heading for Mexico alone. A million miles better. "I'd weigh down any aerolite so much it wouldn't make it two feet off the ground."

"Only for a little bit," he said. "Until the ninth earl is born."

"Not the ninth earl," she said sharply. "Baby Morrow. That's all."

"How about Baby Lord?" he asked. "Does that make sense?"

"I…" She stared at him in confusion. "I don't know."

"We have heaps of time to think about that," he said, and turned on the ignition. "Meanwhile, if we're getting married today—"

"Today?"

"Can you think of a good reason why not?"

"I…"

"Didn't think you could," he said smugly. "Okay, Jenny, let's go find us a preacher."

THEY HEADED for the border.

"El Paso," Michael said as he turned his car onto the highway. He was thinking as he moved, discarding plan after plan and coming up with the one that made most sense. "It's the only place we can get everything done."

"I thought… Can't we marry here? In Austin? Or even Las Vegas? It'd be simpler."

She was still afraid, Michael thought as he turned the car toward the border. She was expecting any minute that the men in suits would come at them with sirens blazing and cart her forcibly away to the dreaded Gloria.

"By the time you see any immigration official—or Glo-

ria—we'll be married," he said softly. "The advantages of
El Paso are twofold. First, there's a judge near there I know
from my days on the force. If it's for me personally and I
tell him the baby's on the way, he'll waive the three-day
license period so we can marry right away. He'd even enjoy
it. Second, it's a border town, so we can fill out all the
immigration forms and get the rubber stamps and signatures
you need to make you legal. By the time you get back to
Austin we'll be so legally correct, officialdom won't have
a chance."

"But..." Her voice faltered. She still looked pale, and
he couldn't help noticing how many times she glanced behind them.

"Jenny, don't worry," he told her gently. "They're not
after us, guns blazing. This is not a bad movie. Sure, Gloria
will have told them you intend overstaying, but you're not
illegal yet. No matter how much money and influence she
has, she can't bribe the department to throw the entire
weight of the law into finding someone who hasn't broken
the law yet. Even if they found us—"

"They'd deport me."

"They wouldn't." He put a hand out to touch hers.
"You're my intended bride, and we're heading off to get
ourselves married before our son in born. There's not a way
in the world they can stop us."

"Then why aren't you stopping off to collect your toothbrush?" she asked, and he grimaced.

"Sharp, aren't you?"

"I have a lot hanging on this," she told him. "And I
need honesty here."

"Okay." He put his hands on the steering wheel and
focused on the road. He still had the top down. The sun
was on their faces, and they were heading toward the border
for all the world like a married couple on vacation.

"It's just that I don't know Gloria," he confessed. His
brow was furrowed, his red eyebrows beetling in concen-

tration. It was a gesture that was peculiarly Michael, and Jen was discovering how much she liked it. And the sound of his voice...

"Gloria sounds like an elderly, aristocratic nutcase, and my first reaction is to discount a heap of your fear," he said. "I can't figure her intentions, but I'm trained never to underestimate an enemy I don't know. So I'm assuming the worst—that she has the resources to fight for what she wants."

"But—"

"Once we're safely married, there's no way she can touch you," Michael said, cutting across her protest. "I know how to look after my own. But let's get married before we go taking any chances."

THEY ARRIVED at El Paso late, far too late to get married that night. They'd stopped briefly to eat, but Jenny was so nervous Michael had barely time to bolt a burger before she was edging him back to the car.

"I told you, Jenny. There are no blazing guns."

"I just don't trust her. She's known all along what I was doing. Now she'll be thrown right off track, and I don't know what she'll do."

Her nervousness was infectious, and by the time they reached the decent, plain hotel Michael knew, it was as much as he could do not to look over his shoulder.

He felt crazy to be worrying about an elderly aristocratic female half a world away.

Never underestimate an enemy you don't know.

"Do you have a suite with two bedrooms?" he asked the woman at the hotel desk, and Jenny looked at him, startled.

"No, sir," the woman said primly. "We have adjoining rooms with a communication door."

He thought about that for all of two seconds and rejected it absolutely. "Nope. A twin room, then."

"Certainly, sir." She cast a curious glance at Jenny.
Married couple having a fight, the clerk's face said, and
the tension in Jenny's eyes confirmed it.

"You sleep well, then," she told them as she handed
over the key. "And…" She took a deep breath and beamed
at the pair of them. "If I can butt in here… You're such a
lovely couple and with the baby so close, well, whatever's
bothering you, you try real hard to sort it out. Those twin
beds are on rollers. If you want, they roll together real
quick."

"GREAT!"

"What's the problem?"

Jenny had plunked herself on the farthest bed and was
glaring at her intended husband as if her life depended on
it. "She thinks we're married," she snapped.

"Get used to it, Jenny," he said lightly, but there was
an underlying seriousness beneath his words that had her
staring. "We're going to have to play this as if we mean
it."

"Why?"

"The immigration officials won't give you a green card
unless they think this marriage is real. The judge we see
tomorrow has to waive the three-day license period. He
won't do that unless he thinks this is a real marriage and
we're only rushing it because of the baby. So we convince
everyone we've been falling in love over the last few
months, and the day before you were due to walk out of
my life, I proposed and you fell into my arms."

"But—"

"And we don't convince them by sharing separate bedrooms."

"We're not married yet, Michael Lord," she said with
asperity. "I don't see why we have to share tonight."

He paused, but there was no room for dishonesty between them. This was too important.

"You're afraid of what Gloria can do," he said. "I don't know Gloria and I don't know what her resources are, but I don't trust what I don't know, and I want you where I can look out for you. I don't want you down the hall."

"You think…"

"I don't think anything," he said wearily, "but I'm taking no chances. We're a couple, Jenny. Get used to it."

EASIER SAID than done. Jenny was so tired she should be asleep on her feet, but she was so aware of Michael that every nerve in her body was still wide awake and screaming that there was a man in her bedroom—a very large, very…well, very *male* man.

A man who for the past few months had been her boss and was now to be her husband.

It was too unnerving for words. She went into the bathroom, washed, changed into her pajamas and made a dive for the bed. Safely there, she hauled the bedclothes up to her neck and then glanced over to see Michael sitting on the other bed laughing at her.

"Very sexy," he approved, his eyes dancing. "Baggy pajamas wide enough to hide a small house. Just what I'd always dreamed my bride would wear."

"Yeah, well, you try being eight months pregnant and figure how to be sexy," she snapped, glowering. "Go get your own pajamas on."

"I don't have pajamas," he said soulfully. "The drugstore only carried toothbrushes and razors—not pajamas."

"That's your problem." Her voice was breathless. "I'm going to sleep."

"You do that, Jenny," he said, his voice gentling. "You must be beat."

She was, at that. Why else would the sound of the concern in his voice make her want to weep?

It was too strange for words. She lay with her eyes closed

as she listened to him head for bed—listened to him wash and use his brand-new toothbrush and then secure the room.

He didn't just lock the door. He was taking no chances. He hauled his bed across the doorway so no one could enter without stepping right over him. Surely the precautions were unnecessary, Jenny thought sleepily, but she felt safer all the same.

She lay still until she heard him slide beneath the sheets, pummel his pillows, then settle down. The sound of his deep, even breathing was infinitely reassuring.

She shouldn't let him do this, she thought, but there was no way she'd stop him. Not now.

"Michael?"

"Mmm." He sounded half-asleep already.

"I—I appreciate this," she stammered. "You don't know how much."

"Don't mention it," he said sleepily. "You wanted rescuing and I rescued you. You have no idea how satisfying it is. Maybe I always knew I wanted to be Sir Lancelot and rescue a few damsels in distress."

She furrowed through her memory bank. "I thought Lancelot was taken up with Guinevere—the king's wife." She frowned. "Did Sir Lancelot rescue damsels, as well?"

"Sure he did," Michael said easily into the dark. "In his pre-Guinevere days he was quite a boy. He dashed around on his white charger rescuing maidens all over the place."

"What, lots of maidens?"

"Yep."

She smiled into the dark. "Didn't it get a bit crowded? Up on his horse, I mean?"

"It might have," he agreed reflectively. "I guess he must have had some sort of system. You know, when the horse got crowded, the damsel on the back fell off, the dragon got her and he had to rescue her all over again."

Silence.

"I don't think, then," she said at last, staring at the darkened ceiling, "that I want to fall off. Not quite yet."

"Then you just hang on for all you're worth, Jenny," he said, and he chuckled into the darkness. "And let's see where this dratted horse takes us."

THEY WERE married at eleven the next morning.

It was the strangest wedding Jenny had ever attended, though in fairness she'd only been to the formal white weddings the British were so good at. Although her wedding to Peter had been quiet, they'd done it in a church, she'd worn white, and a vicar had married them in his crimson robes.

The man who married Michael and Jenny was a portly little judge in a too-shiny suit. He'd known Michael from way back and greeted him like a long-lost friend.

"I never thought I'd see you facing a shotgun marriage," he said jovially, and Michael grinned.

"Have you any idea how hard it is to persuade a girl to marry you these days? Independent, single-minded females—"

"Hey, she sounds just like the sort of wife you need." The judge beamed at Jenny. "Step right up, girl, before he changes his mind. If there's one thing I'd like to see this boy do, it's marry."

So they married, exchanging rings bought half an hour before at a cheap jeweler's in the next block. A secretary witnessed their signatures, and the entire process took just fifteen minutes.

"And not a moment too soon, by the look of it." The judge inspected the last of the documents and nodded his satisfaction. "That's that, then, and I'm glad to make your little one legal." He fixed Michael with his sternest look. "You look after them, you hear?"

Michael smiled and took Jenny's hand, for all the world as if he was a real-life husband.

"Yes, sir," he said softly. "I intend to do just that."

"Then there's only one thing left." The judge grinned.

"What's that?" Michael asked.

"You may now kiss the bride, boy." He chuckled. "My favorite part. My wife says it's the only reason I aimed to be a judge. Go ahead, boy. Kiss her like you intend to kiss her five times a day for the rest of your lives. Or more."

He had no choice. Michael looked into Jenny's confused eyes, and he knew this was what he must do. He must kiss her.

But for an obligation, it didn't hurt one bit. He gathered her into his arms, and his mouth met hers, and what was meant to have been a formal kiss of acquiescence suddenly became much more than that.

He felt her softly yielding to him—but he sensed the tremor running through her and tried to kiss away the doubts and the fears and the uncertainty of what lay ahead.

And somewhere in that kiss, something changed between them—something that would stay changed for all time. Because when he pulled away—finally—after a kiss that had gone on forever and must have satisfied any onlooking judge, it felt as if he was tearing himself apart to let her go.

It was as if in her touch, he was where he needed to be, he thought dazed. Forever.

That was crazy. He needed emotional attachment like a hole in the head!

And Jenny… She looked at him while their hands were still linked. He could see the faint indentation where his mouth had pressed against hers—like a shadow—and he could see matching shadows of doubt and fear in her eyes.

And the fear had deepened.

IT DIDN'T END there. There was a day of legal formalities in front of them. "One of the reasons I brought you to El Paso is that we can do everything at once," Michael told her. "We'll get your immigration forms filled in here and take the first steps to get you legalized. That way if immigration officials are waiting when we get back to Austin, they won't have a leg to stand on."

"Or Gloria."

"Or Gloria," he agreed gravely.

"She'll be so angry. She seems so demure, so ladylike, but she has such power." Jenny shivered in the warm sunshine, and Michael's hold on her arm tightened. She'd been subdued since they'd left the judge's office.

"There's nothing she can do to touch you now, Jenny. Nothing."

"I know that." But still she shivered.

MARRYING WAS EASY compared to immigrating. The forms Jenny filled in were endless.

She and Michael went from one bureaucratic counter to another, and her guilt deepened all the while.

"You shouldn't be here. You should be at work. You know you had appointments today," she told him.

"You sound like my secretary," he teased, and she glared at him.

"That's what I am underneath all this pregnancy-bride stuff. Ellie won't know where you are. She'll be worried."

"I called this morning and told her secretary I wouldn't be in."

"Did you tell her why?"

"I didn't give her a reason, no."

"But you're always in," Jenny said, alarmed. "She'll be worried sick, especially if you're not at home if she tries to contact you. You call her right away."

"I don't need—"

"Michael, people care about you," she said sternly, finding a shadow of her old autocratic self. "Even if you don't believe in emotional attachment, they do. Call."

His eyebrows rose, but the look on her face told him she

wasn't kidding. It was her best schoolmarm look, and he answered accordingly.

"Yes, ma'am."

HE DIDN'T leave her. Michael wasn't letting Jenny out of his sight, not until the last of the legal documents had been signed. Instead, as she sat with head bent, plowing through questionnaire after questionnaire, he sat at the back of the office and used his cell phone.

Ellie answered on the first ring.

"Michael!" He could hear relief echoing in her voice, and he felt a twinge of guilt. Okay, he should have phoned earlier, he acknowledged. Jenny was right. It never occurred to him that anyone worried about him—it never had, which was a side of his personality that drove his sisters nuts. "Where on earth are you?" Ellie demanded. "I've been calling everywhere and you've had your phone turned off."

"I'm not in Austin," he told her obscurely. "I'm out of town on business."

"And would this business have anything to do with Jenny Morrow?"

"It might."

"Then don't tell me," she said hastily. "I don't need to know. What I don't know I can't be forced to tell."

"We're not talking torture here, I hope, Ellie," he said, startled, and she gave a reluctant chuckle.

"Not quite. But the people asking questions…they have all the right authority and they're very insistent. They say Jenny's taken off and plans to stay in the country illegally."

"Ellie, how many illegal immigrants do you guess are in the U.S.?" Michael asked slowly. "Rough guess? Ballpark figure?"

"I don't know. Thousands?"

"That'd be my guess." He frowned into the phone. "So why do you think there's all this interest in our Jenny?"

"*Our* Jenny?"

"She's my secretary," Michael said, stifling the impulse to lay claim to a closer relationship. That could wait. "I'd like to know what the heck is going on."

"I thought *you* might know," Ellie said thoughtfully. "Being away from work and all."

"Ellie, when did I last have time off work?"

"Beats me," she said. "I don't think you have. Not since you started here two years ago."

"Permission to take the rest of the day off, then? With that and the weekend... That should do it. I'll be back at work on Monday."

"Should do what?" Her voice rose. "No. Don't hang up. I take back what I said about not wanting to know. I do. Michael, what's going on?"

"I want you to find out. You're closer to the action than I am."

"There's a strange woman here," Ellie said suddenly, as if she was looking around reception as she spoke and her gaze had rested on someone. "Not a bureaucrat. English, upper crust. Mid-sixties. Looks like Wallace Simpson on a good day. Not a hair out of place. Expensively dressed and smooth as silk. You know the type—or maybe you don't. It's a female thing—on the surface polite and sweet and a little bit helpless, and underneath as tough as nails. She's questioning all the staff about where Jenny might be—says she's Jenny's mother-in-law, and she's worried sick."

"Is she now?" Michael turned away so Jenny couldn't hear him. "What's she saying?"

"She thinks Jenny's run away because the immigration officers have come. She says Jenny's pregnant and alone, with practically no money. She told me the immigration officials are trying to deport Jenny, and she's desperate to help her daughter-in-law and her poor little unborn grandchild. So do I know anything I'm not telling the immigration people?"

"What did you tell her?"

"I didn't tell her anything," Ellie said frankly. "When she asked the staff in accounts where Jenny might be and they didn't know, she offered them money. A heap of money. To be honest, she gives me the creeps. So no, she has nothing from me except blank stares. I can be a real dope when I try."

"Good girl."

"Don't patronize me, you toad. Just tell me—"

"Watch her, Ellie," Michael interrupted. "You're right not to trust her. I don't understand yet if there's just cause, but Jenny's frightened of her, and Jen doesn't scare easily. And don't worry. I'll see you at work on Monday."

"Michael!" Ellie's voice rose in a wail, and Michael grinned and disconnected.

For a change, it wouldn't hurt Ellie not to know what he'd eaten for breakfast that morning.

Or that he was married...

CHAPTER FOUR

"RIGHT. That all appears to be in order." The gray-haired woman pushed her glasses down her nose and stared across the desk at Jenny and Michael. Her eyes bored right through them. "But there are a couple of questions I need to put to you both."

"Yes?" Michael took Jenny's hand and exerted gentle pressure. *Leave the talking to me,* his hand said, but he didn't mind admitting he liked the feel of her fingers in his.

"Why did you delay marrying for so long?" she asked. She fixed Jenny with a stern look. "You're aware your permit to stay in this country expires on Monday." She glanced at her computer screen. "We've been given advice that you didn't intend leaving the country. On the basis of information received, we have officers checking your whereabouts right at this minute."

"Who gave you that information?" Michael asked, as though surprised, and the woman shook her head.

"I can't tell you that."

"If it's Jenny's family in England, maybe we can understand it." Michael smiled, and his grip on Jenny's hand tightened. She was so tense. "They wanted her to come home when her husband was killed but she thought she'd get over his death better if she stayed out of sympathy range. And now... Maybe Jen's thrown out a few hints that she was thinking of staying here after the baby's born and that's what's worrying them. I guess they have reason to worry. Jenny's a young widow, she's alone, she's vulnerable, and they don't know me.''

"I'm not vulnerable," Jenny said, but no one was listening.

"So you've been thinking about marriage for a while?"

"We've been working side by side for the last five months," Michael said easily, as if pulling the wool over official eyes was something he did every day. "Jen applied for her work permit and came to me as a temporary secretary, trying to keep busy to get over her grief at Peter's death. The arrangement was to have been for only a couple of months, but it kept being extended. By me. It didn't take me long to realize Jen was special."

That much at least was true. She was the best secretary he'd ever had.

"But Jenny was newly widowed," he went on smoothly. "It's taken time to convince her to look at anyone else." He grinned engagingly at the woman behind the desk. "Five months, in fact. I must be a very slow convincer."

The woman didn't smile back, but she glanced again at the computer screen, as though what it told her conflicted with Michael's story. Then she looked again at Jenny.

"My information says that you are desperate to stay in this country," she said, ignoring Michael's charm completely. "Maybe desperate enough to consider marriage as a means to staying?"

"Hey, am I someone you'd have to be desperate to marry?" Michael was all ready to feign outrage, but Jenny returned the pressure on his hand to tell him she was capable of answering the question herself, thank you very much. Vulnerable? Ha!

But she didn't remove her hand from his.

"I nearly went crazy after my husband's death," she said softly. "That's why I wanted to stay here for a while—to be close to where he died and to avoid the crushing sympathy of friends and media back home. You know that my husband—my late husband—came from a titled family in Britain? My baby will inherit that title, and my mother-in-law has promised to support us both in luxury for the rest of our lives. I'm not under pressure to stay in America. On the contrary, my family, my wealth, my son's inheritance, all those things are pressuring me to go home. So it's been a very hard decision to stay here, to stay with Michael.''

She smiled, and reluctantly the lady behind the desk smiled back. It seemed Jenny's charm worked better than Michael's.

''I'd be guessing the person worrying about me—putting pressure on your officials—is my mother-in-law,'' Jenny continued, pressing her advantage. Speeding up the thaw. ''She wants me to return home, and she's a very strong lady. Maybe if she's spoken to you then you know that already, and that she thinks I'm a fool for staying. I intended to go home—after all, there's a lot to be said for living on my ex-husband's inherited wealth—but when I went to the travel agent to book my return ticket I realized...I realized just how much I wanted to stay.''

''And why was that?''

Jenny cast a sideways glance—a loving look that almost shattered Michael's composure—at her new husband. If she was acting, she was sure good at it! ''It was knowing how much I wanted to stay with Michael,'' she said in a voice that was no more than a whisper.

''So you didn't buy your return ticket?'' the woman pressed her. ''But you thought about it. That would be how long ago?''

''A month ago,'' Jenny said, unruffled. ''Nearing the end of the time I could fly.''

''So you've been planning this marriage for a month?''

''I have,'' Jenny said serenely. ''I just delayed telling Michael.''

''Can I ask why?''

''I wanted to make him sweat.'' Jenny's eyes twinkled,

and she gave Michael an affectionate grin, for all the world as though they were longtime lovers and she was teasing him. Then she turned to the woman, and her smile died.

"No." She hesitated. "That's not the truth. To be honest... I don't know if you can understand, but... Peter's only been dead for seven months. It's soon. Maybe too soon. That was why we haven't told anyone of our relationship. We've kept it quiet. Though it seemed so right, it still seemed a betrayal. It has been very hard to say yes to Michael. I only know that I couldn't say no."

There was a trace of sympathy flickering in the woman's eyes. "But you've said yes now?"

Jenny's chin tilted. "I surely have. We're married now, so I guess I'm as sure as I'll ever be. Michael's promised to care for my baby like his own." Her eyes defied the woman to doubt her. "An offer like Michael's—from a man like Michael—doesn't come along every day. I'd guess that my mother-in-law is very upset. I can understand her reasons, though we don't always get on. But I'd be a fool to go home to England and to hope that Michael would follow."

"I would follow," Michael said, playing his part to the hilt. He put his arm around her waist. "I certainly would. It'd be me who'd be the fool if I didn't."

And suddenly it was over. The woman was rising and smiling, her frost giving way to a thaw. "Well, this seems satisfactory. There will be follow-up visits, checking on you on your home territory, so to speak, but it seems a formality. We'll give you notice." She cast a look of dislike at her computer screen, as if it had betrayed her. "Enough of my time's been wasted on this. I seem to have sent my officers on a wild-goose chase."

"Your officers?"

"There are two of our people searching Austin for you right now," she told Jenny. "I suspect they'll be annoyed when I tell them I've had you here all along." She pursed her lips. "Of all the useless…"

"Was that because of us?" Jenny said, distressed. "Should I have let people know sooner? I didn't think— I mean, I thought we had until Monday to let people know. I thought if we applied now…"

"No, my dear, it is not your fault," the woman told her. "You go off and enjoy your honeymoon, and I wish you the very best of luck for your life together."

"I DON'T THINK," Michael said carefully as the door closed behind them, "that Gloria is in for a very good reception if she tries to exert more pressure on you through immigration."

"Don't be so sure." Now that she was out of the office, Jenny felt her knees turning to jelly. Michael had hold of her arm, and she was grateful for his support.

"Why? She clearly seemed to be on your side."

"Gloria has influence everywhere, right up to royalty and congress. We'll be checked out thoroughly."

"Then there's nothing to worry about," Michael said, tucking her hand firmly into his. "We're a staid married couple, off to take our honeymoon before we start our life together. Come on, Jenny. Forget about your mother-in-law. Come to think of it, you don't have a mother-in-law anymore. Only me. So from now on, just think about us."

THEY HAD their wedding dinner at a restaurant where Michael said the food was better than anywhere else in the States. He made her eat migas, a very different form of scrambled eggs, and try Carta Blanca, a Mexican beer. She tasted the beer but went back to lemonade in a hurry, pleading her pregnancy, but he knew he was on a winner with the migas. She ate like a starving person.

She'd hardly had any breakfast or lunch. Now, though,

her color was returning and she looked as if she might be able to face the world again.

"We'll stay here tonight," he told her. "Drive back to-morrow."

"I don't mind when we go." She didn't, she decided. She felt light-headed and free. It seemed the weight of the world had been lifted from her shoulders. Or at least most of it.

"I guess," she began, then looked across the table at her new husband. He really was impossibly good-looking, she decided, with his dark coloring and wonderful red hair. There was a trace of chest hair showing at the throat of his open-necked shirt, and she felt an almost irresistible urge to reach out and touch it. To trace it downward.

Too good-looking…

Strange how she'd hardly noticed it before, but she did now. He'd gone out and bought a casual shirt for their wedding because he always wore a shirt and tie for work and decided he wanted his wedding clothes to be different. She wouldn't buy anything new—it was a total waste when she was this pregnant—but she loved his casual look. And she loved the fact that he'd bought something special for their wedding.

He really was…special?

"You guess what?" he asked, and she had to drag her thoughts back to where they'd been. Or to where they should have been.

"I guess we'll have to face your family." She frowned into her lemonade. "Will you explain things? That our marriage is just a formality? We don't want them thinking…"

"That we're really married?" Michael frowned. "We are really married. We need to be, Jen."

"But we won't be living together."

"Yes, we will. She said they'd check."

"She also said they'd give us notice."

"That's true. Still…"

"So we tell your family the truth. Otherwise…" She ran her finger around the rim of her glass, troubled. "They might accept me as part of the family."

"So?"

"So it wouldn't be honest. Or fair."

"Jenny, you're my wife," Michael said firmly, so loud that people turned to stare. He grinned and lowered his tone. "Okay, our marriage isn't what most people think of as a marriage. We don't love each other and we'll lead independent lives. But it's still a marriage. We've signed a contract, and we play by the rules."

"But…"

"If either of us decides we want out sometime in the future, then that's okay. People understand divorce, even if they don't like it. But for now, we tell people we're husband and wife and let them decide what to make of it. I guess my brother and sisters might have to be told the truth—they'd guess anyway—but for the rest…"

"The rest?"

"The rest as in everyone else," he said. "They need to know as much as Gloria needs to know. We'll send a notice to the local paper. We won't tell people that we fell in love, but we won't tell them that we didn't. Love has many different faces. There are lots of couples who don't stay tied to each other. Who travel independently. Sleep independently."

"Watch separate TVs?"

He grinned. "That, too. I bet you don't like watching football."

"I do, actually." She smiled, but the trace of uncertainty remained. "In moderation. Like once a year for half an hour with plenty of chocolate on the side. But I see what you mean. It's only…"

"Only what?"

"I don't like telling lies."

"We're not. We're married, Jenny. How hard is that to accept?"

It sounded totally reasonable.

But still the worry remained.

"At least let's insist on a few basics. Like no presents. No party. This really is crazy." Her brow furrowed. "I mean, if people think it's romantic, well, we'll be in for all sorts of things."

"Then we say—firmly—that we don't want it. No fuss. But otherwise, we treat each other as husband and wife. An independent couple, but a couple for all that."

She smiled then, though her doubts remained. "You might not know what you're saying. When I tell you off for the sixtieth time for drinking beer out of the can... Speaking of which." She reached forward to grab his can, which had been supplied with a glass beside it. He'd elected not to use it.

He was faster than she was, hauling the beer out of reach. "Not so fast, woman. Have you no respect? I might have asked you to marry me, but if you start interfering with my beer-drinking habits..."

"There'll be all sorts of things I'll want to interfere with," she said, her worry returning. "I wonder... Maybe we went into this too fast."

"We didn't have a choice."

"I know that, but..." She shook her head. "I don't want to cause trouble for you, Michael."

"You won't." He smiled. "Hey, I was brought up with two sisters and a brother. I'm accustomed to leading my own life surrounded by chaos. Family doesn't touch me."

"Why not?"

"It's just easier to turn off. I always have. That's what makes this whole thing feasible."

Somehow that only made her feel worse.

THAT NIGHT was difficult.

Once again they shared a hotel room. "After all, the

authorities would be surprised if we didn't sleep together tonight,'' Michael told her, and Jenny had to agree. Tonight, however, he didn't pull the bed across the door.

"If Gloria's as smart as you think she is—and she's obviously paying a bundle to keep informed—then she'll know what's happened by now. The officials in Austin will have been called off, and they'll have told Gloria why.''

''I guess.''

''She can't touch you, Jenny,'' Michael said, and he stroked her face gently as she sat on the bed. ''Don't start looking for threats. You're safe.''

Safe, but at what price?

She climbed into her appalling cotton pajamas and snuggled under the bedclothes, then lay in the dark with Michael three feet from her side. He went straight to sleep, his low, even breathing sounding softly across the room.

It should have been reassuring, but it wasn't. It was unsettling, strange.

What had Michael said? *Family doesn't touch me.*

It touched her. People touched her. What Michael had done for her, what he intended to do for her—it moved her to tears.

She was so indebted.

She should never have agreed to this. She knew better than Michael what sort of reception would greet them in Austin when people found out. How would his family react to her? She could guess. They'd react with horror—and they'd be right. His sisters would want a nice local girl to marry their wonderful brother. Someone he loved, not someone he felt sorry for.

The baby stirred within her, and she was achingly aware of the new little life waiting to be born.

''I've done this for you,'' she whispered into the dark, her hands resting on her belly. ''I've married Michael for you.''

It wasn't totally true.

She stared at Michael's silhouette in the dark and felt emotions that had been repressed for a very long time.

He was letting her close. Not too close, but closer than he'd ever let anyone else. He'd married her.

"For better or for worse," she whispered into the night. "Well, Michael, this is my worst, and this is your best. I just hope that sometime in the future we can balance things out a bit."

AT THREE in the morning she scared the living daylights out of him.

He'd been solidly asleep, dreaming, and his dreams hadn't been half bad. Jenny was in there somewhere, and her smile.

Her low moan had him sitting bolt upright. Jenny was standing on the other side of the room, leaning on the wall and rocking back and forth with pain.

"Jenny!" The light was on and he was over there faster than should have been physically possible, gripping her shoulders and turning her to face him. "Jenny, what is it?" Hell, if it was the baby…

It wasn't the baby.

"Oh, Michael, I'm so sorry," she whispered, and there was agony in her voice. "I didn't want to wake you. It's not the baby. It's okay."

"What is it?"

"It's just cramps. My legs…they seize up some nights. I tried not to wake you."

"Cramps?"

"It's a side effect of advanced pregnancy," she said, closing her eyes in pain. "One of the things you don't hear about until it's too late. Like varicose veins and heartburn."

"Let me help."

"There's nothing you can do. It'll pass."

"Lie down, Jenny," he told her, pushing her to the bed.

Before she could say a word, she was lifted and laid gently on the pillows, and he was sitting on the bed beside her. He took her legs onto his knees and pushed the loose cotton up. "This one?"

"They're both bad, but that's the worst."

It had to be. Her calf muscles were rock hard, knotting in vicious spasms. "Hell," he muttered. "Jen, this is some cramp!"

"You're telling me. Leave it, Michael. Go back to sleep. It'll pass."

"Yeah, so I just lie in bed and snore while you pass out in agony. In your dreams! I'm not completely without feeling. We need some cream. Moisturizer or something."

"There's cream in my bag. In the bathroom."

"Coming right up." And he left her, diving for the bathroom to search her toiletries.

This felt wrong, he thought as he lifted her toothpaste and hairbrush and rifled through lipstick, cosmetics, toiletries. It was strangely intimate, as if they really were married.

That's what it felt like, he realized. He felt married, and he wasn't at all sure he liked the sensation. He'd been alone for so long, and now the woman out there needed him and he was responsible. This was taking him someplace he wasn't all that sure he wanted to be.

But this was no time for regrets. Decisions had been made, for better or for worse, and he had to live with them. He found what he was looking for and headed back to Jenny.

To his wife.

SHE SHOULDN'T let him do this, Jenny thought as she struggled against the pain. She shouldn't let him near. She'd tried so hard to be quiet, not to wake him.

Because she didn't need him. She didn't!

But the last few months had been so long and so lonely,

and to know that he was here and was prepared to stand by her...

The thought was infinitely comforting.

She didn't love him, but she needed him. Dear heaven, she didn't have the strength to hold him away. Even Michael was better than the bleak future she'd faced two days ago.

Even Michael?

Maybe...maybe especially Michael.

MICHAEL TOOK all the time in the world. It was almost an hour before the cramps eased, and the entire time he sat at the end of the bed and massaged her calves as if he wasn't tired—as if the most important thing in the world was to use his big hands to gently soothe the aching hurt in her legs. He applied moisturizer to soften the skin, gently working his fingers into each knot, one after another, over and over again.

He could feel how much pain she must have been in. She'd only made that one tiny groan, which had woken him, but for her legs to be in this mess, she must have been awake for hours. He swore into the night as he worked, thinking over the past few months. She'd put in long hours at the office for him, and he hadn't granted one concession to her pregnancy. In fact he'd hardly noticed his secretary had been pregnant. And each night, she must have gone home to this.

Alone.

"Let's forget about driving tomorrow," he told her. "I want you checked by a doctor first." Hell, had he caused problems by driving all the way to El Paso in one shot? He should have stopped often. Made her walk. Hired a larger car than the Corvette.

"I'M FINE," she whispered. In fact, it was as much as she could do to get her voice to work at all. She felt wonderful.

The pain had eased to almost nothing, and to lie here with her head on the pillows while Michael's fingers worked their magic... While his hands eased the pain, taking away the desolation and loneliness of the last few awful months... She was feeling so grateful she could almost burst.

She was feeling as though she could almost reach out and take him to her, take him as her true husband.

Which was really, really stupid. She was eight months pregnant with another man's baby. Peter. Her husband.

No! Not her husband. Peter was her first husband, and that was over. Her husband now was the man massaging her legs with such infinite gentleness that she wanted to weep.

Michael was being kind. Nothing more. Heavens, he'd done enough for her without her placing emotional obligations on him. Somehow she forced herself to lie still and she pushed her errant heart into order.

You've got yourself a marriage of convenience, she thought. *A green card marriage. That's what you need, so don't you dare mess it up by letting your heart get involved.*

FINALLY SHE SLEPT, and Michael went back to bed. But he lay awake staring at the darkened ceiling, wondering just what he'd let himself in for.

For better or for worse, he was married, and he was starting to realize this wasn't just the solution to one problem at all. It was the start of a whole heap more.

And it was the beginning of a brand-new dimension to his existence.

THEY TOOK the entire day to drive home, with Michael insisting on so many stops that Jenny was starting to go nuts.

"I don't need this."

"I don't want you cramping again tonight."

"At least I won't be waking you up."

"That's another thing. You're not staying in that lousy apartment."

"It's where I live, Michael," she said stolidly. "They said they'll give us warning if they check, so I'm staying there."

"We have to act married. Besides, it's a dump."

"Dump or not, it's my home," she snapped. "It's nothing to do with you. You've offered me marriage and I'm incredibly grateful, but I have no intention of interfering with your life. Or of you interfering with mine."

"It's not sensible. They'll check."

She shook her head, her curls flying in the wind. "They won't check yet, and it's not sensible to be anything but independent. You're my boss, Michael, and I'm one of your employees, who from now on happens to be on leave to have a baby. We have a green card marriage. Nothing more."

Michael glanced at her set face, and his head told him she was partly right. He'd offered marriage on the spur of the moment, and she'd accepted with gratitude. She was asking nothing more, and there was nothing more he wanted to give.

Was there?

Maybe not, but living together... It wasn't negotiable. Whether he wanted it or not, they had no choice. Immigration officials weren't stupid.

"Give me a day to clean out the spare room," he told her grudgingly. In truth, his spare room was fine, but maybe she needed space, and maybe he could do with a day or two to get used to the idea of her living with him. "But you need to move in with me if we're going to make this work."

"No."

"Don't be stubborn," he accused, but she shook her head and looked away.

Maybe it would take the warning of an immigration visit to make her see sense, Michael thought. Meanwhile, he could hardly cart her to his place screaming. And did he really want to?

HER APARTMENT looked exactly the same as he'd left it—somewhere between dreary and awful. Michael carried her baggage up the three flights of stairs—the elevator was out of order—and stared around with distaste. He wanted her out of there.

"You can't stay here."

"Of course I can." She smiled as he put her bag on the bed. There wasn't anywhere else to put it. "I've been living here for months and haven't been mugged yet. I told you—I like it. There are nice people here. Would you like some coffee before you go?"

"I...no." His brow furrowed. "This is only for a couple of days at the most. Do you have coffee?"

"Hey, I'm not exactly starving in an attic," she told him, exasperated. "I live simply because I need savings to support myself while I can't work, but I know how to look after myself. And I'll stay here until we hear from immigration. You don't need to worry. I've eaten every vitamin and done every exercise Dr. Maitland's given me."

"You're seeing Abby?"

"Of course I'm seeing Abby." She flushed defensively. "Obstetric care is one of the perks of working at Maitland Maternity. There's no way Ellie would employ me unless I was looked after by the Maitland obstetric staff, and my baby's too important for me to take stupid risks."

"Yeah, right." He tried to make his voice sound as if he hadn't been worrying, but it didn't come out right. Okay, he had been anxious. He'd had visions of her without health insurance, and not having seen a doctor since she'd left England.

But why on earth was he worrying now, when he hadn't

so much as thought of her pregnancy since the day he employed her?

For one reason and one reason only, he told himself grimly. Then she was his secretary.

Now she was his wife.

The realization slammed home hard, and with it came an overwhelming sense of responsibility. It was a feeling so vast it almost knocked him sideways. He hadn't expected this. He hadn't asked for it and he'd never dreamed he'd feel like it. Now, though, it was as much as he could do not to pick up her bag and haul her out of there. Carry her out in a fireman's hold if he had to.

But she was asking him to leave.

"Thank you, Michael." She was smiling. "You've been wonderful." Her voice trailed off, but the look she gave him was direct and honest. "I was in a mess, and you've rescued me in true hero style. You don't know how much it means to me, but... Well, thank you." And she took two steps forward, reached up and kissed him very lightly on the lips.

It was a feather kiss, a kiss of gratitude and relief, no more, and there was no reason in the world it should pack any charge at all.

But pack a charge it did, a million volts slamming through his body, leaving it seared and shaken to its core.

It was the shock, he told himself, dazed, as she drew back—the shock of acknowledging responsibility. He took a step away from her, and she was still smiling with her lovely green eyes, as though she hadn't felt the charge at all. He figured he'd better get out of there fast. It was their second kiss—and he didn't dare risk a third.

"I...well...I'll be off."

"Yes. You'd best leave. You'll have things to do."

"I'll see you Monday." His voice sounded lame. Spineless.

"No, Michael, I won't see you Monday," she reminded

him gently. ''There's only four weeks before the baby's due. Abby told me to quit. Ellie's hired you a new secretary. You met her last Wednesday, remember?''

That's right. This had all been organized. He knew it—sort of. So why the heck was his head fogging up like soup?

''I guess…''

''If immigration contacts either of us, then we'll get together,'' she said. ''But after our performance yesterday, they might not even check.''

''Jenny, they're not stupid. They'll come, and I don't know how much notice they'll give.''

''I'm not going anywhere.'' She gave a self-mocking smile. ''So call me. I'm a cab drive away.''

There was something else gnawing at him. ''When the baby's born… What will you do when you go into labor?'' It was impossible to keep a note of anxiety out of his voice.

She heard it and smiled. There was no need for his anxiety, but she liked it all the same. ''There's no problem,'' she assured him. ''I'll take a cab or I'll call an ambulance to take me to the hospital. I'll even walk, if there's time.''

''Don't you dare. Call me.''

''Hey, I'm only eight months pregnant, and I don't need—''

''Call me!'' He barked the command, and she blinked. And then she smiled again.

''Okay, Michael. I'll call you.''

''At two in the morning if necessary,'' he growled. ''Anytime. You swear?''

''I swear.''

''There's nothing else you need?''

''Nothing.''

''I told you, I can afford—''

''There's nothing else,'' she said, with a lot more confidence than she felt. She opened the door, then stood waiting until he passed through it. ''Thank you for everything, Michael. Goodbye.''

SHE'D SOUNDED so firm.

Jenny closed the door after her husband and stood for a long, long time with her back against it, staring at nothing. There was nothing else she needed.

Except someone.

Except Michael.

Unconsciously she traced her fingers where his mouth had touched hers, remembering the feel of his harsher skin against the softness of her lips. Nice.

Michael was nice.

''The girls at work would have kittens if they heard me,'' she said into the silence, thinking of the reception staff and the female nurses at the hospital. Michael Lord had a reputation as a hunk of the first order. But nice? That was the last word they'd use to describe him. He was cool, aloof, demanding...

''But nice,'' she said softly, and fingered the ring on her finger. She'd moved Peter's rings to her right hand. The new band of gold lay light and strange on her ring finger.

Different.

She touched Peter's rings and tried to conjure up his face. She couldn't. Frowning, she crossed to her bag and found his picture, put the photograph on her bedside chair, where it belonged.

''Because Peter's my husband.''

Peter.

She closed her eyes, pain and guilt washing over her. Peter's title was this baby's birthright. If she did what Gloria wanted, the baby could inherit it right away.

No. That way was madness. To barter what she knew was right for this new little life for riches and a title...

''I'm sorry, Peter,'' she whispered bleakly into the silence. ''I can't do it. It just seems so wrong. I'm sorry.''

She opened her eyes, and there was no one there. Nothing.

Except tomorrow and tomorrow and tomorrow...

CHAPTER FIVE

MICHAEL LEFT HER and drove to the river. They'd had dinner on the road, so he wasn't hungry. It was nine at night. He should go home, get some sleep.

But he was married.

What did that have to do with anything? He didn't feel married. He stopped the car and got out, walked to the riverbank. The night was fresh, pleasant, but there were no other people around. Maybe it was too early for the town's lovers to be out walking. Saturday night, most of the local kids would still be at the movies, and older couples would be dining in one of the city's restaurants.

Single people didn't tend to come here.

But he did. This was a place for quiet, a place to get his thoughts in order. So much had changed.

Only it hadn't changed, he realized. He was free to go home as he always did, and Jenny expected nothing more of him. On Monday there'd be a chirpy secretarial replacement sitting in Jenny's office, and life would go on as usual.

But he was married.

This was stupid, he thought savagely. Jenny was acting as if they could go on as before, but their marriage had to be made public if she wanted immigration status. She couldn't stay in that apartment.

She intended to. She didn't want to put him to any trouble.

So what would she do with herself, in the weeks of waiting for the baby to be born? If she had her way, if immigration didn't bother to check, she'd stay in that dump of an apartment, speaking to no one.

It was none of his business. He touched the gold band on his finger. According to Jenny, he could take it off. He needed to keep it close in case there were questions, but he didn't need to wear it. Jenny was making no demands.

Unconsciously he started to remove it, then let it slide back.

Better not. If officials came asking questions... If he lost the damned thing...

What if the baby came early? he thought suddenly. What if it came tonight? His mind was heading off in all directions.

"She has a phone," he said into the night. "She's not irresponsible.... She's not irresponsible but she's too damned independent.... Why too independent? Do you *want* her to live with you? No, but..."

His voice trailed away. Of course he didn't want her to live with him, but a vision of her face flashed into his mind. Her skin too pale, as if she didn't spend enough time in the sun. Her eyes creased with worry, but her face set and resolute.

She'd been through too much.

And if she has cramps again tonight...

"Butt out, Lord," he told himself savagely. "You've done enough. She needs space, so get back to where you left off."

The phone on his belt buzzed into life, and he quickly grabbed it. If she needed him...

"Mike?"

"Garrett." Michael's breath came out in a rush. It wasn't Jenny.

"Hey, who were you expecting? Marilyn Monroe?"

"Yeah, right. What do you want?" It was impossible to eliminate the impatience in his voice, and he could imagine

Garrett's eyebrows doing a hike upward at the other end of the line.

"You were invited for dinner."

"What?"

"Tonight," Garrett said patiently. "We've had steak and salad, and Dylan and I have drunk most of the beer, but if you're fast you can have some of Shelby's pumpkin pie."

Jenny doesn't like pumpkin pie.

Somehow he didn't say it. With a mental shake, he managed to get himself into the conversation. Into reality. "I'm not coming."

"Are you with someone?"

"No."

"As usual. You're neck deep in work, maybe?"

"No, but…"

"Then we're expecting you." Garrett's growl matched his. "The girls are disappointed. Or are you planning on staying out of family life completely now?"

"No."

There was a pause. Something had caught Garrett's attention. Something different? His voice lowered a notch, and Michael heard worry come into it. "You sound… You're not down in that damned casino?"

"No!"

"Then get your butt over here, little brother," Garrett demanded. "Before I drag you."

Yeah. Okay. It seemed sensible enough, or more sensible than standing on the riverbank having conversations with himself. Besides, there was no point worrying Garrett and his sisters.

He took a deep breath, gathered his wits, turned into a single man again and went to face his family.

"THERE'S FIVE LEADS."

Michael was sitting on the sofa at Garrett's ranch, a can of cold beer in his hand. He'd refused Lana's offer of a glass. He sat there trying not to think that Jenny would be shoving a glass at him regardless. He was trying not to smile at the thought.

"Are you with us, Mike?"

Michael blinked and focused. Garrett was standing in the center of the room. Their sister Shelby was on the floor at his feet, playing with Lana and Dylan's baby, Greg, and Lana and Dylan were sitting way too close on the other sofa. The way they were looking at each other, there'd be another baby before too long.

"Oh. Um, yeah. Right."

Garrett fixed him with a big-brother look that said, Pay attention or take the consequences, and continued.

"As I said, we need to do something concrete."

What the heck were they talking about? They looked like they were waiting for an intelligent question. "We?" he said weakly, and hoped it was appropriate.

Apparently it wasn't. All it earned him was a glower from Shelby.

"Garrett and me. Michael, you're not listening. Shut up and concentrate."

"Yeah, right."

"We found five sets of triplets born around our birth dates," Garrett repeated, frowning at his brother. Something was up with Michael, and he didn't know what. His eyes stayed watchful as he kept talking. "Without fertility drugs, there weren't as many triplets born then, and most didn't survive. There are only five registered in Texas as making it."

"So?" Two intelligent questions in one night! He was doing well. He nudged Shelby, and she glowered again.

"Shut up, Michael."

Garrett's frown deepened. Yeah. Something was definitely up with his baby brother, but all he could do was keep talking while he tried to figure it out.

"There was one set of triplets born to a LeeAnn and

Gary Larrimore three towns from here at Lorretta Free Clinic. That seems the most promising lead, mostly because the hospital records are so scant, but there are four more around Texas. We thought if we split up… Mike, if you can help…"

Michael sighed as he finally figured what they were talking about. Their birth mother again! He might have known. They were asking him to get involved, and he didn't want to.

"Why would I help?"

"Because we want to find our mother, Michael," Shelby said, exasperated. "With your resources…"

"Sheila Lord was our mother, and that's the only mother I want," Michael said flatly. "Our natural mother dumped us." Immediately Jenny came to mind. She wouldn't have dumped her baby. No way! "Terrence and Sheila were the world's greatest parents," he went on. "They're who I think of as Mom and Dad. I don't need anyone else."

"Most of the time you don't need anyone at all," Shelby snapped. "But some of us do."

"There are easier ways to find someone to care about than searching for a woman who dumped us."

"She cares." Shelby's voice rose. "Our mother cares. You read the note."

"I know she's having a guilt trip all these years later," Michael argued. "So she sent Megan a stuffed toy and three cute little sweaters. It means nothing. She doesn't suggest getting in touch."

"The note said she loved us. Maybe she feels too guilty to ask about getting in touch."

"Then maybe she's right to feel like that. After all, she dumped us. She had no guarantee we'd be looked after."

"Oh, right." Shelby was angry, and on her high horse. Fighting with Michael had been her chief pastime since she was three. She swiveled on the floor and fixed Michael with a withering look. "She dumped us at Maitland Maternity, where Megan was in charge. Even back then, the press coverage on the place would have told her that Megan would move heaven and earth to get us cared for, and cared for together.''

''If she loved us, then she'd have stuck around to find out that we were okay.''

''She had reasons she couldn't.''

''Well, I'm not interested in them,'' Michael said flatly. ''Terrence and Sheila did their best to bring us up. They gave us everything we needed and more, and it seems disloyal to them to go hunting for some woman who took the easy way out.''

''You're too hard, Michael.''

''I'm not hard. I just see the facts. There's no room in our lives for someone who never showed the least interest in being our mother.''

''There's no room in your life for anyone,'' Shelby snapped.

Now, that was a bit much. Michael considered her words while his siblings glared at him. He had everyone he needed right here in this room, he thought, and he really was fond of his hotheaded sister.

''Hey, except you,'' he told Shelby, trying to prod her into smiling. He tweaked her hair as she sat on the floor beside him. She glowered, and he tweaked again.

''Cut it out!'' Shelby protested.

''Then cut out being mad at me. You know you don't mean it.''

''You're so darned aloof. You don't care.''

''Hey, I care about you guys.''

''Not enough to help us.''

''Nope.''

''Because you're selfish.''

''Because you're wasting time.'' He paused. ''And maybe because searching for this woman might be opening yourselves up to a whole lot of grief.''

"Aren't you even interested?" she demanded hotly. "How can you not want to know?"

"Easy. I mind my own business. Not like some sisters I know."

"Oh, you are so—" She grabbed the cushion she'd been using to support tiny Greg on the floor. Greg was lying flat on his back now, surveying his toes, and he had no need of it. In a practiced maneuver, Shelby took aim and swiped the cushion across Michael's head.

Cushion swiping had been a skill Shelby had practiced since she was a toddler. Michael knew it and expected it. He rose and, catching her wrist, hauled her to her feet. He pushed her easily backward so she fell onto the sofa, then laughed into her indignant face.

"Some things never change," he said fondly. "Isn't this you all over, Shel? When all else fails, resort to violence."

"And some things about you never change," she retorted, hauling her arm back without success to aim with another cushion. "Here's Michael Lord, resorting to indifference because he might just get hurt if he gets involved."

"That's deep, Shel," he said appreciatively. "You been doing a psychology course on the quiet?"

"I don't need a psych—"

And she stopped dead.

"I don't need..." he prompted, but she was no longer concentrating on what she was saying. Her eyes had grown as huge as saucers, and she was staring at his hand as if it had grown another thumb.

"Michael," she said, and her voice sounded strangled and far away.

"What's wrong?" It was Garrett who asked the question. Michael had seen where she was looking and gave an inward groan. He knew what was coming. How could he have thought they wouldn't notice?

"Shel, what's happening?" Lana was distracted enough to pull away from Dylan's arms and rise in instinctive protective mode. The siblings might fight as much as they liked, but if there was the faintest thing wrong with one of them, the rest of the brood sensed it in an instant. And reacted accordingly. "Shelby?"

"He's wearing a wedding ring," Shelby whispered in horror. "Michael, you're not married!"

Michael considered this for all of ten seconds. He stared at his family, thinking of one smart reply after another.

None seemed right. In the end, there was only one thing he could think of to say. After all, they had to know sometime.

"Well, yes," he said softly. "I guess you could say that I am."

LANA SAT DOWN. It was as if her legs had suddenly gone from under her. She opened her mouth to say something, but nothing came out.

On the floor, baby Greg looked up in wide-eyed interest. The world was a wonderful place, his infant eyes declared, and his uncle Michael was fascinating if he just stood still.

Which was what he was doing. As were his siblings. Michael looked around at his family, and they stared back like so many frozen statues.

"It's someone…" Lana gave a soft moan, finally recovering her voice. "Oh, no. It's someone from the casino?"

"Hell, Lana." Michael shook his head in disbelief. This at least he could handle. "Will you get it into your head that I hit the gambling scene for a whole three months after Dan was killed? Sure, I was off the rails, but that's over. You and Shelby have spent the last two years worrying about me."

"I've been worrying, too," Garrett volunteered. He took Michael's beer can from his hand. "It's the Morrow woman, isn't it?"

"The Morrow woman?" Michael's eyes narrowed. What sort of a description was that?

"The Morrow woman?" Lana moved. She grabbed Michael's beer can from Garrett's hand and thrust it at Dylan, as if it was getting in the way of what was really important. She was practically gibbering. "What Morrow woman?"

But Michael was no longer listening. He was facing Garrett head-on. *The Morrow woman?* It sounded like an accusation.

"Who told you about Jenny?" he demanded, his voice dangerous.

"Jenny?" Shelby's voice was practically a squeak. "Who's Jenny? You've married a woman called Jenny? I don't know any Jenny."

"Ellie was looking for you on Friday morning," Garrett told Michael, ignoring his sisters. His eyes didn't leave Michael's face. "She called me and told me there'd been a problem with your secretary."

"Your secretary?" Lana gasped. "Jenny, as in Jenny-your-temporary-secretary? You're married to Jenny, your secretary? I know Jenny. She's lovely. But she's pregnant. She's huge. Michael, she's—"

"Well, there you are. I don't have to tell you anything about it," Michael interrupted dryly. "You've figured it all out for yourselves."

"Catch me, Dylan," Lana said dramatically. "I'm going to faint." And she collapsed with theatrical effect onto the sofa and into her husband's willing arms. There was laughter in her eyes, but there was no matching laughter in Shelby's. Lana's world had expanded with her husband and child, but Shelby's life still revolved around her brothers and her sister. Her eyes were filled with undiluted horror as she struggled from the sofa to face him.

"Michael, you haven't…" Shelby was staring at him as if he'd been caught walking naked at midday. "Of all the… No. Tell me you haven't."

"Surely there were alternatives," Garrett said uneasily. "Ellie said the woman's life is in a mess, but…"

"You know, Garrett," Dylan said conversationally from the sofa, his arm holding Lana comfortably against him, "if I were you, I'd stop calling Michael's new wife 'the woman.' I'm watching Mike from down here, and every time you say it his face turns blacker."

That stopped them dead. Garrett and Shelby stared at Dylan, then turned to stare at Michael.

His expression was like a thundercloud.

Lana made a noise that was somewhere between a squeak and a gasp, then somehow collected herself. She hauled herself out of her husband's arms and bounced up to stand before Michael. She took his hands in hers and fixed him with the Lord look—the look that told him he wouldn't get away with anything but the truth, the whole truth, and nothing but the truth.

"Of course she's not 'the woman.' She's Jenny and she's really, really sweet," she said warmly. "And you've married her. So tell us all about it, Michael. Don't leave a single thing out, and don't tell us any lies. Just tell us."

Michael looked at his sisters' troubled faces and gave an inward shrug. What the heck? They needed to know. These guys were his family. And somehow…so was Jenny.

So he did as ordered. He told them everything, while they stood and took it in with various degrees of disbelief and incredulity.

"Well," Lana said at last, plonking herself down at Dylan's side again. "Well."

"She's eight months pregnant?" Shelby asked in a distant voice. "You mean, she's found herself a father for her child? When you had nothing to do with it? Of all the conniving—"

"Sort of like me and Lana," Dylan said softly, holding his wife. "Like me finding a mother for Greg when Lana had nothing to do with it. Conniving like that, do you mean? Careful, Shelby."

"It is *not* like that," Shelby snapped. "You guys love each other. She—she trapped him."

Michael's brows lowered. "I offered, Shel."

"But you don't love her?" she demanded, wheeling on Michael with anger. "Of course you don't love her! Where is she now?"

"I don't know. Home, I guess."

"Your home?"

"No, her home."

"You don't plan on living together?"

"Not yet." He frowned. Not until he could make her see sense. Tomorrow maybe?

"Well, that's something." Shelby looked relieved, but Garrett was shaking his head.

"Mike, do you have any idea what sort of legal minefield you've put yourself into?"

"I can handle it."

But Lana's mind had gone off on another tangent. "You're married to a woman who's eight months pregnant and you don't know for sure where she is?" she demanded, bouncing up from her husband's hold again to face Michael head-on. Her indignation was palpable. "What if she goes into labor?"

"She has a phone."

"She knows where you are?"

"I have the cell phone."

"She'll call you?"

"I...yes." He fell silent. Would she? She'd promised. Maybe she wouldn't.

She would.

"You're worrying about her, aren't you?" Lana said triumphantly. "You care about her."

"Lana, she's my secretary. She might have been hired as a temp, but she's the best assistant I ever had. This way...this way I get to keep her."

"As your secretary?"

"Yeah. Why else would I want her?"

She stared. "How about as a wife?"

He sighed. "How often do I have to say it, Lana? This is a business arrangement. She needs to stay in the country, and I appreciate her secretarial skills. There's no way I want to marry anyone else, so what's the problem?"

"Does she have anyone else?" Lana demanded. "Friends? Family? Or is she completely alone?"

"I guess she has friends." He didn't know. Hell, he didn't know!

"Are you bringing her to the wedding?" Lana had moved into organization mode.

"Wedding?"

"Camille and Jake's wedding," Lana said patiently. "It's here. Tomorrow. Remember? Don't tell me you didn't notice the marquee on the front lawn."

"Yeah, but…" Okay, he'd forgotten. After all, Jake and Camille had had a civil ceremony a few months ago, but Megan had convinced them to hold a formal ceremony so the whole family and their friends could attend. A wedding. Heck, why had he ever accepted the invitation? He hated them. He'd barely gotten over Lana's wedding. Or his own.

"Bring her, Mike," Lana said firmly. "Let us all meet her. I know her a bit from popping in to see you at work, but I don't know her well. She's always friendly, but just efficient friendly, if you know what I mean. We need to get together."

"Why? Lana, she's not my wife."

"Is that what you're going to tell the authorities?"

"No, but—"

"And if immigration asks questions, and Garrett and Shelby have never even met her?"

"There's no real need—"

"She's alone, Michael. I'm assuming she's finished work until the baby's born, so what's she doing for the next few weeks?"

"I have no idea."

"In my shop I see heaps of pregnant women," Lana told him. "They all say the last few weeks of pregnancy seem endless. They're full of fears and anxieties—and you're just leaving her by herself."

"I told you, Lana, she has nothing to do with me. That's the way she wants it."

"You've married her, Michael," she snapped. "For better or for worse, she has everything to do with you."

"Lana..."

"Enough! We're going home now," she said, bending to scoop her small son from the floor. "Come on, Greggykins. Let's take your daddy home to bed. And tomorrow...tomorrow you and me and Daddy are coming back here to see Camille marry her Jake and meet your new aunty Jenny and make your first contact with your new cousin."

"Cousin?"

"Greg's my son, Michael, and your new wife's about to have a baby," she said serenely, standing on tiptoe to give Michael a sisterly kiss on the cheek. "Like it or not, brother mine, you've just expanded our family. So shut up and get on with it."

THERE WAS nothing else to say.

Lana and Dylan left, Lana giving Michael her unsolicited advice, Dylan following with amused pride.

"Go with the flow," he told Michael as he passed him on the way out. "You can't fight City Hall."

"City Hall meaning Lana?"

"One and the same." He grinned and headed out the door.

That left Shelby and Garrett. Unlike Lana, Shelby was close to tears.

"I don't know how you could do it," she said. "Oh, Michael, I wanted you to marry—but not this way."

"Shelby, you know I never intended to marry."

"Yeah, but I'd hoped you'd meet someone who would change your mind."

"I already have. Her name's Jenny."

"I mean someone you love."

"Like I love you guys? I don't think so." He gave her a hug that was meant to be reassuring, but her eyes were still troubled.

"Oh, Michael…"

"Don't fret about him, Shelby," Garrett said roughly, putting an arm around his sister and giving her a squeeze—almost as if he was protecting her. "Our Mike's a big boy now. He's got himself into this mess."

"It's not a mess," Michael protested, but Garrett shook his head.

"This mess," he repeated. "He may not see it yet, but it's a minefield. But don't worry, Shel. If there's one thing Mike's good at, it's minefields. He's not security chief of Maitland Maternity for nothing."

Garrett hesitated, then sighed. This evening had got sidetracked, and he'd called them together for a purpose. "I suppose there's no chance of you helping us look for our mother now, Mike?"

"No."

"You being so busy with your new wife and all?"

"Get off my case, Garrett."

"Yeah, right. But you'll squeeze in Jake and Camille's wedding tomorrow?"

"I don't—"

"You'd better," Garrett warned. "You've married the woman, and now it's time she meets your family."

"It's not as if—"

"Just bring her tomorrow, Mike," Garrett said heavily. "We'll judge your new wife for ourselves."

CHAPTER SIX

MICHAEL LEFT, and he should have gone straight home. He was tired, wasn't he? The last sleep he'd had seemed days ago, in a hotel in El Paso.

With his wife.

The words kept drifting into his mind and staying. *His wife.*

She wasn't his wife, he told himself savagely. She was just some woman he'd done a favor for. She had nothing to do with him.

The car nosed itself toward her apartment all by itself.

What was he doing? It was close to midnight. Jenny'd be asleep, and he had no business being there.

He'd just drive by to see.

To see what? He was being a dope.

But he'd just drive by, all the same.

HER LIGHT WAS ON.

He couldn't see Jenny's apartment from the street. It had one lousy window looking out over the fire escape at the back, but Michael knew it well enough by now. He'd just sort of head his car down the back alley where he'd parked it before and look up, and— Her light was on.

So what if it was on? So what if she was having a sleepless night?

Maybe she was having cramps again.

It had nothing to do with him, he told himself, a note of desperation entering his logic. Tomorrow he'd convince her to move into his place, but for now she didn't want him. If her muscles cramped, then she'd just walk around until they eased. It was only for one night.

That was that. He should never have come here. He backed his car onto the street again and turned away from—

No. He didn't turn away. His car slowed to a crawl. Another car was parked in front of the apartments.

Not just a car. A Mercedes.

This wasn't the sort of neighborhood where you parked a Mercedes, Michael knew. For one thing, no one in this neighborhood owned such a pricey car. For another, it was careless. On Saturday nights, vandalism was at its worst, and parking expensive cars in this low-income district was asking for trouble. Michael had left his Corvette here two days ago, in broad daylight with Jenny inside, and even then there'd been trouble.

But why was the Mercedes here? And why was Jenny's light on?

Maybe there was no connection at all. Still… Edgy, he drove slowly past the car and noticed the tiny sticker on the edge of the windshield. It was a stylish *S*, so small and discreet that thieves weren't supposed to know what it stood for, but Michael did. He'd been a cop. He was trained to notice such things. The *S* stood for Sparchan's Rental Service—suppliers of luxury rental cars for the well-heeled tourist.

So what was a well-heeled tourist doing parked outside this dump of an apartment block at midnight?

When Jenny's light was on?

He didn't like it, and suddenly his logic wasn't driving him. Instinct was. It took him ten seconds to park the car, ignoring the threat of thieves and vandals, and another ten to race up three flights of stairs.

Jenny…

At the top of the stairs he forced himself to pause. He'd

been trained too well to rush in without thought. *Stop, think and live.* That was his legacy from Dan. It was a hard-learned lesson, but one he'd never forget. He paused and slid along the wall, his eyes on Jenny's door.

It was wide open, and a woman was speaking. Not Jenny. An older woman with an aristocratic English accent. Measured, controlled and icy with contempt.

"You're coming with me, my dear. Now! If you believe I'll allow my grandchild to be born here, then you're even sillier than I think you are."

Michael frowned. There was real venom behind the words.

"I'm not coming with you, Gloria." That was Jenny. Her breathing was too fast, and it was all he could do not to rush in. "You can take your thugs and leave. I'm staying right here."

Thugs!

Wait… Force yourself to wait, he told himself harshly. Rushing could do more harm than good.

The thugs wouldn't be doing any physical harm, he figured, his thoughts racing. If it was Gloria, she wouldn't allow Jenny to be hurt—not while Jenny was carrying the baby she wanted so much. Somehow Michael forced himself to keep still, straining all the time to hear.

"You're not staying here." Gloria's voice lowered, became silky smooth. Michael slid silently along the wall until he was beside the doorway. He could hear but not see. Thugs, Jenny had said. How many? "It's time this nonsense was over. I have a plane waiting to leave. The immigration people were ready to escort you there for me, and then you had to be so foolish as to take such drastic measures to avoid them. You might have known it wouldn't work. What did you pay to have someone marry you?"

"I didn't pay Michael. He wanted—"

"Of course you had to pay. No one would want you like this." The woman's voice was disdainful. "Look at you.

This place is a disgrace, you're fat and unattractive, and your breeding's appalling. What my son saw in you—''

"Peter wanted me."

That stopped her for a moment. "Oh, yes," Gloria said at last, her voice an angry hiss. "My esteemed son. He wanted you. For about five minutes. You know very well the only reason he married you was that you were so low-class he knew it would upset me. You were a grubby bit of boyish rebellion, nothing more."

"Get out," Jenny whispered, and Michael could hear fear mixed with her anger. "Get out now, this minute, or I'll call the police."

"You just try it, my dear." There was a pause, then Jenny's breath rasped inward, as if something dreadful had been placed before her. "This is for you, my sweet daughter-in-law. We need to be sure you come quietly. Unless you agree to accompany me like the meek, quiet mother of my son's heir."

"*No.*"

"But yes, my dear."

He'd heard enough. Michael spun into the doorway and faced them.

There were two thugs, men built like stud bulls. They were dressed in immaculate suits, but the image of civility stopped right there. They looked like bouncers at some seedy nightclub, and he thought he recognized one of them from his days on the force. They were thick-necked and heavy-jowled, and seemed to have been squeezed into their suits. With one glance Michael understood Jenny's fear. One of the men had a syringe, and he was holding it toward Jenny like a gun.

What the hell? Michael's mind raced. He'd seen syringes in his time, held by drug addicts and wielded like weapons. This one was different, though. These people wanted Jenny's baby. At worst the syringe would contain an an-

esthetic and, unless Gloria was a complete fool, it wouldn't
be harmful to an unborn child. Or its mother.

There was no sign of any gun, and why should there be?
They wouldn't need one. Two large men and one woman
against a very pregnant Jenny? What were the odds?

Jenny would be no match at all.

Nor was there any guarantee Michael could do better, he
thought grimly. He wasn't carrying his gun. He was fit and
well trained, but he wasn't as tall or as heavy as either of
these guys. He moved into the room and stepped aside,
leaving the doorway clear. Then he stood still, loose-limbed
and watchful.

Unnecessary violence wasn't his style. Besides which,
there was a really good chance he could lose. What he
needed here was logic.

"That's enough," he said flatly. "You're scaring the
lady, and she'd like you to leave." His voice was soft, with
just the faintest undertone of menace. "Now."

"Who—" He'd caught them by surprise. Gloria wheeled
to face him. "Who are you?"

"I'm Jenny's husband," Michael told her. "I'm asking
you to go."

There was a long, drawn-out moment of absolute silence
in which it seemed the whole world stood still. Jenny's face
was drained of all color. She'd backed away from the men
and stood with her hands behind her to hold the table, as
though she had need of its support.

Her eyes had flickered once to Michael as he entered,
but her gaze returned to the first thug's hand. They were
fixed on the syringe.

She wouldn't be thinking the way he was, Michael knew.
She'd be terrified of the syringe for her baby's sake.

But the threat was fading. The guy wielding the syringe
hadn't moved. He was the one Michael had recognized, and
there was a trace of uncertainty in his eyes.

"Bruno," Michael said. "What the hell are you doing here?"

Bruno's hand dropped to his side. "He's a cop," he said into the stillness. "I know him." It obviously made a difference. Bruno would do a lot for money, Michael thought grimly, but violence—kidnapping and assault—in front of cops was out of his league. Michael had arrested him in a drug bust years back. Just as well Bruno didn't know he had left the force.

Bruno's eyes were on Gloria, and Gloria was obviously thinking fast. The lady was diminutive and beautifully groomed, dressed in an immaculate soft gray suit that must have set the estate back thousands. Her dark hair was perfectly coiffed, her eyebrows penciled into lines of permanent astonishment, and her pearls looked to be worth a king's ransom.

She had the appearance of a woman in charge of her world.

She wasn't in charge now. Michael could see a whole gamut of emotions race across her features as her sharp, intelligent eyes summed him up. She cast a quick glance at Bruno and saw his uncertainty. It added to her own.

He saw her other henchman's muscles tense and involuntarily tensed his own. He had to deflect the violence fast. Michael was superbly muscled and trained to use his body to good effect, but there were two against one here, and he was no Superman.

"Yeah, I'm a cop, and I wouldn't do anything stupid," he said into the silence. "It's not worth it. It will achieve nothing and get you into so much trouble your heads will spin. All the money in the world won't get you out of it."

And then he waited.

While Gloria thought.

What were her options? he asked himself, his eyes not leaving her face. Keep going? Make her men bash him— if they would—and take Jenny by force?

"Even if you hurt me," he said pleasantly, "I have a large extended family who will move to protect Jenny, plus the police force. She's not alone. She has me—her husband—and she has in-laws and connections. If you succeed in taking Jenny out of the country, we'd invoke the full force of the law in having her and her baby returned. The Lords and the Maitlands are a powerful force in Austin. This is our territory, and you're not welcome."

Silence. The woman's face contorted in fury.

"What are you being paid?" she demanded at last, her voice furious.

"I'm sorry?" Michael showed polite surprise, nothing more. His eyebrows arched as if he couldn't make any sense of what he was hearing.

"What has the girl promised you?"

"I don't understand."

"You won't get any of it. The child stands to inherit, but the girl herself... She's as poor as a churchmouse."

"If we're talking about Jenny—"

"Of course we're talking about Jenny. My daughter-in-law. But if she's—"

"You know, I don't think she is your daughter-in-law anymore," Michael said evenly, his eyes flicking to Jenny and then moving away. Hell, she looked dreadful. If he kept looking at her, he'd slug someone. "She was only your daughter-in-law while she was married to your son. But she's no longer married to your son. She's married to me."

"You really married her?"

He didn't just want to slug *someone*. He wanted to slug *her*. "I really married her."

"Why on earth—"

"That's none of your business." Michael's voice was flint hard. "Get out."

"No." Gloria smiled then, and at her nod, Bruno carefully replaced the cap on the syringe. He placed the sealed syringe in his pocket, and Jenny's breath came out in a rush of relief. "Not quite yet."

"Now." Michael took one dangerous step forward, but Gloria put up two beautifully manicured hands.

"There's no need."

"There is."

"How much do you want?"

It was a raw demand, thrown bluntly into the room, and it had the effect of making Michael stop dead.

"What?"

"I assume there's money in here somewhere." Gloria cast a disdainful look at Jenny. "I have no idea what terms you've agreed on, but I'll make it worth your while to forget them. You can say you married her when you were drunk. I'll pay you off, and we'll have your marriage annulled. You'll find me more than generous."

"Generous?" Michael's eyes were watchful, carefully assessing.

"More than generous." Gloria's mouth twisted into the self-satisfied smile of someone who knew everyone had his price. "Say two hundred thousand?"

"American dollars?"

"Pounds sterling." The smugness grew more pronounced. "That's about three hundred thousand of your—"

"I know what it's worth." Michael's eyes narrowed. "You'd pay that much? You must really want her."

"I want nothing about her. I just want the baby."

"I'm not—" Jenny spoke from the other side of the room, but Gloria turned on her like a snake.

"Quiet, girl. We're talking business."

"How high will you go?" Michael asked idly, and waited.

Gloria looked at him assessingly.

"I have to assume you'll go higher. If Jenny has offered me more than that—"

"She hasn't." Gloria swiveled to stare at Jenny incredulously. "She doesn't have a penny to her name. I've seen to that. If she's said she has, then she's lying."

"How much?" Michael asked. "Half a million pounds?"

"I don't—"

"You really want the kid. Do you want him half a million pounds' worth?"

"I don't—"

"Get out, then," Michael said indifferently. "Half a million pounds, or we're not talking at all."

"Michael!" Jenny's voice rose in dismay. She was staring from Gloria to Michael, and her face reflected her sense of betrayal. "You don't mean—"

"Quiet, Jenny," Michael said kindly. "Can't you see your mother-in-law—or your ex-mother-in-law—and I are doing business?"

"I don't wish—" Gloria said, but Michael interrupted.

"That's not the way to talk. Not when you're trying to buy a man's wife from him. Half a million or out!" He took a step toward Gloria, and Gloria fell back as the thugs stepped forward. Neither of the heavyweights seemed to know what to do.

"Very well, I agree," Gloria said weakly. "Half a million."

Silence.

"You'll pay that much?" Michael demanded.

"I said I agreed."

"Half a million pounds," Michael said blankly. "You have to be kidding. Certified check?"

"If you must."

Jenny gave an angry, desperate gasp and headed for the door. Michael moved to block her, holding her lightly against him.

"No, Jen. Stay."

"I'm not a possession," she said furiously. "To be bartered."

"No." He looked thoughtfully into her furious eyes and smiled, then looked at Gloria. "She's right. Jen's not a possession. Besides, she's real cute. You know, I have a mind to keep her."

"For half a million—"

"I know. I'm nuts. But a wife like this doesn't come along every day."

"You know you don't want her. It's just a marriage of convenience. How much?"

"You mean you'd go higher?"

"I..." Gloria looked incredulous. Then the venom returned in force. "If I must. But not—"

"She's not for sale."

"You'll have your price. Everyone does. And if you don't sell..."

"Are you threatening me?"

"If you like. It's my son's child."

"No." Michael's arm held Jenny tight. "Jenny's carrying my son. That's the end of it."

"Your son!" she hissed. "Any DNA testing in the world will tell that's nonsense."

"I think you'll find," Michael said smoothly, "that since I've married Jenny, any court in the land will uphold my right to claim fatherhood—with or without DNA testing. As long as Jenny doesn't dispute it, and I don't think she'll do that." He looked into her confused eyes and smiled. "Will you, love?"

"No."

"I didn't think so." His thoughtful gaze returned to Gloria. "Now get out and stay out. Take your hired men and your filthy little syringe and your private jet and get the hell out of this country. If Jenny and I never see you again it'll be too soon."

"You can't—"

"Oh, yes, I can," Michael said softly, dangerously. "Jenny's my wife, and I know how to look after my own. Get out. Now."

THEY DIDN'T SPEAK.

They didn't speak while Gloria and her thugs took themselves down the stairs, Bruno giving them a nervous backward glance. They didn't speak while the trio gunned the Mercedes into action and drove out of sight, rubber burning on the road behind them. Michael could have bet Bruno was behind the wheel. Jenny stood numb while Michael crossed to the bed and reached under it for her suitcase.

Finally she stirred to life again. A couple of kids—a boy and girl of about sixteen, draped around each other in obvious lust—had stopped at her open door and were staring in. Their curiosity was obvious.

"You heading to the hospital?" the boy demanded, looking with fascination from Jenny's belly to where Michael was placing things in her suitcase. "Looks about time. My mom said you went on Thursday. False alarm?"

"I...yeah."

"Gee, you're big," the girl breathed, and Michael suppressed a grin and turned to face them.

"That's what happens when you let your heart take over from your head," he told the entwined couple. "It'll happen to you, too, if you're not careful."

"We're not that dopey. He's got protection," the girl retorted. "Don't you, Bob?"

But Bob, it seemed, hadn't. He gave a shamefaced grin. "Aw, we don't need it, Mary. It's safe."

The girl wrinkled her nose in horror and turned to look at Jenny. Her eyes widened. Obviously Jenny's condition didn't appeal one bit. "You moron. You think I want to be as fat as that? Get real."

"Aw, Mary..."

The girl turned and fled downstairs, and Bob followed,

bleating protestations of eternal love. He hadn't caught her by the time he reached the street, and his protests echoed faintly into the night.

"I think we might just have done our bit for population control," Michael said, grinning. Then he glanced at Jenny's white face and tried to think of something to ease the strain he saw there. She wasn't smiling. "Hey, it's okay, Jen. Don't worry. I'll look after you."

"I don't want to be looked after." She closed her apartment door and leaned against it, breathing fast. "Nor do I want to be an advertisement for safe sex. Michael, what are you doing?"

"Packing."

"I can see that. But why?"

"You know you can't stay here."

"Or you'll sell me," she said bitterly. "For half a million pounds."

"That was some offer!" He tried to make her smile. "Just lucky I'm already loaded."

"Lucky." She winced. "You sounded interested."

"Yeah." He left what he was doing and put his hands on her shoulders, holding her at arm's length. Her eyes were full of worry. "Sure, I was interested in seeing just how far she'd go."

"And?"

"And it seems the sky's the limit. If she's prepared to pay half a million for this baby, then you move into my place right now. I thought we'd have a couple of days' grace from immigration, and maybe we do, but it's not safe for you to stay here."

"Gloria's gone."

"If you stay here, then she'll be back."

"No."

"Yes, Jenny," he said, his eyes locking on hers. "She wants your baby, and she wants it a lot. Her offer told me that. The woman has no scruples. You need to be out of her range.''

"I'll go to a hotel.''

"You think she can't find you? She has serious money, Jen. She can bribe and she can buy whatever she wants.''

"But I'm married. I have the right to stay here. She can't touch me. Even if she forced me to go to England tonight, do you think I'd stay there?''

"What would you do if she succeeded in getting you back to England? You have no money, and she has influence there. If she manages to get the baby to England and applies to the courts for custody, Lord only knows what dirt she'll dig up against you. She can pay whoever she wants to say whatever she likes. Since the baby stands to inherit the title, then an English court may order that the baby stays with her. So...''

"So?''

"The only thing to do is to stay with our original plan,'' he said, still holding her shoulders. His gaze was intent and sure. Jenny's world was crumbling, so he had to sound confident. "I understand why you had to run, but the threat's not over. We make sure our marriage sticks. It's a legal contract, but Gloria will be down at immigration first thing tomorrow telling them our marriage is a sham. She'll shout it to the rooftops, and if necessary she'll bribe them to get their interest.''

"But...''

"Jen, if she's not back here tomorrow, the immigration officials will be. That's almost guaranteed. Either way, you can't be here. Our marriage has to seem real. You have to be with me. You need my protection, and so does your baby.'' He gave a self-mocking smile. "Maybe it's time for me to be a real hero.''

She didn't smile back. "Michael, I don't want to live with you.''

"Jen, we started this,'' he told her, and his voice took

on a note of steel. "You knew you'd have to stay with me, whether you want to admit it or not. To do otherwise is stupid, and Gloria's proven that tonight. Now, let's get your gear packed and move you where you legally belong. Living with your husband."

JENNY SAID NOTHING on the drive, but Michael was growing accustomed to her silences. He liked them, he thought. When his sisters were upset they let him have it with both barrels. Jenny withdrew into herself, holding her trouble close.

They had packed all her belongings into the Corvette. There was nothing personal left in her apartment.

"The break has to be complete," he told her.

"I can't stay with you forever."

A couple of years, he thought, but he knew if he said that, she'd bolt like a startled rabbit. "Let's take one day at a time," he said instead.

Or even one night at a time, he thought as he watched her worried face. Her absolute weariness concerned him. His first priority was to get her to sleep tonight.

The responsibility he'd taken on was growing heavier by the minute, he acknowledged bleakly. It seemed he had himself a wife in truth, as well as on paper.

At least she had a calm nature, he decided, trying to look on the brighter side. She wouldn't disturb his bachelor existence much.

"I'll try not to be too much trouble," she whispered into the dark, as if she guessed his thoughts. "I never meant to do this to you."

"I offered," he said, and managed a smile. "Don't be grateful, Jen. Just do what you need to do to survive and go from there."

MICHAEL'S HOME couldn't have been more different from Jenny's. His multilevel town house was part of a new housing development built on a tree-lined avenue overlooking the bike trails by Town Lake.

Michael hit his remote control and the door of his garage slid silently up. The Corvette entered the garage, and the door slid closed behind them, and Jenny had the sensation of being trapped. Crazy or not, she had to suppress an impulse to get out, thump on the garage door and demand to be let out.

But Michael was holding open the door to his house, and she had nothing to do but walk inside.

And gasp.

His home was white!

Jenny stopped dead and stared around with astonishment. Of all the places she'd imagined Michael could live, this wasn't it. This was no messy bachelor pad. The place was stark and coldly white, with the occasional splash of black for dramatic effect. White tiles, white chairs and sofa, white wood furniture with glass-topped tables to reflect the white tiles. White walls, with black and white prints on the walls. White drapes.

Michael put down the first load of her belongings and pulled the drapes wide. Outside was parkland and the river beyond. The lights of Austin were twinkling against the night sky. Gorgeous.

She turned to the room—and shuddered.

"Michael?"

"What's wrong?"

"This room." She gestured helplessly. "I can't..."

"You can't what?"

"I can't live here," she said honestly. "I don't think I can even stay here."

"Why not?" He smiled at her. "It's in better shape than your place. That was a real dump."

"There's no need to get personal."

"But it was. Admit it."

Her anger flared. "If we're talking of dumps..."

"Are we?" He was watching the spark behind her green eyes. She came alive when she was angry.

She really was lovely.

"What's wrong with this place?" he asked, and watched while she tried like crazy to be polite. And failed.

She took a deep breath. "Michael, it's awful."

"Oh, yeah? Who are we kidding here? Your place was awful. This place has serious money spent on it."

"I can see that, and of all the wasteful—" She bit her lip, and Michael grinned. She was so transparent.

"Go on."

"I'm too polite."

"No. Come on, Jen." He was enjoying this. "I've been honest about your place. You owe me the same."

"You don't want to know."

"Yeah, I do." She was fascinating. Her eyes were roving around the place as if she were mentally pulling it apart, and he could see her courage returning. "We're married, remember? You're going to have to show immigration officials around and admit you like living here."

"You think I could do that in a million years?" she asked incredulously.

"Why not?"

"Oh, yeah, as if I could ever like white. I'd rather face Gloria again than admit I had anything to do with this place. Where do you relax?"

"I'm not here much."

"I can see that. It looks like the photographer's just left. But when you are here, where do you watch TV and drink beer?"

"Mostly I do my beer drinking at Garrett's ranch," he admitted.

"No wonder. It's so cold here. Who decorated the place?"

"A woman I went out with."

"How many times did you go out with her?" Jenny demanded, fixing him with a look. Michael stared at her. She was transforming in front of his eyes. This wasn't the quiet Jenny he thought he'd married.

"Beats me. Twice, maybe."

"She obviously didn't know you. This isn't decorating. This is a vacuum!" She went to the sofa and stared in disgust at its gorgeous white surface. "You don't sit on this thing!"

"Of course I do." He was stung.

"How often?"

"I don't know. Sometimes."

"Like never," she said flatly. "I tell you, Michael, if you sat here now you'd leave a mark that'd take a chemical arsenal to remove. I bet your housekeeper has an awful job keeping it clean."

He glared, cornered. "How do you know I have a housekeeper?"

"Hey, I just guessed." She grinned. "Sherlock Holmes, that's me. And I'll bet she comes once a day. Or more. What's her name?"

"I don't..." Michael frowned. "What the heck does it matter what her name is? It's an agency. Whoever's available comes. I don't know names."

"Then that's easy. Michael, you don't really like this stuff, do you?"

Did he? He tried to find words to defend his decor, but they weren't there to find. There was something about this woman that demanded honesty. "No, but..."

"Let me fix it for you." Her eyes gleamed with challenge, and he found himself starting to laugh.

"Hey, I didn't bring you here to work."

"And there's no way I'm sitting here idle. I'm scared to sit down. This stuff is the pits, and if I have to stay here for a month I'll go nuts. You remember what I did with your office?"

Did he?

His office had been a bit like this, all chrome efficiency. Five months ago—it must have been about the time Jenny started—it was suddenly transformed. His glass desk was replaced by a vast antique wooden one, his swivel chair became old leather, the chrome disappeared, and someone painted the walls a dusky pink instead of gray.

He hadn't realized she'd done it until now. He'd thought it was part of an office renovation ordered by Ellie. Come to think of it, though, it was a darn sight more comfortable place to work now than it had been before.

But... She was starting on his home?

"We'll talk about it in the morning."

"There's no problem." She was staring at the furniture as if it were poison. "I'll be able to sell these for heaps and replace them with items that are much more comfortable. You won't even have to write a check."

"Jen..."

She fixed him with a look, and for the first time he felt like a—like a husband! "Tell me that you like this stuff, and I won't touch it."

"I don't like it, but...it's home."

"You watch TV at your brother's."

"Yeah, but—"

"Let me have carte blanche to fix this place, and I'll feel happier living here. It'll be a project for me." She smiled at him, her most charming smile. It was a smile that made him blink. Made him take a step backward. "Please?"

"You haven't even seen your bedroom yet. Maybe you won't want to stay," he said weakly, knowing he was defeated before he started.

"I don't want to stay," she said honestly, her eyes sparkling at the sound of defeat in his voice. She knew she'd won. "But if I must stay then I'll be useful, and I'll run replacements past you before I buy them. I'm not taking over your life, Michael. It'll be your choice."

"Hell, Jen." He stared at her, baffled. He was so far at

sea here he was almost drowning. That's just how he did feel, as if his life were being taken over—by a tidal wave.

"You do what you want," he said heavily, humor fading. "You're my wife, so this is your home. Do what you want."

HER BEDROOM was the most comfortable place in the house.

"Shelby stayed in it while her place was being redone," Michael told her as he showed her in. Jenny had fallen silent again, and it was worrying him. It seemed there were two Jennys—the one who'd been kicked so many times it was hardly worth getting up again, and the stronger Jenny who was only allowed to escape for brief airings and then put firmly back in her box. "She added a few of her own touches."

There was a bright patterned quilt on the bed, a floral print on the wall and a large framed photo on the bedside table. The picture showed a middle-aged couple, parental and proud, with their children. The two girls and the younger boy looked to be about four years old, and there was an older boy of about six.

There was no mistaking who they were. Michael's grin, even then, was unique.

"I'd forgotten you're a triplet," Jenny exclaimed, finding her voice. "Who are the others?"

"That's Lana sitting down. I gather you've met her. Shelby's behind me and has my arm twisted behind my back—that's because I was going through a phase of sticking my tongue out at the camera. Garrett's the big guy."

"They all live here? In Austin?" She frowned in concentration.

"Lana runs the baby shop, and Shelby owns Austin Eats Diner, next to the hospital. Garrett lives on his ranch a few miles out of town."

Jenny was frowning. Something about the picture didn't make sense.

"You all have red hair," she said slowly. "But your parents don't."

"We were adopted."

Something in his voice warned Jenny she shouldn't take it further, but she was so far past exhaustion she didn't pick up on it. "That's right. You said your birth mother abandoned you. But your adoptive parents took all four of you? That's wonderful."

"They were wonderful people."

"Were?"

"They died some time ago."

"Oh, Michael, I'm sorry." She hesitated. "And your birth parents?"

"I know nothing about them." His voice was clipped and tight, but she was still too tired to pick up on it. "As I said, my birth mother abandoned us when we were babies."

"You've never tried to trace her?"

"Why would I want to do that?"

"It must be the most awful thing," she said, her hands moving unconsciously to her stomach. "To give up your baby. And to give up four babies... It'd be like tearing yourself apart."

"Not everyone feels like you do."

"Maybe not." Her eyes were clouded, doubtful. She obviously couldn't see how anyone would feel different.

His birth mother had, Michael thought bitterly. She'd just walked away.

"There must have been some dreadful reason. It'd probably be easy enough to trace her—"

"Leave it, Jen," he said roughly. "Let's leave it."

The force of his words took her by surprise, and she backed off. "Okay. I'm sorry."

She was hurt. He could see in her eyes that she was

flinching inside, wondering what she'd said. He hadn't meant to snap.

"We're both tired," he said, a note of contrition in his voice. "Let's turn in now. The guest bathroom's just here. If there's anything more you want..."

"No, thank you, Michael. You've done enough." It was an odd, formal little speech and sounded wrong to both of them.

"I'll go to bed then," he said.

"Good night."

Damn, she sounded so forlorn he wanted to take her in his arms and...

He didn't know what. He just knew he had to get out of that room while he still had the strength to resist.

"Good night, then, Jenny. Sleep well." And he walked out of her bedroom and closed the door so fast you'd think there were demons after him.

CHAPTER SEVEN

MICHAEL WOKE to the smell of pancakes.

He lay for a moment in his stark white bedroom, sniffing the air, wondering if he was mistaken. Nope. Definitely pancakes.

There were pancakes being made in his kitchen.

How long since anyone had cooked in his kitchen? Shelby had when she was here. When was that—eighteen months ago? He'd eaten at home then, but mostly he ate breakfast down at her diner. The rest of his meals, too, come to think of it. He used the kitchen for making coffee and heating TV dinners.

But pancakes. Jenny was making pancakes?

What time was it? He lifted his wrist and inspected his watch. Seven-thirty. He stared at the dial as if it must be a mistake. What was she doing up?

It had been well past midnight when she went to bed. She should still be sleeping. He shoved back the covers and headed for the door—and then remembered that he wasn't alone. Swearing, he grabbed his pants as a knock sounded on the door and it started to open.

He yelped and dived for the bedcovers.

Whether he'd made it in time or not, he couldn't tell. When he turned to face his visitor, his sheet decorously up to his neck, she was in the room. A twitching muscle at the corner of her mouth and a twinkle lurking at the back of her eyes made him suspect that he hadn't.

"I'm sorry," she said apologetically, the twinkle growing. "I shouldn't have disturbed you, but I've made you breakfast. It'll spoil if it stays in the oven."

But Michael was no longer focusing on breakfast—or on his modesty. What on earth was she wearing? He blinked, and blinked again. He was accustomed to Jenny in the plain navy or black shapeless dresses she wore to work. They looked like something out of the welfare bin from thirty years back, he thought grimly. He'd grown accustomed to the idea that his secretary spent no money and no time on her clothing.

But what was she wearing now? There'd been a pile of clothes in the bottom of her suitcase. This must have been among them. Traces of a previous life, he thought.

And the traces were stunning! She was dressed in bright crimson leggings, an oversize T-shirt that practically reached her knees, with crimson, purple, yellow and white stripes, and brilliant yellow trainers on her feet. With black laces!

Her shoulder-length curls, usually held demurely back, bounced happily in a ponytail, tied up with a huge crimson ribbon.

"What the…" She still looked pregnant—very pregnant—but she seemed about ten years younger. She looked amazing.

She looked gorgeous!

"You don't wear clothes like that," he said, and she grinned, bouncing over to put his pancakes on his bedside table. Her ponytail bounced in unison.

"I do. Well, mostly I do. In my past life I did. When I'm doing office work, when I'm eight months pregnant and when I don't have any money to spend on clothes, then I don't. I wear sacks that I make myself. But these leggings are Lycra. See?" She held up her T-shirt so Michael could see where the Lycra stretched to dangerous limits. He blinked again. "This is what I wore for jogging before I was pregnant. It's the only outfit that still fits me, though

118

whether or not it will after my baby's born..." She looked thoughtful. "Maybe I've ruined my leggings, but I guess I can always wear suspenders." She smiled happily at him, supremely unconcerned. "Anyway, I'm off. Here's your breakfast."

"You're off?"

"For a jog." She grinned. "Well, a joggle, more like. I'm not very fast and I'm not very elegant."

"Are you supposed to be doing that?"

"Yep. Abby says so. There's more pancakes in the oven if you want them. I've eaten six."

"Six?" He was starting to sound inane, and Jenny was aware of it. She couldn't know he was just plain dumbfounded.

"You don't sound very bright this morning," she said, peering at him anxiously. "Maybe I shouldn't have woken you." She looked at him with maternal concern. "You just eat your pancakes—there's a nice cup of tea here, too— and then snuggle under the covers. I'll come in very quietly when I return, so I don't wake you."

"Jenny." Goaded, he started to throw the covers off, then thought better of it. Jenny chuckled.

"Very wise."

"Wait and I'll come with you."

"Why on earth would you want to do that?" she asked in amazement. "It's Sunday morning."

"Why on earth would *you* want to do it?"

"That's easy. It's a gorgeous morning. The river's calling. I've been so worried for the last few weeks that I've been making myself ill, but suddenly, thanks to you—" her smile softened so much it made his gut kick in "—I'm no longer worried. All's right with my world and I'm off to feel the sun on my face." She stooped, and before he knew what she was planning to do, she kissed him lightly on the forehead. Then she whisked herself over to the doorway, smiling at his baffled expression.

"Jenny," he began.

"Yes?"

He stared. He stared at her some more. Then he stared at the beautifully prepared tray—the stack of pancakes, the maple syrup and whipped butter, the little teapot he hadn't even known he had.

Then he stared at her, this stunning, laughing woman he hadn't known existed under his staid, plain secretary.

"I'm—I'm sorry I didn't get up when you started to cook," he said at last, sounding pathetic even to himself. "I'm not much into domesticity."

"Then that's a pity, Michael," she said softly, the twinkle still in her eye. He had an overwhelming impression he was being laughed at. "Because, like it or not, you've married into all the domesticity I can muster."

FOR ABOUT fifteen minutes after she left, he stayed in bed. He ate his pancakes—well, he ate four and couldn't figure out how she'd managed six—and then lay back and stared at the ceiling.

Sunday morning he usually joined up with a couple of buddies who were into basketball. Like him, they were cops or ex-cops. They shot a few baskets, had a couple of beers and shared some laughs, and generally reassured themselves that the bachelor life they led was exactly what they wanted.

Once upon a time there were a dozen or so guys who showed up. Lately he'd been thinking they were becoming an endangered species.

If he didn't go, he told himself, they'd be even more endangered.

So why shouldn't he go? He'd given Jenny a key last night. There was no need for him to stay here and wait for her to return. He could head off to the courts, and she could let herself in. There was no need to wait.

She shouldn't be long.

He rose and showered—slowly—and dressed, and she wasn't back yet.

He took his breakfast dishes into his pristine kitchen and loaded the dishwasher. He collected the newspaper and read a few headlines.

She still wasn't back.

The guys would be waiting. They'd be on the court. He paced and swore.

She wasn't back even then.

Okay, he'd just wander down the road, take the path by the river. Heck, it was as good for him to take a river walk as it was to shoot baskets, and the guys wouldn't miss him this once.

He started walking. But since he was wearing runners, it wasn't long before his feet started a jogging rhythm.

What if Gloria's thugs had been waiting for her?

Logic told him he was being unreasonable. There was no way Gloria's hired men would be lying in wait for her down by the river so early on a Sunday morning. There was no chance they could have guessed she'd go there.

But if they'd been driving by…

"You're getting paranoid," Michael said crossly, but his feet hastened their pace all the same, his jog turning to a run. Finally he could see the wide riverbank and…

She was there.

If there was one thing that could be said for yellow, crimson, purple and white stripes on a very pregnant lady, it was that they could be seen from a long way off. Jenny stood out like a striped beacon. She appeared to be…

Playing hopscotch?

She couldn't be, Michael thought. But that was exactly what she was doing. "Home," she yelled triumphantly. She was surrounded by a sea of little girls—half a dozen six- or seven-year-olds—and they had a hopscotch court marked with stones. They'd been egging her on. She held up her stick, triumphant, and waved. "You bet I couldn't make it. How's that for a pregnant lady?"

The girls fell into a fit of giggles, and an elderly lady rose from the park bench and clapped her hands. "That's wonderful, my dear. But should you be jumping? I mean, the baby…"

"My baby's jumping so much that his mother needs to get her own back." She grinned at the girls, and then she caught sight of Michael, who just happened to arrive breathless. "Michael."

He said the first thing that came into his head, and his first thought was the same as the elderly lady's. "You shouldn't be jumping."

"Are you an obstetrician?"

"No, but…"

"Then I'm jumping."

"Nope." He reached her and pulled her away from the hopscotch court, then stood glaring into her laughing eyes. "Honestly, woman, have you no sense?"

She laughed at him, her face glowing with exercise and sunshine. The October morning was clear, with the promise of a gorgeous day to come. "I'm not feeling very sensible," she admitted. "I'm feeling pretty happy right at this minute. Michael, this is Mrs. Eldbridge and her granddaughter Susan, and Susan's friends, Lucy and Veronica and Louise and Carrie and Rebecca. It's Susan's seventh birthday, or it was yesterday. We're still celebrating. Ladies, this is…this is Michael."

"Is he your husband?" A child with a hole instead of a front tooth and two extremely long pigtails looked at him with interest. For the first time, Jenny faltered.

"Yes. This is my husband."

"And your husband says you shouldn't be playing hopscotch," Michael growled, and the little girls giggled. They clearly didn't think much of his ferocity, but they seemed to think Michael himself was just fine.

The little girls obviously thought he was a hunk, Jenny observed. Her husband.

Somehow she made herself concentrate on something other than his body. "Michael, I was thinking…"

He still held her. His hands were on her shoulders where he'd pulled her from the hopscotch court. She looked into his face and smiled, and suddenly she was too close for comfort. Way too close—but there was no way he was releasing her.

"Can we all come back to your—to our place for pancakes?" she asked.

That stunned him. "What, everyone?" He looked around the sea of expectant faces, and Jenny put an entreating hand on the collar of his shirt.

"It's just… Mrs. Eldbridge lives in a one-room apartment with her granddaughter, and Susan really wanted a sleepover for her birthday party. So that's what they had, but the girls woke up very early and there's a man who sleeps in the apartment above who…who doesn't like being woken up early and was rude."

"He yelled awful things," the little girl with pigtails said, wide-eyed.

"And the girls aren't being collected by their parents until eleven, so Mrs. Eldbridge brought them down to the river. But she still has more than two hours to fill."

He gave an inward groan. "Jenny, I don't see…"

"We have enough to give everyone breakfast, don't we?"

"I don't think I do," Michael said. "I mean we. For a start we don't have enough plates." For heaven's sake, what was he saying? This was nothing to do with him. He didn't want to be part of a child's birthday party!

"Of course you don't have enough plates," Mrs. Eldbridge said. "That's nonsense. We're fine. We'll keep walking, won't we, girls? Let's see if we can see some boats."

The girls' faces fell as one.

"I've walked enough," one said sadly. "These are my party shoes." She gulped, sticking one shiny red shoe in front of her. "Actually," she said carefully, "they're my sister's party shoes, and they pinch my toes. They hurt."

She looked at Michael with huge, mournful eyes, and Jenny gazed at him with eyes just as pleading. Cocker spaniel eyes. Eyes a man could drown in.

Good grief!

"We don't have enough plates," he repeated weakly. It sounded pathetic, even to him.

"We could share," the little girl with the pinching shoes said.

No! The thought of a seven-year-old birthday party in his bachelor town house was almost claustrophobic. But every eye was on him, including Jenny's. Clearly she'd offered hospitality, and she expected him to back her. He was wedged into a corner, and he said the only thing possible.

"Why don't we go to Shelby's?"

"Shelby's?" Jenny was as confused as the children.

"My sister runs a diner. It's not too far from here." Yep. That's what they'd do, he decided. After all, what use were sisters if they couldn't bail you out once in a while? "Shelby makes the *best* breakfast."

"You want to go to your sister's diner?" She stared at him and then at her stripes. "Now?"

Hey, maybe it wasn't such a good idea, he realized, but he'd already suggested it, and the kids were looking as if they'd been offered Christmas. This wasn't a privileged group, he decided. Most of the little girls looked as if they were dressed in hand-me-downs, and Susan, the birthday girl, was almost waiflike. She obviously lived with her grandma, and Grandma didn't look as if there was any money to spare at all.

Okay. So Jenny's heartstrings had been tugged, and he

was expected to come to the party. He didn't even know if Shelby would be at the diner herself.

"We'll need two cabs," he said in a voice that sounded more sure than he felt. He'd get this over with and then he'd give Jenny a very firm talking-to about what she should expect of him. Maybe it was okay for her to get involved, but she couldn't involve him. He didn't need this in his life. "We'll take two cabs, and we'll drop you back at your home at eleven."

"There's no need for you to do that, young man," Mrs. Eldbridge said with quiet dignity. "The girls and I are just fine walking by the water until it's time to go home."

He should agree—but they were all looking at him. One elderly lady in a worn dress and six small girls with bright, expectant faces. And one Jenny.

All of a sudden it was easy. "There is a need," he said, smiling at the elderly lady with his most heart-stopping smile. "It would be a real pleasure for Jenny and me to be included in Susan's birthday. If you'll permit us."

She smiled then, a huge, relieved smile that almost made him glad he'd offered. "Well, young man. That's so nice of you, you and your lovely wife. I'd almost forgotten that such nice young couples exist." She beamed at Jenny. "You're so lucky, my dear. He's really special."

Jenny beamed right back, and tucked her hand proprietorially around Michael's arm.

"Don't I know it?" she said. "I'm feeling luckier by the minute."

SHELBY was at the diner.

It only took five minutes to get there by car. Michael and Mrs. Eldbridge went in one cab with three of the girls while Jenny and the other three followed behind in a second taxi. They assembled on the pavement, and Michael opened the door to usher them inside.

Shelby looked up from behind the counter—and nearly dropped the plate she was carrying.

"Michael," she said, in a voice that sounded like she'd been hit with a hundred volts.

"Hi, Shel. What do you do in the way of birthday breakfasts?"

"Birthday?"

"It's Susan's birthday," Michael told her patiently, in a voice that suggested she'd better treat this as normal—or else. He motioned to Susan. "Here she is. The birthday girl herself. I thought pancakes. Or doughnuts. Or..."

"Or both?" Susan said wistfully, staring around in appreciation at Shelby's cozy eatery. The smells coming from the kitchen were mouthwatering, and Michael could see lights coming on in all the little girls' eyes.

"Or both," Michael agreed gravely. "Could you manage that, Shel? And maybe hot chocolate all around?"

"With marshmallows on top," Jenny added from behind him, working up courage. She bit her lip. It wasn't the time, in front of this birthday group, to admit she was meeting Michael's sister for the first time. "Hello, Shelby."

"Jenny," Shelby said, dazed, her eyes wandering to the amazing stripes. "You're..."

"Jenny and I met Mrs. Eldbridge, her granddaughter and their friends on the riverbank while we were jogging," Michael said quickly.

"You were *jogging?*" Shelby could barely make her voice work as she tore her eyes from Jenny to stare at her brother.

"We were jogging." His eyes dared her to say more. "Jenny invited everyone home for breakfast, but I thought there'd be more choices here. What do you think?"

There was silence while Shelby almost visibly gathered her wits.

"I do a very nice birthday breakfast," she said at last.

"I'm only here for a couple of hours before I need to leave for the wedding, otherwise I'd have missed this."

"Very fortunate," Michael said dryly, and his eyes met hers. Steel meeting steel. "Shelby..."

"Hot chocolates coming up," she said faintly. "With marshmallows." And then under her breath she added a rider. "Just as soon as I've phoned Lana and Garrett and told them to come over and take a look at this miracle."

IT WAS A RIOT of a birthday party. Once she got over her shock, Shelby did them proud. After they drank their hot chocolate, she ushered everyone into the kitchen to flip their own pancakes. Once they'd eaten, they were each allowed two choices on the jukebox, and Jenny had them all dancing, much to the bemusement of Shelby's other customers. After half an hour's dancing she even had a few staid adults jiving their legs off.

A couple of interns from the hospital wandered in. They were given free coffee and directed to a seven-year-old partner. Michael, who was dancing with the birthday girl at Jenny's direction, felt his mind spin at what his wife had accomplished.

Then there was the birthday cake. Rising nobly to the occasion, Shelby produced a snake of doughnuts in the shape of a huge S for Susan, with seven candles she'd found. Partied out, each little girl was finally ushered into a cab clutching a bag full of warm doughnuts for home.

"I can't believe you did this," Susan's grandmother whispered as they filled the second cab with her charges. Her eyes brimmed with tears. "Susan and I...well, we don't have very much, but she wanted a birthday party so badly. This morning everything was going wrong." She took Michael's hands between hers and squeezed. "Your wife, she's just the loveliest girl, and she deserves...well, you look after her, do you hear?" She gave his hands a last squeeze, cast a teary smile at Jenny and disappeared into the morning with her swarm of little girls.

Michael turned away to find Jenny watching him.

And Shelby.

And Lana and Dylan and Garrett and Greg. They were all out on the sidewalk, and every single one of them had big goofy grins on their faces.

"What the heck?"

"I thought they needed to come down and see," Shelby said innocently. "Garrett was neck deep in wedding chaos, but even he had to come. I knew they'd never believe me if they didn't see it for themselves."

"How long—"

"We've been here half an hour," Garrett said, grinning. "We've been in the back spying on you. You're a great dancer!" He turned to Jenny. "So, I guess you're Michael's Jenny."

"I..." She flushed. "I'm not...."

"You're not?"

"I'm just Jenny," she said simply.

"Nope." Garrett shook his head. "You're not Just Jenny." His eyes were warm, and there was laughter lurking somewhere behind them. "If you can get my brother to put on a birthday party for a bunch of kids he doesn't know—"

"That's enough, Garrett," Michael said roughly. "There was hardly a choice. Jenny was right. The kids were getting restless down by the river."

"Yeah, and you'd have noticed without Jenny."

"Anyone would." Jenny took a deep breath, searching for courage. "You must be—"

"Garrett. Michael's big brother."

"Of course." She gave him a shy smile. "You still look like your picture. Same red hair. Same big-brother look."

"What's a big-brother look?" he demanded, and Jenny's smile widened.

"I guess sort of proud and worried, both at the same time."

Garrett let his breath out. Whoa. "I think I just stopped worrying," he told her, and reached forward to give her a hug of welcome, bulging stripes and all. "I think I stopped worrying right this minute. Welcome to the family, Jenny Lord."

"Jenny Lord?" She cast a doubtful look at Michael. "Oh, yeah. I guess I am."

"I guess you are," Garrett told her. "And I'm wondering whether my little brother knows just what he's let himself in for."

BY THE END of the afternoon, he was beginning to find out.

They went to the wedding. Camille and Jake had decided they wanted a low-key affair—"just those we love in a place we love"—and there wasn't a chance of Michael getting out of it.

"Jake'll personally come and get you if you don't show up, little brother," Garrett told him. "And so will Camille. You're part of their family, and Jenny's your wife."

Michael had cringed inside. He did *not* want to go. He had helped Jake defend Camille from her ex-husband, Vince, but the events of those few short months ago were still nightmare fresh. The shoot-out at Garrett's cabin. The dreadful moment when he'd thought Garrett was dead. He should have prevented it, he thought savagely. He should have realized how desperate Camille's ex-husband would be.

He hadn't—and Garrett had been shot. The love that Camille and Jake shared had blossomed from that near tragedy, and the family had moved on, but for Michael it had been one more reason for self-imposed isolation.

And now, sitting beside Jenny, who looked lovely in the white dress Lana had borrowed for her, he felt so constrained he wanted to bolt for freedom.

The wedding ceremony started. Camille, exquisite in her beautifully embroidered gown of soft raw silk, gazed into Jake's face with love and total trust, and she gave him the answers he so longed for with sureness and with pride.

"I, Camille, take you, Jake, for richer, for poorer, in sickness and in health…"

Michael looked away. He glanced at Jenny and found her expression as strained as he felt. She'd done this twice before, he thought. She'd married—and now Peter was dead. She'd made those vows again. To him. What had these new vows meant for her?

Had Peter looked at her the way Jake was looking at Camille?

Something stirred inside him that could almost have been envy. He glanced at Jenny's hands, which she clasped and unclasped in her lap. His ring encircled her finger, but she wore Peter's rings on her right hand.

He had an almost irresistible urge to still those restless fingers with his own, but such an action would signal a commitment, he thought fiercely, and that's exactly what he didn't want.

Commitment meant pain. She would walk away, as his birth mother had, as Barbara had.

So he kept his hand to himself. But afterward, as the Maitland and Lord families and their friends milled in the afternoon sunshine, reveling in the happiness of the bride and groom and checking out Jenny with stunned amazement, he finally took her hand.

Not to comfort. To escape.

"Let's get away," he told her. "I've had enough of this."

Wordlessly she agreed—she'd said nothing for most of the afternoon—and they left as soon as decently possible.

Once in the car, with Jenny sitting white-faced and silent beside him, all he felt was an overwhelming claustrophobia. Why? he demanded of himself as he drove. The afternoon couldn't have gone better. Jenny had been welcomed and embraced into the family. Garrett had even hinted she might help in the search for their birth mother. Michael had nixed that one pretty fast.

Then Shelby and Lana had started grilling Jenny mercilessly about her past. What they learned they must have liked, because by the time they left, his sisters were starting to talk about turning Michael's spare room into a nursery and who was the best baby-sitter around.

To her credit, Jenny had mostly listened. She hadn't agreed to Garrett's request for help but had deferred to Michael, and she'd seemed content to have Shelby and Lana make plans around her.

However, quiet or not, she hadn't refuted anything. She hadn't come right out and said, "We're not turning Michael's spare room into a nursery because that's where I sleep. Michael and I don't sleep together! We're not a proper husband and wife."

It would have been hard to say it in the face of their enthusiasm, he acknowledged, but maybe she could have tried. It was important.

And what would she have done if she'd been faced with the Maitland clan's attention? The two of them made their escape while most of the Maitlands were still with the photographer, so Jenny had been spared Megan's welcome, Ellie's shock and Abby's concern.

That was to come. Now that they'd heard the news, their curiosity would be aroused.

Even Garrett seemed to assume things had changed, Michael thought as he drove his wife toward town. Sunday nights Michael usually spent at the ranch, and he and Garrett played pool on their dad's old pool table. After the wedding celebrations that's ordinarily what would have happened. But Garrett hadn't even raised the possibility. He'd helped Jenny into the Corvette and waved a hand in farewell, as if he wouldn't be seeing his brother for a while.

"See you around, Mike." Then he'd looked sideways at Jenny. "I'm sorry you need to go, but I understand you must be tired, Jenny. You take care of the lady, now, Mike. She's quite something."

She was, Michael thought bitterly, glancing sideways at Jenny.

But she wasn't really his wife!

"I'm sorry, Michael." She sounded tired, and when he checked her out again, he saw that her face had sagged. "It wasn't meant…"

"What wasn't meant?"

"Everything," she whispered. "I mean, when I saw those little girls this morning, I felt so sorry for their grandma that I just offered without thinking. You'd think I'd have learned not to be so darned impetuous by now. And then, when it ended up with me having to go to the wedding with you and all your family being so welcoming… You've hated it, and I don't blame you."

"I didn't hate it."

"You did. I can see that you did." She sighed. "You mightn't know it, but you get a sort of look—the same one you get when some sales rep comes in with a security system that bores you to snores, yet you still have to listen. That's what you looked like today."

"What, all of today?" He was shocked. Surely not.

"No," she said. "Not all. Most of the time you tried not to. You were truly wonderful with the children this morning. It was mostly this afternoon, and maybe…maybe it's only because I know you well." Her voice faded to a whisper. "Anyway, I'm sorry. And I'm sorry you're stuck with driving me home. Don't you and Garrett normally spend time together on Sunday night?"

"How do you know that?"

"You've told me," she said. "Lots of times. When I've asked you about your weekends."

Had he? Michael frowned. He couldn't remember telling her about his weekends.

But maybe he had. In the past few months, Jenny had become part of the furniture around his office. He could very well have talked to her, he decided. He'd never had to watch his tongue when she was around. He'd learned fast that anything he told her went no further, and he'd relaxed in her presence.

But he wasn't relaxed now. He was edgy. Chafed by the ties he'd never expected.

But she was untying them. "There's no need to stay home tonight on my account," she told him. "Just drop me off and go on back out to the ranch. Say I need to sleep. It's a family celebration. You should be there."

"Garrett won't expect me."

Jenny took a deep breath. "Then maybe Garrett should. He knows this is just a formality."

"Our marriage?"

"Yes. Our marriage."

"I hope he does," Michael said, and he couldn't keep the note of bitterness from his voice. "It's obvious my sisters don't."

She hesitated, thinking. "I wasn't sure what you'd told them," she said after a pause. "I didn't like to..."

"To dispel the romance?"

"Michael, I wouldn't presume..." She hesitated and cast a nervous look at him. "I don't want this, you know."

"Don't want this marriage?" The strain of the afternoon was still with him. "You're not making that very clear."

There was another silence, longer this time. She fingered the rings on her right hand—the rings she'd moved the day she wed Michael.

"I don't... Michael, Peter's only been dead for seven months. There's no way..." She took a ragged breath. "If you think I'm..."

Damn, now he had to feel guilty as well as trapped. "I

don't think anything,'' he said wearily. ''I don't think a darned thing. It's what my sisters think.''

''Which is?''

''That I'm finally domesticated. Trapped.''

It was the wrong thing to say. He knew it the minute he let the words leave his mouth, but it was too late to retract them. They hung in the silence between them like a threat.

''Then that's just stupid.'' Her voice rose a notch, anger filtering through it. Her anger matched his. ''I didn't trap you into marriage, Michael Lord. That would have been unfair. You offered. You came into this with your eyes wide open. I was amazingly, incredulously grateful for your offer, but if I'd thought for a moment that you believed I'd engineered this…''

''I don't think that.''

''That's what it sounds like,'' she said.

''Then I'm sorry.'' But he couldn't get rid of the edge of anger in his voice, no matter how unfair he knew he was being.

More constrained silence. Michael glanced at her. Damn, she did look tired.

''Jenny…''

''Michael, let's just leave this,'' she said wearily. ''I feel so guilty anyway that I can't bear it. At least not tonight.''

''There's no need for you to feel guilty,'' he told her, his own guilt still there. ''You're right. I offered. What my family does to me is no fault of yours.''

''Any family would do just what they're doing. They're right. And I should never have agreed to marry you. I need to—we need to do something.'' She sighed. ''But for now, heaven knows what the answer is. I seem to be getting deeper and deeper into a quagmire. Just drop me off at your house and go out to celebrate with your family. Please, Michael?''

''I don't want—''

"If you weren't married, would you ever stay home for dinner on a Sunday night?"

"No, but—"

"Then there's your answer," she said flatly. "You're not married, not really. So do what you always have done."

CHAPTER EIGHT

HE WENT OUT, but he didn't return to the wedding. He'd be grilled within an inch of his life if he did. The look in Ellie's eyes as she'd headed for the family portrait session warned him he was in for it. But the interrogation could wait.

Besides, he was convinced his brother and sisters would give him a hard time if they thought he'd left Jenny alone. Garrett and Lana had seemed far too fond of Jenny, and even Shelby seemed to be coming around.

So…

So he drove to his friend Harvey's, drank a few beers, watched a ball game on TV and tried to keep his hand out of sight so Harvey wouldn't notice the ring.

Not that Harvey would. He wasn't into wedding rings.

Nine o'clock. The ball game ended. There was time to watch another, but just as Harvey flicked the remote, the phone rang. Harvey gave an apologetic grin and took the phone into the kitchen. He came back a couple of minutes later, a sheepish expression on his face.

"Sorry, but I need to kick you out, Mike," he said. "Something's come up."

"Like…" Michael stared at his friend's face, confounded. He'd never seen Harvey look like this before. "Like a woman?"

"Rose," Harvey said, a dreamy expression drifting into his eyes. "I took her out last week. It was the first time she's agreed to date me, though I've been asking her forever. It was worth the wait. She's really something. She needed to go to Vegas to see her parents for the weekend, but I said if she got back in time, maybe we could go out together tonight—grab a burger or something.'' He paused, and the sheepish grin intensified. ''So she called. Guess this means she's interested, huh?''

''I guess it does,'' Michael said slowly. He rose. ''Well, I'll be off then.''

''I knew you wouldn't mind. Hey, this morning when you didn't show, that had to be a woman, right?''

Michael hesitated.

''I knew it,'' Harvey said, interpreting his silence as confirmation. He clapped Michael on the shoulder and beamed. ''Must be something in the water and we're all catching it. See you next week, buddy—that is, if you're not busy. Or if I'm not busy. But hey, I hope we are.''

OKAY, fate was telling him it was time to go home, Michael thought, and maybe it was. Nine was late enough. Jenny would most likely be in bed by now. He'd hit the cot himself, then get up early tomorrow and be at work before she woke. They'd start their independent lives together as of this moment.

Was Harvey right? Was there something in the water? He didn't think so. He sure didn't feel like a dose of domesticity.

He felt…trapped.

He drove his Corvette into the garage, his mind filled with dark thoughts. He entered his darkened house the same way and looked around as if he was expecting a wife in curlers, with rolling pin upraised. Which was crazy. No one was up. The lights were all off, and Jenny's bedroom door was shut.

So. This was what he wanted, wasn't it? He didn't need to check on her. She'd be fast asleep.

He flicked on the living room light, frowned at the white

sofa—she was right about that!—then went into the kitchen to make himself a coffee. He sure didn't feel like sleep, though he didn't know why. Just then a knock sounded on the outside door.

Who?

He opened the door, and it was Gloria.

There was a Gray Suit with her.

Michael's first instinct was to slam the door shut on the pair of them, but the official beside Gloria looked just official enough to make him pause. This wasn't one of Gloria's thugs. It was the older of the two immigration officials who'd started this whole mess.

Even so, he only opened the door wide enough to speak, not to let anyone in.

"Mr. Lord?" It was the official speaking. He held out a card. "Henry Harness from Immigration. Can we come in?"

"No." Short, blunt and to the point. The man took a step back and stared. Apparently he wasn't used to people saying no to him.

"I beg your pardon?"

"You heard," Michael told him. "No."

"Can I ask why not?"

"Because you're with the lady." Michael nodded perfunctorily at Gloria. "This woman has been causing my wife grief, and she's not welcome here."

The man flicked an uneasy glance at Gloria, which made Michael wonder just how much he was being paid to take an interest in these proceedings. Where on earth had Gloria dug up an immigration official at nine-thirty on a Sunday night?

"There've been allegations of wrongdoings in relation to your marriage," the man said, and Michael grunted.

"Yeah. Let me guess by whom."

"I just need to satisfy myself that your wife is with

you," he said. "Unless I can do that, then tomorrow I'll instigate investigations."

"At whose request?"

"I don't understand."

"You'd better try harder then," Michael said flatly. "My wife and I have filled out every required form and satisfied all criteria. But this woman…" He raised his eyebrows and gazed at the elegant Gloria as if she was some form of pond scum. "This woman came around to my wife's old apartment last night while we were in the process of packing her belongings to come here. She made certain threats, and some of them were physical. She upset her so much that my wife hardly slept last night. Tonight, Jenny's barely asleep, and here she comes to upset her again. My wife's eight months pregnant. This is harassment and—"

"She's not here," Gloria said triumphantly. "I told you. The marriage is a sham."

"Do you have a warrant?" Michael demanded of the official, ignoring Gloria completely.

"A warrant?"

"To search," Michael said patiently. "I assume you know what a warrant is?"

"I…" The man was right off balance. "No, but—"

"Then go away and get one. And while you're at it, I'd take out some insurance on events that may happen if you badger my wife into giving birth prematurely. Because I'll sue you for every cent you'll ever earn and then some."

"I didn't mean…" The man was flustered. "I'm sure if we inquire—"

"She's not here." Gloria was vitriolic in her certainty. "I tell you…"

"I'm sorry," the official said heavily. "I can't force my way in, no matter how—"

"How much are you being paid?" Michael asked, and the man flushed.

"There's no need to take this further this evening. Good night, Mr. Lord. I'll come back in the morning."

"If you bring my wife's ex-mother-in-law with you, then you're not welcome."

"We'll act through the proper channels," the man said stiffly. "I don't believe this lady is central to our inquiries."

"I'm sure she's not," Michael said pleasantly. "And if I were you, I'd make sure those channels of yours are legitimate, or I won't answer for the consequences." And he closed the door on the pair of them.

SHE MUST HAVE HEARD.

As he closed the door, Michael expected Jenny's bedroom door to fly open. She had the downstairs room. The front door and her bedroom door were only feet apart. Unless she was sound asleep, she must have heard every word that had been said.

There was nothing. Only absolute silence from within. He heard Gloria's car start and disappear into the night. They'd well and truly gone.

So why didn't Jenny come out?

She must be exhausted, he told himself. She'd been up way before him this morning, and the wedding had been both a physical and emotional strain.

He didn't want to wake her, but...

"Jenny?" he said softly, trying to fight his increasing sense that something was wrong. "Jen?"

Nothing.

She was asleep, he told himself firmly. Her bedroom door was closed, and that was that.

But he couldn't for the life of him go to bed without checking. He was being stupid, paranoid, intrusive, but he opened her bedroom door just a crack.

Her bed was still beautifully made up, and it was empty. So was her bedroom.

Where on earth was she?

Michael stared at the untouched bed for all of two minutes, his mind racing in every direction.

Had she left him? His eyes roved around the room, taking in her folded pajamas on the pillow and her husband's photograph in the frame beside the bed.

She wouldn't have left that behind. So where?

The conversation on the way back from the wedding played uneasily in his brain. *I seem to be getting deeper and deeper into a quagmire. I should never have agreed to marry you.*

She was confused, she was depressed and she'd been alone all night.

Hell, he never should have left her!

Where could she have gone? His head was spinning as he tried to find answers. She didn't have a car. She didn't have any money, and if she was leaving, then surely she'd have taken her few possessions. So where?

The river.

The answer came so suddenly it was like a bolt out of the blue, and it scared him stupid. No! She couldn't be that depressed!

I should never have agreed to marry you. I'll have to do something.

She wouldn't be so crazy, so desperate!

But he was already moving toward the door, and he was starting to run.

HE SEARCHED for half an hour without finding her. He was close to breaking point, as angry and frustrated as he'd ever been in his life. And scared. Surely she hadn't done anything stupid, he told himself over and over. Surely she couldn't...

He forced himself to slow down, walking along the hiking trails, methodically searching every park bench and every twist and turn of the water's edge. His eyes searched the shadows under the trees. If she was here, then he'd find her—if she wanted to be found.

An autumn fog was settling over the water, making the pools of light from the lamps strange and distorted. The bats that made their home under the bridges were swooping low over the water, and the stillness was almost eerie. If he called her name, the sound would echo up and down the river and achieve nothing—except make him feel like he was going mad.

Which was just how he was feeling. Crazy! This was unbearable. He thought back to the Jenny of this morning, bouncing up and down on the hopscotch court in her wondrous clothes, dancing with her little girls, helping light the candles on the birthday doughnuts.

She'd felt great. Free. And this afternoon he'd made her feel so guilty she'd wanted to end it.

But not like this. Surely not like this.

He'd call the cops.

No. They wouldn't come. He knew enough of police procedure to know what would happen if he called. "How long has your wife been missing? Maybe only an hour? Was there any disagreement? Oh, right. Well, then, we suggest you sit at home and wait it out."

He couldn't sit at home. He'd go nuts.

Where the hell was she? She had so few options. No friends. No family. Just Gloria waiting to force her back to England.

"Jenny?"

Finally he couldn't help himself. He stood on the bank, staring at the black, slow-moving water, and he called. Her name echoed back to him, over and over. *Jenny... Jenny... Jenny...*

No Jenny answered, but there was a whimper from below.

A whimper? It wasn't a human sound, but it was enough to make him peer where the bank steeped sharply forward.

There was a huddled figure right at the water's edge. Dark and large.

Dear God... He clambered down with a speed he didn't know he possessed, put a hand on the figure's shoulder—and Jenny's face turned to greet him.

FOR A MOMENT the relief was so great he couldn't believe he'd found her. He stood, stunned, with his hand on her shoulder, her white face looking at his. Jenny was here. She was safe. She was alive!

"Dear God, Jenny..."

His legs wouldn't hold him anymore. He sat down hard beside her and shoved his head between his knees. For the first time in his life he came close to passing out.

"Michael?" A soft hand ran through his hair, and her voice, when she spoke, was thick with concern. "Michael, what's wrong?"

"What's wrong?" He gasped and sucked in a great lungful of fog-filled night air. "What's wrong? Jenny, have you any idea what..." He gave another gasp and shoved his head down again.

Silence. He sat, recovering from fear, and she didn't say a word. Just waited.

Finally he raised his head. He stared at the water, where the scudding mist was moving and swirling in shredded ribbons and the bats were flying low. The river was black and mysterious beneath, hiding all. If she'd been in there...

"How long have you been sitting here?" he asked at last, his voice detached. He didn't look at her.

"A couple of hours. Michael, I'm so sorry if you've been worried."

"A couple of hours?" He sighed. "Can I ask why?"

"I came down here for a walk," she told him. "I'm—I'm sorry if you were worried, but I was sort of upset after you left me. And then I found Socks and I didn't know what to do with him. It all just seemed too difficult."

"Socks?"

He looked sideways, then really looked and saw what he'd been too upset to see until now.

She was wearing a coat—a garment he vaguely recognized as his. It was the black trench coat he used for night work. The coat was vast and dark, ideal for checking security at three in the morning when he didn't want to be seen, when he wanted to check that his outdoor security guards were doing what they were supposed to be doing. The coat had been hanging in his back entrance, and it disguised her bulk, but there was something apart from Jenny and baby underneath. Her pregnant bulk was... bigger?

"What," he asked fascinated, "do you have under your coat?"

"I told you," she said patiently. "Socks."

"And Socks is a..."

"Dog."

"Right. A dog." He nodded sagely, tossing the idea around in his head while his heart rate settled to almost normal.

"What sort of dog?" he asked at last, cautiously. His head was starting to work again, recovering from blind panic.

"A big dog."

"A big dog. Right. Any more specifics?"

"Well, he's a sort of..." She hesitated. "I guess a lot's gone into his breeding," she said at last. "Maybe that's all I can tell."

He nodded again. "So. We have a big, nondescript dog of uncertain parentage called Socks." He was buying time. "Jen, can I ask why he's sitting under your coat?"

"He was cold."

"I see." He didn't, but he wasn't confessing that for a minute. "Do you think he's warm now?"

"Maybe."

"Then do you think you could let him out now so we can go home?"

"He's still frightened. He's shivering."

"Jen…"

"I don't know what to do with him," she said in a small voice. "I can't take him back to your place—I mean, you've done so much for me already. And I can't leave him here."

"You mean he's a stray?"

"I guess so. He has no collar and he looks starving."

"Right. A stray." Michael was still having trouble keeping his heart beating in any sort of normal rhythm, but a stray dog was something he could deal with. Practical. "It's okay, Jen. We can handle this. If you don't want to leave him here, then we'll take him to the city pound."

"No."

"No?"

"Michael, look. You need to see him." She hesitated, then unfastened the top three buttons of the coat. "Come on, Socks. Come on, boy."

Socks came out—sort of. Two eyes peered from beneath her coat, brown pools of misery and distrust. The eyes looked warily at Michael, decided they didn't much like what they saw, then disappeared again into the coat's vastness.

"It's okay, Socks. He's a friend." Jen unfastened a couple more buttons, and the dog's head was revealed in its scraggy splendor. It was the head of a definitely peculiar dog, Michael thought, dazed. Scruffy, to say the least, with matted hair that was a dirty golden brown. The dog's ears drooped down like a cocker spaniel's, but his head looked more like a Labrador's—a Labrador on a bad hair day.

As Jenny had said, a whole lot had gone into this dog's breeding, but she was obviously seeing something Michael couldn't.

"He's just lovely," Jenny breathed, hugging him close. "Oh, Michael..."

"No." Michael shook his head with certainty. "You're wrong there, Jen. This dog is not lovely. This dog is weird. Seriously weird. I've never seen a dog like this in my life."

The dog looked at him reproachfully, and so did Jenny.

"Why," Michael asked carefully, still buying time, "are you calling him Socks? Is he wearing a collar?"

"No collar. You should see his ribs." She held the dog closer, as if he needed protecting. "He's truly a stray. No one wants this dog."

Michael could see exactly why.

"Then why Socks?"

"He has white socks. Or they might be white after a bath. And he reminds me of a dog I had as a kid."

"You had a dog like this?"

"Well, no." Jenny broke into an involuntary chuckle. "Socks One was a basset hound. But he looked at me the same as Socks Two." Her smile died, and she stared over the river. "My aunt had Socks One put down when my parents died."

"When was that?" Michael asked, startled. He knew nothing about this woman, he realized. Nothing!

"When I was ten."

"Your parents died when you were ten?"

"Mmm. In a car crash. I lost them—and then I lost Socks."

His heart twisted, and he put a hand on her shoulder. Socks looked up as if he wasn't the least bit sure he wanted to share, but Michael wasn't in the mood for dealing with a jealous dog, especially one with ears like this. "I'm sorry, Jen," he told her, and she shrugged.

"Things happen. I guess you know that as well as anyone. You were adopted, too."

"So your aunt adopted you?"

"Sort of." Jenny's tone changed, hardened. "My parents

left me a house, you see, so my aunt and her boyfriend moved in. They took over my life, and that was the end of Socks. They had him put down. It was also the end of my house. I was shunted off to boarding school, the house somehow got sold, and the funds disappeared into never-never land.''

"Oh, Jen..."

"You had better luck with your adoptive parents, though."

"Yeah." Michael thought back to his childhood. There was no chance of a dog like Socks being put down in the Lord household. If anything, there'd been pets to spare. There was certainly love to spare.

"Yeah, I guess."

"And Lana says your birth mother loved you."

"I wouldn't know about that." His voice hardened. "I know nothing about her."

"And you don't want to know?"

"The past is history. There's no need to rake it up."

"It stays with you, though," she said softly, staring again at the river. Socks stared with her. Four reproachful eyes. "You can't let it go completely. If my parents hadn't loved me, and if I hadn't known that and remembered it in the bad times, then I don't think I could have gone on. It's part of who I am."

"It's dead and buried." His voice was unnecessarily harsh, and he bit his lip, but Jenny looked bleak.

"Is it?"

"It has to be."

"Dead and buried." She took a jagged breath. "I just wish it was," she said bleakly, her face twisting in remembered pain. Her voice cracked, then she seemed to catch herself. "I'm sorry."

"Jenny, what's wrong?" He stared, puzzled, but she shrugged, pushing away remembered nightmares.

She took a deep breath. "No, that's enough of that. I'm

just— I was thinking of something I told Peter. But I don't know what I'm thinking of now. You've come down here in the dark just to find me, and here I've taken your coat without even asking.'' She made as if to pull it off, but he stopped her. The dog whimpered against her, as if expecting to be hauled out and thrust away. His big ears disappeared inside the coat. Socks was staying put.

But Michael was no longer thinking of Socks. ''Why did you come down here?'' he asked gently, watching her face. The emotion in her eyes was tearing at something deep in his gut. She was so lost, so at sea.

''I came out for a walk to try to decide what to do,'' she said with quiet dignity. She had herself in hand again. ''I can't figure how we can stay together in your town house. It's crazy.''

''There's no choice.''

''There is. I just need to find another place to stay, somewhere Gloria can't find me. Then if immigration comes, you can contact me.''

He thought this through and found an immediate flaw. Or rather, the flaw was looking at him again. ''You intend on taking Socks with you?''

''I...'' She faltered. ''I guess I'll find a place where I can take him.''

''There's no landlord that'll take a dog like this.''

''I don't need to stay in the city,'' she said calmly, as if this was a decision she'd made hours ago. ''I can go out into the country somewhere. Get a place to stay on a farm or something.''

''Oh, sure,'' he mocked. ''Farms take in dogs like Socks all the time. And you can always race from a farm to my place at a moment's notice when immigration officials arrive asking questions. They were here tonight.''

''Here!'' Her eyes widened. ''You mean at your home?''

''That's right.''

''Oh, Michael.''

"It's okay," he said, flinching at the fear in her eyes.
"They think you're safely in bed. In my bed. They had no
right to search, and I didn't let them in. But if you think
you can stay someplace else…"

"I must be able to," she said in distress. "I must!" The
fear was still there, with a hint of something else. The
knowledge of being trapped?

That was pretty much how he was feeling, Michael acknowledged bleakly. Claustrophobic. Closed in. Hell,
they'd done this in such a rush they hadn't thought it
through.

But if he'd had time, would he have acted differently?
Michael found himself searching his heart as he watched
the misery on her face. Would he have done the same
thing? Or would he have waved her off to Mexico alone,
to face childbirth and her future with nothing and nobody?

No way! He saw the courage in her eyes and knew he
would do no such thing. He'd hurt her this afternoon, he'd
hurt her badly. She'd come here to try to figure out a way
to get out of his life—for his sake, not her own. Here she
was, distress on her face, and it was all on his account, not
hers. He'd caused it by showing her how unhappy he was
with their situation.

"Hey, Jen." Reaching out, he touched her face. It was
cool, as if the damp and fog had penetrated. She gave an
involuntary shiver, and he flinched. Guilt swept in like a
physical kick in the rear. Hell, he was being a total jerk.
He'd suggested this. He'd married Jenny, despite her
doubts. His sense of honor was telling him to accept that
fact and move on.

"Come on, Jenny," he said gently. "Let's take Socks to
the pound and get you home."

The fear and distress changed in an instant. Her eyes
searched his, and her mouth tightened to stubbornness.
"No, Michael, I can't."

"Can't?"

"Socks is not going to the pound. I'm sorry, but…"

"You're not seriously suggesting we keep him? Jenny, that's impossible."

"I *am* keeping him."

"But…"

"If you won't let me move to the country, and if I have to stay with you, then I'm sorry, but he'll have to stay with us, too." She took a deep breath. "Okay, I know I'm being a pest and I know you don't want me to stay, but you're out all day. He won't cause any trouble. You'll see. You'll hardly know he's there. And it's only for the next few weeks…while I need to stay."

"Jenny, I am *not* a dog person."

"You're kidding." She put her hand down and brought the dog's face out from where it had been pressed against her breast. Gently, she raised it so those great brown eyes were looking straight at Michael. He stared down and tried to look away—and couldn't.

"How can you say you're not a dog person?" she asked reproachfully. "You look Socks in the eye and tell me that. He's the most wonderful dog."

"You know nothing about him." Michael glared, and the dog—Socks—looked soulfully back. "He's probably vicious."

"Oh, yeah!" Her voice was mocking. "You see how terrified I am."

"When he's been fed he might have a totally different personality."

The dog whimpered and licked Jenny's hand. Good grief, he really was the strangest-looking mutt. His golden-brown hair was straggly and moth-eaten, and he looked as if he hadn't had a bath in years. But he gazed at Jenny with a slavish adoration that said if he had a choice of half a side of beef or Jenny, he'd choose Jenny any day. Vicious? Well, maybe not.

"Yeah, one sniff of red meat and he turns into Attila the

Hun!'' Jenny was seeing exactly what he was seeing. She chuckled and ran her fingers under the dog's ears. The dog looked mutely at her. ''I'd like to see that.''

''Well, I wouldn't,'' Michael said bluntly, trying not to think about what her fingers were doing. Trying not to imagine what those fingers could do if they touched him. ''For Pete's sake, Jen, you're probably catching all sorts of diseases right at this minute.''

''I must have already caught 'em,'' she said cheerfully. ''I've been cuddling him for hours. He's staying.''

''There's a no-pets clause in my title,'' he said, driven against the wall and still fighting, but Jenny shook her head. Her eyes were mischievous. Honestly, she was like a chameleon, flashing from one mood to the next.

''Nope. Nice try, though. The lady living next door to you in the very same block has a pug called Basil. I met her this evening and was introduced to Basil in person.''

''You met Mavis?'' He stared at her, appalled.

''Yep. Is there anything wrong with that?''

Michael groaned. ''Jenny, Mavis is the biggest busybody in the neighborhood. What on earth did you tell her?''

''What do you mean?''

''Did you tell her we were married?''

''Well, I sort of had to,'' she confessed. ''She kept asking, and what was I supposed to say? So I did, but it made me feel dreadful. Like it was an invasion of your privacy— to have some strange woman running around saying she's your wife.'' She struggled to her feet, still holding the dog, rejecting Michael's hand as he made to help her. ''No. I can manage on my own.'' She took another deep breath, searching for words. ''I'm sorry, Michael, but I'm afraid that's the last time I'm going to say it. If I keep feeling guilty I'll go under. So let's forget the sorries, forget the guilts and just take Socks home and get on with it.''

''Take Socks home?''

''And me. And the bump.'' She smiled, but there was

lingering anxiety behind her eyes as if she was expecting to be slapped. This woman had been slapped more than once in her life, Michael realized, and the thought made him feel ill.

"Jen..." But she was still speaking.

"Take your wife, our unborn child and our dog home to bed," she said gently. "Welcome to domesticity, Michael Lord. We somehow seem to have jumped right in at the deep end, but I'm afraid there's nothing for us to do but to swim. Together."

CHAPTER NINE

SWIMMING was a very good description of what came next. Michael carried Socks home. "He's too weak to walk, and I'll carry him if you won't," Jenny decreed, so he had no choice but to carry the misbegotten bag of bones. By the time they reached the front door they were both scratching. Socks, it seemed, came with friends. Jenny fed him four TV dinners, which appeared to hardly ease his hunger, and then they had no choice but to fill the tub and soak off the unwanted visitors.

Socks had agreed entirely with his dining arrangements. The bathroom plans, however, were not so much to his liking. Jenny had been right in deciding there wasn't a vicious bone in his body, but Socks had his own way of objecting. By the time he was up to his neck in water and soaped to the eyebrows, his two new owners were soaked to the skin.

"There's no need for you to stay," Michael insisted, aware that Jenny must be exhausted after sitting for so long on the riverbank. "Go shower and change."

"You can handle him?"

"Sure I can handle him." Michael fixed Socks with a look. "Can't I, Socks?"

In answer, Socks shook himself again, and water sprayed from one end of the laundry room to the other.

"I'll leave you boys together then—to bond." Jenny chuckled, and retired to her own room.

BOND. HA! The only thing bonding was dirt. Socks was filthy, with ingrained grime that looked as if it hadn't been touched for decades. Michael used laundry soap and elbow grease, and more laundry soap and more elbow grease, and after fifteen minutes of scrubbing, he finally figured he had nice clean fleas. Too bad about the dog. Still he scrubbed on, knowing it was expected of him.

Which was truly strange. He didn't do things because women expected him to. Did he?

Finally Jenny reappeared, flushed from a hot shower. To Michael's amazement she was enveloped in *his* bathrobe and was holding a bottle of dog shampoo and a container of flea powder like trophies of war.

"How about this?" she asked gleefully, bouncing into the room. It was hard to believe she was eight months pregnant. "It's courtesy of Mavis. I figured we needed proper stuff to kill the little suckers."

Michael stared. He was feeling itchy and scratchy. He was soaked to the skin—he'd decided to hold Socks under until every flea was drowned—and his eyes were suddenly riveted to this bright-eyed, triumphant, pregnant waif of a woman. Wearing *his* bathrobe.

She took his breath away.

"You didn't visit Mavis like that?" His voice came out sounding like a croak.

"I sure did, and I even woke her up." Jenny's eyes twinkled with guilty mischief. "But she doesn't mind. Mavis hasn't had so much excitement in years. What with your callers earlier this evening—I gather they were sniffing around asking questions—and me wearing your bathrobe and announcing we were married, I doubt she'll get back to sleep all night."

He groaned. "Great! It'll be all over the neighborhood by dawn."

"Mmm." She cast a doubtful look at him. "Does that bother you?"

"No, but…"

"I'm not saying sorry anymore, Michael," she said resolutely. "We're in this together. Can I shampoo him now while you have a shower?"

"No." He took the shampoo from her and emptied half of it into the tub. Socks almost visibly flinched. "I'm soaked to the skin already, and there are fleas doing the backstroke in here. Hunting and killing is man's work. Clear out, lady, while I do the dreadful deed. I'll bring him out to you after I've toweled him dry."

"Are you sure?" Jenny gazed doubtfully at her bedraggled mutt, who looked even more doubtfully at her. "Poor Socks. He looks so sad."

"*He's* sad!" It was all Michael could do not to utter an expletive. "I'm itchy, I'm half drowned and I've been told I'm adopting a dog who's half Shetland pony and half goat—and *he* looks sad!"

"I guess I can leave you to your fun," Jenny said, chuckling. "I'll plug in the hair dryer in your doggy salon—I mean, in your living room—and wait for you there."

She ducked and bolted for cover as a sodden towel whizzed straight at her head.

DOG SALON or living room? Ha! It was neither. Michael's living room looked as if it had never been used in its life. White shag carpet, white sofa, glass coffee table with designer fruit bowl and designer fruit.

Jenny picked up an apple and took a bite, amazed to find it was real. His housekeeper must go to heaps of trouble with this fruit bowl, she thought, selecting and arranging each piece like an artwork. She grinned as she looked down, suppressing an almost irresistible urge to take a bite from every piece and leave it like that.

"Cut it out, Jenny Morrow," she said. "You let Michael's beautiful artwork be."

But the fire was a different thing. It, too, looked designer perfect, with pine cones and logs set in artful symmetry. The firebricks in the back were still white. It really hadn't been used. Austin's climate was mild in fall and winter, but Jenny was still feeling the dampness of the riverbank, and the thought of crackling logs was definitely appealing. After all, she was going to live here, too.

No more apologies.

She took a match from the beautiful white ceramic container on the white mantel and watched guiltily as the flames flickered into life. Then she stuck her bare toes out to the warmth and sighed with sheer sensual pleasure. Yes!

That was how Michael found her when he hauled the towel-dried Socks in from the laundry room. She was sitting staring into the flames, and for once, his living room looked lovely.

No. Jenny looked lovely.

She glanced at him, her eyes dancing in the firelight. When she held out her hands to greet her wet dog, Michael felt his gut wrench in a way it never had before.

"I... He's all yours." Heck, his voice sounded strangled. "I'll just go take a shower myself."

He practically bolted out the door, with Jenny looking strangely after him.

IT TOOK MICHAEL twenty minutes to shower, anoint his various bites and regain his composure. When he returned, he found a transformation of gigantic proportions.

Dirty, flea-ridden and starved, Socks had looked appalling. When he was wet, every rib had stood out and he looked bedraggled and sodden, all big eyes and droopy ears.

But now, blow dried and brushed with love... Michael stopped at the living room door and stared.

Socks would never win any pedigree dog prizes, but his coat was a gorgeous honey color. His ears were a mass of rippling silken fur, and the rest of his coat would soon

match. Jenny was lying full length on her side on the carpet
before the fire, still in his red bathrobe, gently stroking the
dog's matted fur over and over. The two of them made an
amazing splash of color in the golden firelight.

Jenny had a brush in one hand and a hair dryer in the
other, and there was a pair of businesslike scissors on the
floor beside her. She picked them up as he walked in and
waved them in his direction.

"Great. We need one person on brush and one person
on scissors. He has king-size mats under his tummy. They
stink like crazy when you put them on the fire."

Michael blinked. The tableau before him was almost sur-
realistic.

Socks, however, was enjoying himself to the hilt, sitting
up in front of the fire as if he was on show. When Jenny
mentioned his matted fur, he tucked his head under his
chest and looked down, as if inspecting his belly for himself. And then he returned his gaze to Jenny.

Good grief. The dog was practically purring.

I would be, too, Michael thought, dazed, staring at them
in stunned amazement, *if Jenny was brushing me!*

It was a ridiculous thought. Somehow he shoved it aside
and knelt to take the scissors from Jenny's hand. Their
fingers brushed briefly as she passed them to him, and the
feeling was like an electric shock striking right through his
body. It was as much as he could do not to pull away as
if burned.

"Oh, Michael, you're flea-bitten." She looked sympa-
thetically at the red splotches on his chest. He'd hauled on
a pair of jeans but left his chest bare, all the better to apply
calamine lotion. She reached out a finger to touch, but he
pulled back. *No way.*

"You…you must be, too." He sounded like an embar-
rassed schoolkid. Why the heck wasn't she feeling this
strange charge between them?

"Nope." She grinned. "Or not very much. You must be fatter. They always chew the fat ones first."

"Right."

"It's true," she said seriously. "My dad always said that."

"And he was a flea expert? I though you said he was a miner."

"His hobby was entomology." She gave him a cheeky look. "An entomologist is someone who studies insects."

"I know what an entomologist is," he said, goaded.

"Sorry." She didn't sound sorry at all. "I just thought, you being American and all…"

"You're saying my knowledge of the Queen's English isn't all it ought to be?"

"I expect you'll get it right sometime," she said kindly. "Just as soon as you learn to spell."

"Yeah, right." It had been a major source of conflict between them in the months she'd been his secretary. She'd type *center* as *centre*. He'd change it, and she'd patiently change it back again. He'd given up in the end, letting her spell as she darn well pleased, and he gave in now. Anything for a quiet life!

"Okay. Okay. So what's a coal miner doing with a hobby like entomology?"

"Contrary to what Gloria believes, being a miner didn't make my father ignorant," she said. She glared, defying him to argue. "There was no money to educate him, so my dad left school after grade eight, but he kept right on learning."

"He studied insects in his spare time?"

"So did my mother," she said proudly. "They wrote a great research paper that's still widely acclaimed all about the habits of bumblebees. I remember hours and hours with my parents, tracking individual bumblebees—only we kept getting them confused. It's very hard to tell one bee from another, you know. Unless…'' Her voice grew thoughtful. "Unless you're another bumblebee, I guess."

"You're probably right."

She didn't seem to notice his amusement, or the way he was watching her. He couldn't keep his eyes from her.

"In the end my father roped them with a piece of fine thread, and we'd run around the garden with our chosen bumblebee tied on our line like a kite,'' she told him. She chuckled. "It was a good piece of research. There aren't many kids whose dad gets home from work, grabs his string and heads out to the garden to rope bumblebees."

"I can see that,'' Michael said faintly. He hesitated, still watching the firelight flickering over her face. "It's a good memory to have."

"It's part of me,'' she said softly, lifting a tuft of Socks's hair for inspection. "Cut here, Michael. I wouldn't have missed it for the world. I mean, my parents—they're part of who I am, and if this little one inside me starts following bumblebees, then I'll be really proud. I'll know where it comes from."

She paused, as if unsure whether to continue. But she did. "Don't you feel that about your own birth parents? That you need to know them—that there's a part of you missing?"

"No,'' he said flatly. "I don't need them."

"I've learned not to need my parents, too,'' she told him sadly. "I had no choice. But every morsel of information I could ever find out about them was important to me. I can't understand why it's not important to you."

"It's not."

"It's all to do with not letting people close, isn't it,'' she probed, still gently stroking Socks. "Not needing anyone. Pretending you can stand alone—that you're you and you're not part of anyone else."

"Jenny, get off my case.'' He sighed. "I do let people close. My brother and sisters."

"You love them?"

"Yeah, but..."

"But you tell yourself that you don't need them."

"Look, this is getting a bit personal," he said tightly. The emotion in the room was supercharged, and his reaction to emotion was to bolt. "Do you mind if we just concentrate on Socks?"

She looked at him for a long moment, her green eyes shrewd and assessing, and Michael thought suddenly—even more uncomfortably—that she saw more than he wanted her to. Finally she nodded.

"Well, at least we know he needs us," she said cheerfully, looking at the dog. She cast another sideways glance at Michael. "Tell me," she said. "If you were down on the riverbank just now—alone and not with me—would you have brought Socks home?"

"No!"

"Really?" Her eyebrows shot up.

"Definitely not."

He looked at Socks, and Socks looked at him. Michael felt a pang. Reproach was something this dog had honed to a fine art.

Maybe he wouldn't have abandoned him entirely, he thought. He would have at least taken him to the pound.

Jenny was shaking her head in disgust. "Then it's just as well I'm here," she told him with asperity. "Michael Lord, you need humanizing."

"By humanizing, you mean turning me into chief cook and bottle washer for a misbegotten mutt?"

The mutt rolled over on his back, exposing his newly dematted tummy. Socks closed his eyes in bliss and waved one back leg, begging to be scratched. Michael glared at the dog, glared at Jenny, then scratched.

And Jenny grinned.

"That's exactly what I do mean," she said smugly. "It's very therapeutic. She lifted another tuft for Michael to clip, but she winced as she did it.

"What's wrong?"

"Nothing. I'm fine."

"You winced."

"I did not wince. I never wince."

"You winced." He frowned. "Cramp?"

"No."

"It's not a labor pain?" he demanded, startled.

"Yeah, right. One labor pain and I intend to start yelling my lungs out. That was a 'my leg's been stuck in one position for too long' wince—*if* there was a wince. And if there was, then it was a very little wince, and I'm denying it, anyway."

"Methinks the lady doth protest too much." He was sure she was hurting. "Jenny?" What was he thinking of? She'd had one heck of a day, and it was late. "Go to bed, Jen," he said sternly.

"No. I want to finish this—and we haven't decided where he'll sleep."

"I'll organize it. I'll finish his brushing. Go to bed."

"I am tired," she admitted. She paused. "I'll go soon. But I want to watch."

"Then lie on the couch and watch. Now!" He turned his voice into a roar, and her eyes twinkled—just the way he liked them most.

"Yes, sir." She started to rise, but staggered, and he moved like lightning to help her, holding her hands, pulling her up then supporting her as she lowered herself onto the couch.

"Ten minutes of watching," he said sternly, reluctantly releasing her hands. She felt nice. "And then bed."

"You sound like my father."

"That's exactly what I feel like."

ONLY IT WASN'T at all what he felt like, he thought as he brushed Socks. Jenny's father? That would make the feelings he was having paternal. Ha!

The dog was asleep, abandoning himself to Michael's ministrations with absolute trust. Michael had found the very spot on a dog's belly that needed scratching most, and he'd thus been deemed a friend for life. He could do anything he wanted, and it was okay with Socks. Socks was fed and clean and flea-free, and he was with belly scratchers. Friends. He could afford to sleep because he was in doggy heaven.

And it suddenly seemed like that for Michael, too, though he couldn't quite figure out why.

It was midnight on Sunday. He should be still over with the guys or else sleeping the sleep of the dead, he told himself. Instead, he was sitting by the fire, gently brushing a starving mongrel and watching a very pregnant and very lovely woman drift off to sleep beside him. She'd watched and watched for a whole four minutes, and every minute her eyes became heavier.

And now she slept with Socks.

It was strange. Surreal.

He should stop brushing, he told himself, his hand still rhythmically stroking. He should boot Socks into the laundry room and send Jenny to bed. But he wanted her to wake up the next morning to a perfectly groomed dog. He knew she'd expect it of him.

And he was content exactly where he was.

So he brushed on into the night, woman and dog sleeping beside him. And when he finished brushing, he sat and stared into the flames for a very long time.

SOMETIME about two in the morning he decided he should go to bed. He was three-quarters asleep himself, the dog settled on his knees with his long ears draped onto the floor, and he was resting against the couch with Jenny's sleeping face just inches from his. The fire had died to a heap of glowing embers, and there were no more thoughts left to think. There were only feelings, and feelings were threatening to overwhelm him.

So...bed.

"Come on, boy," he told Socks. "Let's get you settled." His body was lethargic, unwilling to stir, but he forced himself upright. The dog whimpered in protest. Michael stood firm, then stooped and lifted Socks into his arms.

"Let's introduce you to the garden and then show you your sleeping arrangements." He cast one long, lingering look at Jenny and left her to her slumbers.

The garden was entirely to Socks's satisfaction. He did what he needed to do in the manner of a well-trained dog, then headed indoors and directed himself straight for the living room again.

"No way," Michael told him. "The laundry room's where dogs sleep."

Socks looked reproachfully at him as if he'd just taken offense. He sighed—heck, the dog's sigh was almost human—and then trod heavily to his designated sleeping place. He eyed a couple of dry towels Michael had laid out for him as if they were an affront to his dignity, sighed again, then watched with mournful eyes as the door was closed firmly behind Michael, locking him in.

WHICH LEFT JENNY.

He could leave her in the living room, Michael thought. It was warm enough. She could sleep on the couch for one night.

The couch wasn't quite long enough, he decided. Her legs were bent. She'd be better off in bed.

But there was no way in the world he intended waking her, so he stooped and gathered her gently into his arms, lifting her to lie against him.

She didn't stir. Her body was warm against his bare chest. His bathrobe seemed far softer against his skin now than when he wore it himself. She was totally relaxed in sleep. And she smelled of something. What?

He couldn't place it. He didn't know what she smelled of. He knew enough of Jenny now to know she wouldn't be wearing some expensive perfume, but whatever it was, it was lovely. Lavender water, maybe? Or maybe the smell was just Jenny.

This was ridiculous. He was growing sentimental in his old age. He got a grip—metaphorically as well as literally—and carried his lovely burden to her bedroom.

She still didn't stir. He lowered her onto the bed, pulled the bedclothes away, and then rolled her over so she was lying on the sheet. Then he unfastened her robe and stared for a second, his mouth twisting at the sight of her pregnant body in her shabby pajamas. She looked defenseless. Young. Poor.

His sisters wouldn't be seen dead in clothes like these, he thought grimly. Maybe he could call Lana tomorrow and ask what women wore when they were pregnant, something soft and pretty and—

What was he thinking of? Jenny wouldn't thank him for criticizing her clothes!

Enough. He stooped to pull the bedclothes over her, and as if he'd spoken her name, she stirred and opened her eyes. She looked at him as if she was dreaming. Her eyes crinkled into a smile of pleasure, but they had that look that told him she wasn't seeing him. She was seeing some lovely thing in her dreams.

He touched her eyelids, closing them gently.

"Sleep," he told her. "Sleep, Jen."

"Love…" It was a husky whisper. Her eyes didn't open. She wasn't seeing him—heaven knew who she was seeing—but her arms came out and her hands reached for his face, urging him down to her. He was so surprised that he let himself be propelled toward her.

"Love." The word was whispered in the dark, and her

lips found his as he froze into stunned submission. He let himself be kissed.

Her lips were so soft, urgent, even in sleep. They tasted like nectar, and he couldn't believe what she was doing. Her hands were holding his face against hers, and her mouth was searching, searching...

And finding. She had what she wanted in the touch of his mouth against hers. She had...what?

Whatever it was was indefinable. The touch was like fire between them, a fierce, burning pain that threatened to overwhelm him. He felt his gut tighten, and it was all he could do not to gather her body against his and sink beside her on the soft, welcoming bed.

No! For one long moment Michael froze, but she was too sweet. Like a siren's song, she was impossible to resist. He let himself be drawn in, sinking to sit on the bed beside her and returning her kiss with a passion that stunned him. With a fire he didn't know he possessed. With a need...

No!

This was crazy. Jenny was asleep! She was dreaming of her dead husband, not him!

Somehow he dragged himself back, and her hands fell loosely to her sides. Her eyes were still closed, but her mouth curved into a gentle smile of happiness. She was making no objection. She'd kissed her man, and now the dream could continue.

"My love," she whispered, and she turned, snuggling into the pillows and drifting into dreams in which Michael had no part.

How COULD HE sleep after that?

He couldn't. No man could. He lay and stared into the dark for a long, long time. At about three or four there was a whimper from the laundry room, then another. Not a howl. If it had been a howl, maybe he could have resisted, but the dog sounded as miserable as he was. And lonely.

He swore, then padded through the living room and opened the laundry room door. Socks lay on his towels and looked at him with eyes that expected nothing—he'd lost all hope.

"This is ridiculous," Michael said. "You should be in the pound."

The dog's eyes said he agreed with him entirely. That was what he deserved.

"She wanted me to brush you. I've fed you and housed you. There's nothing else you need."

The eyes said he was entirely right. Socks needed nothing more. Except...

"Come on," Michael said, goaded, holding the door wide. "I guess I'm lonesome, too."

It was the first time he'd admitted such a thing in his entire life.

It was also the first time in his entire life that Michael Lord shared his bed with a dog. Yet still he stayed awake.

Because all he really wanted to do was to share a bed with Jenny.

CHAPTER TEN

JENNY SLEPT LATE—gloriously late. She woke to sunlight streaming in over her bright coverlet and to a snuffling at her side. A moist tongue touched her tentatively on the cheek. She smiled with delight and rolled over to embrace one ecstatic dog.

"Socks! How did you get in here?" And then she frowned, remembering the events of the night before. "How did I get in here? Michael?"

He must have carried her in. Her eyes flew open, and the memory of a dream came back to her—a dream so sweet it made her toes curl and a blush creep across her cheeks. Michael holding her. Michael's mouth on hers, the feel of his body...

"It must have been a dream," she said fiercely, sitting up with a start. Socks looked inquiringly at her and let his tongue loll, waiting for the next move. "I never would have... He wouldn't..."

Unbidden, her fingers came up to touch her mouth, and the taste of him still seemed to be there, infinitely sweet.

Michael.

"For heaven's sake, what am I thinking of? It was probably you doing the kissing, you dopey mutt." She gave Socks a hard, swift hug and swung her feet out of bed—then stopped as a knock sounded at the apartment door.

She froze. Michael would get it. She'd just stay here.

Michael didn't get it. The knock sounded again, firm and sure, and Jenny figured this wasn't someone who'd go away.

She looked at the clock on her bedside table and gasped in disbelief. It was ten o'clock!

She never slept until ten o'clock. Never!

Michael would be at work. He must have left without waking her.

The knock sounded again.

She didn't want to answer it. Not alone. But if it was the immigration people, then the worst thing she could do was to pretend not to be here. She took a deep breath, hitched her pajamas over her pregnant tummy, grasped Socks's scruff and padded barefoot toward the front door.

"This is your job," she told Socks firmly. "I'm the one in charge of TV dinners and you're the one in charge of security around here. You're a guard dog, Socks. Guard!"

He looked adoringly at her and wagged his tail. Yeah, right.

It was Megan Maitland.

Jenny opened the door half an inch without releasing the chain and checked the front step with one cautious eye. Then she gasped and withdrew, fumbling to release the chain. Megan! The CEO of Maitland Maternity—the matriarch of the entire Maitland clan—and here was Jenny looking like…

"Like something the cat dragged in," she told Socks desperately. "Or maybe you dragged in. For heaven's sake, I'm wearing Peter's old pajamas…"

It couldn't be helped. Megan had seen her and Megan was waiting. Pinning on her most welcoming smile and hoping her hair wasn't sticking straight up—which it always did after sleep—Jenny opened the door.

When she finally made her voice work, it came out a ridiculous squeak. "Hi."

"Hello, my dear." Megan smiled, unfazed at the sight before her. She appeared not to notice the pajamas, or the amazing hairstyle, or even the pregnancy, but took Jenny's hands in hers as though welcoming her into the family. "Mi-

chael told me you'd be home and that I could find you
here.''

"I—I don't..." Jenny was floundering like a fool but Megan didn't seem to notice that, either.

"I wanted to catch you yesterday at the children's wedding,'' she said, edging around Jenny and heading straight
for the kitchen. She left Jenny to follow, talking over her
shoulder. "It was so like Michael to bring you to an occasion
like that and then take you away before we could meet you.
Honestly, we were ready to shoot him.''

"I was tired." The squeak was still there. It was all she
could do to get her voice to work.

"I don't blame you for that," Megan said warmly, turning
to face her. "Sit down, child. You look exhausted. Ellie says
you've had quite a time, and your baby's almost due.''

"I—"

"Now I've pieced together quite a lot between Ellie and
Garrett and Lana," Megan said briskly. "But why don't you
tell me all about it yourself? Michael's my godson, you
know, and I've always been an honorary aunt to all the Lord
children. I want to know...''

And then her voice trailed away. Jenny stared.

Megan Maitland. Although Jenny had seen Megan at the
hospital, she'd never been formally introduced, but her reputation as a mover and shaker was daunting.

But now, despite this woman's power, despite her obvious
authority, her beautifully groomed appearance, her confidence and her interest in Michael's life, there was a hint of
appeal in the older woman's voice. It was as if she really
did want to be allowed to come close.

As if she really cared.

"I want to know everything," she said, and her smile
wavered. "Please. I care so much for those children—Michael and his sisters and brother. It's as if they're partly
mine.''

"I don't—"

Megan's hand came out and took hers. "Please, my dear. I care about Michael, and if what Garrett says is true, then I intend to care about you, as well."

Jenny hesitated. For seven long months she'd kept herself apart. Her troubles had been hers and hers alone. But now she had a husband who cared about her, and her husband had family and friends who wanted to know all about her.

Who had a right to know. And who might just care for her, too.

"Let's get you some breakfast, child," Megan said. "And then tell me everything."

To do anything else was impossible.

Jenny found herself talking freely. She talked and she talked, in between tackling the cornflakes and coffee Megan insisted she demolish. After a while she forgot about the baggy pajamas and her tousled curls and even Socks devouring cornflakes under the table. And all the time she spoke, Megan listened, as if every single word was important.

As she told her story, Jenny watched Megan's face, expecting condemnation, but there was no such thing. When she had finished, there was a twinkle in those compassionate eyes.

"Well," she said. "Well, child."

"I never wanted to draw Michael into this mess," Jenny said desperately. "What you must think of me..."

"What I must think? I think you're an incredibly brave woman," Megan said warmly. "The easiest thing in the world would have been to return to England, to surround yourself with luxury and allow your baby to be brought up by others. To stay here must have taken sheer courage."

"But in one way, it's selfishness to keep my baby away," Jenny said slowly, thinking about it, as she'd done a million times before. Thinking of what Peter would have wanted. Her baby's father. "I'm robbing my baby of his birthright so that I can have a say in how he's raised."

"You're not robbing him of his birthright," Megan said solidly. "Are you telling me when he comes of age he can't head back to Britain and claim his birthright?"

"No, but—"

"Then don't be silly. You're his mother. It's your right—your duty even—to raise your son the best way you know how."

"You know—" Jenny hesitated and met Megan's eyes "—I have the feeling that's why Michael's helping me...because his own birth mother didn't do that. Raise him, I mean. I'm starting to feel that Michael's carrying so much anger. And by helping me he's almost thumbing his nose at his birth mother, saying, 'You could have taken care of us.'"

There was a long, long silence as Megan stared across the table at Jenny's troubled face. And then the older woman's face softened. She took Jenny's hand in hers again and held it tight.

"Garrett said you were one amazing lady, and he was right," Megan said. "That's quite an intuition you have there."

"I don't know if I'm right."

"Oh, I'm sure you're right," Megan told her. "That boy... Michael internalizes everything. He was the one who was full of questions about his real parents from the time he could understand what happened. Then, when he was about eight, all of a sudden he got angry. He hated the thought that he'd been abandoned. And now..."

"Now?"

"Now his birth mother is trying to make contact with her children. He doesn't want to know. He's still so angry."

"I'd guess..." Jenny sighed and stirred her coffee. She needed to do something to keep herself from rising and pacing the floor, which was what she felt like doing. This conversation was almost unbelievable.

"His birth mother mustn't have had a Michael to rescue her from her demons," she whispered. "Poor lady. She must have had such strong reasons for walking away from her children.''

Unconsciously her hand touched her pajama-clad tummy in a gesture of defense. She looked up and saw that Megan's eyes had dropped to her waistline, and Jenny was embarrassingly aware of her inelegant outfit.

"Sorry." She hitched the pajama cord tighter over her baby. "This... This isn't me at my best. If Michael could see how I'm entertaining guests in his home, he'd be horrified.''

"I don't think horrified is the word for it." Megan smiled. "When I talked to Michael this morning he seemed just plain befuddled." She stooped to look under the table, checking out Socks and giving Jenny a chance to regain her composure. "To find himself with a wife and a dog all in one weekend. And what a dog!"

"He's wonderful," Jenny said warmly. The dog was something she *could* talk about. "Socks, come here." At the sound of his name, Socks looked at her adoringly, then stood and flopped his big ears across her knees. "He's just the best.''

"You know, after he was eight, Michael would never have a pet of his own," Megan told her, watching Socks with interest. "It troubled his adoptive parents. He hasn't let anything or anyone close to him.''

"No." Jenny fondled Socks's ears and looked troubled, too. "And now he's landed with me. Well, please don't worry, Mrs. Maitland. I won't stick around any longer than I must. As soon as my baby's born and I have residence status...''

"But I don't think you understand, my dear," Megan said. Her hand clasped Jenny's again. Her grip was strong and sure—a woman who knew what was right. "We're not troubled that Michael has—as you describe it—been landed with you. Garrett and I—and as far as I can see, Lana and Shelby, too—are delighted.''

"But—"

"Garrett told me you could do Michael nothing but good, and after meeting you, I think I agree."

"So you'd have him saddled with another man's baby."

"What I'm thinking," Megan said, eyeing Socks with amusement, "is that this baby may well end up being Michael's baby. As Socks may well end up being Michael's dog."

"Now that," Jenny said warmly, grinning despite her trouble, "is really ridiculous."

"What's really ridiculous?" Michael said from behind her, and she jumped about a foot.

"MICHAEL."

It was all so domestic. So cozy. Michael stopped in the doorway and blinked in amazement. Megan was sitting over a mug of coffee, her eyes dancing with laughter, and his Jenny was laughing, too.

Not his Jenny. Not *his* anything.

"Woof!"

Socks broke the silence. He'd obviously remembered Jenny's injunction that he was the guard dog around here, which meant he had to utter one threatening bark before hurling himself across the floor to jump up on Michael's best work suit. Michael caught his paws and staggered under the weight of him as Socks's tongue came out to lick his face.

"Ugh. Stupid dog. Get off. Jenny, I thought you were going to train him."

"Hardly before breakfast on day one," Jenny retorted, turning bright pink.

"Before breakfast?" He glanced at his watch and grinned. "It's almost eleven o'clock."

Jenny's blush deepened. "Just because some people get up early one day in their lives, they think they can gloat.

Not likely. I'll have you know I beat you to work every single day for the last few months.''

"So you did.'' He smiled at his wife, and the pleasure glimmering in his dark eyes made Megan stare. Was this Michael?

"What are you doing home, anyway?'' Jenny asked, and Megan stared some more. She couldn't remember when she'd seen laughter in Michael's eyes. He always held himself so aloof.

"I was in by six. I decided to take an early lunch, so I thought I might come home.''

"Well, that's a novelty.'' Megan shook her head in amazement. "You're honored indeed, Jenny. This is a man who has two-minute lunch grabs in the hospital cafeteria or, at best, five-minute salads at his sister's diner. To what does Jenny owe this pleasure?''

"Hey, I have a wife now,'' Michael said, grinning. "I have domestic responsibilities all over the place, and besides, Jen told me she can cook.'' He checked out his wife's pajamas and shook his head. "I might have hoped for a more appealing outfit, but never mind. I'll excuse it this once. Do we have something for lunch, Jen?''

"Of course we do.'' She hauled her dignity together as best she could, stood and hitched her pajama cord tighter. "The menu is cornflakes. Cornflakes, cornflakes or cornflakes. That's it. We're even out of TV dinners. Socks ate the lot. Sorry. Socks and I need to go shopping.''

"So it's cornflakes.'' Michael sat down, his smile still holding Jenny tight. "My favorite. What a woman! What do you think of my wife, Aunt Megan?''

"I think you're a very lucky man, Michael Lord,'' Megan said in a voice that made Michael's smile die. There was no laughter in Megan's voice at all. She sounded deadly serious. "I'm with Garrett all the way on this one.''

Silence. You could have heard a pin drop. Finally Jenny spoke. "I'm off to get dressed,'' she said. "You think you can manage your own cornflakes? The directions are on the box."

"A dutiful wife would pour my flakes," Michael said, trying for a casualness he didn't feel. Jenny chuckled.

"Where would you like them poured, dearest?" Jenny took a step toward the cereal box, speaking in honeyed tones, and Michael grinned and raised his hands in self-defense.

"Okay, woman. I can take a hint. Leave me with our guest and the dog and the domestic chores while you fritter your time away on your appearance. Marriage! It's not what it's cut out to be, Aunt Megan."

"I can see that," Megan agreed, still serious. "And aren't you lucky that it's not."

Once more there was an uncomfortable silence. Jenny saw the smile die on Michael's face. He was feeling trapped, she thought, and wished suddenly that Megan would go. He needed space. He didn't need to be crowded like this.

She could make him laugh again if Megan left.

The knowledge came to her in a flash—she knew him as well as Megan did. That was crazy! Megan was like family.

But Jenny was his wife.

It was too much to take in.

"I'm off," she said again desperately, and headed for her room—then stopped dead as another knock sounded.

Great!

"Will you excuse me?" Jen asked carefully. "I'm not dressed for visitors."

"You're dressed for Megan," Michael said. "Isn't she a visitor?" And then he looked at Socks, who'd abandoned his pursuit of nosing for errant cornflakes. Socks was standing bolt upright, and the hair on the back of his neck was bristling

The dog growled.

"But he didn't even bark at Mrs. Maitland," Jen said wonderingly, putting a hand down and touching his bristling fur.

"That's Megan to you," Megan said blandly. She had the look of someone who was enjoying herself. "Or Aunt Megan, if you must, and it's a wise dog. Socks knows family."

"But…"

"So if it's not family…" Michael sighed. "Surely it's not official. I've just about had enough of this. Jen, stay where you are." He walked to the front door while Jenny stayed behind, holding Socks by the scruff of his neck. The Gray Suits were back again.

"YOU GUYS don't know when to give up."

Michael stood on the front step and stared at the two men, summing them up. Officials through and through. There was nothing to fear there. Then he looked past them, and there was Gloria—again—standing next to her luxurious rental car. Behind her were the two thugs who'd threatened Jenny with the syringe. Bruno and the other one.

Now what?

Now nothing. The two men on the doorstep were definitely officials. There was no way they could stand by and watch while anything untoward happened—especially since Megan was standing in the kitchen with the door open.

So keep it light.

"Hi, Gloria," Michael called, and waved. "Lovely day. Great day for traveling. You heading to your earldom soon? I don't know how England can be managing without you."

Maybe humor wasn't Gloria's strong point. The woman flushed a deep shade of red, and then her face was shuttered. She was dressed all in black, her hair was drawn into a chignon that stretched every muscle tight in her face, and she looked as if she was about to bust her stays.

Where had that expression come from? Michael wondered irreverently, and only the thought of the thugs beside her kept him from grinning.

"What can I do for you?" he asked, turning to the officials, who were regarding him with caution.

"We're doing a residence check on Jennifer Morrow."

"Jennifer Lord," he reminded them. "My wife." He looked closely at the older of the two men. "Can I see your ID, please?"

He was presented with two ID cards and grimaced. Okay, they were official, which meant he had to be polite. Where did Gloria keep digging them up?

"A residence check?"

"Our information is that Jennifer Morrow—Jennifer Lord—works at Maitland Maternity and she lives with you. The official who came here last night wasn't able to verify that she was here, and she wasn't at work this morning."

Michael sighed. "Nope. She was asleep last night because she was tired. She's given up work now because she's tired. It happens, you know. Tiredness. It goes with advanced pregnancy. Our baby's due in a little over three weeks."

"What does he mean—*our* baby?" The hiss came from the street, and Michael sighed again.

"I told the official last night that this lady wasn't welcome here," he said, motioning to Gloria. "My wife is frightened of her. She's intimidating and she's unpleasant. If this is an official visit, then can we go indoors and leave her outside?"

The older official hesitated. And then he raised his shoulders. "Mr. Lord, this lady—" he indicated Gloria with an expression that told Michael his opinion of the woman was somewhere around the same level of distaste as Michael's "—has been making her presence felt around the department in no uncertain terms. She has people leaning on us all over, and we're not enjoying it one bit. She's swearing to us that your marriage is a sham and that this Jennifer—"

"My wife."

"Yes. Your wife. She says that Jennifer doesn't live here."

"That's ridiculous."

"But it would save us a whole lot of grief if we could

just see her,'' the official said. He gestured to Gloria. "And her mightiness, too.''

"My wife doesn't wish to see her.''

"Hey, Michael!'' There was a holler from the street, and Michael turned to see Lana heading toward him, with baby Greg bundled in a cocoon at her breast.

"What are you doing home? What's wrong?'' she called, anxiety in her voice. "Is there something the matter with Jenny?''

"Jenny's fine.''

"I've got the day off from the store and just came to take her shopping.'' She walked up the street toward them, making a careful assessment of the callers. "Is she busy?''

"She's entertaining guests,'' Michael said, then sighed one last time and stood aside. Why fight what was starting to look like an avalanche? "Jen, we're coming in,'' he called toward the kitchen. "For Pete's sake, hang on to Socks!''

SOCKS WAS NOT amused. The dog allowed Michael in, even giving a perfunctory wag of his tail. He figured instinctively that Lana and the baby were friends. But when he saw the Suits, his hair stood straight up again, and when Gloria and her thugs marched in, his control broke. He snarled and launched himself forward.

Jenny held on for all she was worth, but Socks had strengths she didn't know about. She stumbled against something—probably Lana's foot—and would have fallen except for Michael. He caught her, and then whirled to catch Socks before the mutt went for Gloria's jugular.

And then there was silence.

The silence went on and on, the only sound the low growl of Socks as he strained against Michael's grip. Whatever canine instinct was working here, it was working well. These people wished Jenny ill, and Socks wanted them out of here.

"I agree,'' Michael said at last, as the second of the thugs came in and edged cautiously around the table out of the dog's range. "I don't like them any more than you do, boy, but we have no choice but to talk to them. Now sit."

And to everybody's amazement, Socks sat. He looked resignedly at Michael as if to say, "Okay, I'm sitting. But one word from you and I'll have these guys on toast."

Jenny couldn't see. Her face was against Michael's chest, and she was burning with embarrassment. Michael grimaced, then lightly touched her tousled curls with his lips and turned her to face the assembled company. She made a desperate struggle to stay exactly where she was and then gave up. She stood there, facing Gloria in pajamas…facing the world in pajamas!

They were all looking at her. Megan was watching with kindly approval. Lana was staring with stunned surprise and the beginnings of laughter. The Suits were staring as if she was some sort of peculiar specimen, the thugs were watching with veiled menace, and Gloria was glaring at her with loathing.

And the waist of her pajamas was slipping down!

Before she could do anything, Michael's arms came around her, and one of his hands slipped to the side and her pajama bottoms rose miraculously to their rightful position. She practically sagged with relief. She *did* sag, but Michael's hold tightened, and his mouth once again brushed her hair.

"You're my wife and I'm proud of you," he whispered into her ear, and her blush started all over again. "Remember that." And then he turned to face the company.

"Now."

Michael's gaze took in the assembled company. "Who do we have here? Lana, you're here to take my wife shopping. Very nice. She needs something a little more fashionable in the nightwear line, and I'm counting on you to help out. Aunt Megan, you're here to get to know my gorgeous Jenny. I know you approve."

His gaze moved to the immigration officials. "And you two gentlemen. What are you here for?"

"To satisfy ourselves that this woman is living as your wife," the older Suit said.

"And are you satisfied? I told your colleague last night that my wife was exhausted. She slept late this morning and she can hardly look more domestic than she does now. Or are you saying I telephoned her when I heard your knock, she grabbed a cab and rushed across town and arrived here to greet you?"

"I think we're satisfied now, sir," he said, but the younger man stopped him.

"If I may…"

"What is it, Charles?" his partner asked, and Charles gave a self-conscious grin.

"The old lady says this marriage is a sham and she wants us to prove it. You want proof this lady lives here? Use the dog."

"The dog?"

"It's obviously Lord's dog," Charles said patiently. He addressed himself to Jenny. "Okay. The dog's clearly vicious. Your husband's told it to sit. I want you to grab the mutt from behind and haul it backward away from him." He raised his brows. "There's not many dogs that'll tolerate that—except from an owner. So will you do it? Unless you're afraid, of course. If you're the least bit unsure, then don't even try."

"This is ridiculous," Megan said, startled, but Michael was grinning. He'd seen what Jenny could do with Socks last night. They'd bonded like two soul mates.

"I don't want to," Jenny said with dignity. "It's not fair to Socks to tease him like that."

But Michael propelled her forward.

"Just do it, Jen. Then never again. Let them all see that Socks is yours as much as he is mine." He grinned.

She didn't grin back.

Her humiliation level somewhere above her eyebrows, she stalked around to stand behind Socks. Socks was still sitting, as ordered, gazing at Michael with love. His dopey face was a huge question mark.

"It's just me, Socks," Jenny said, then grabbed his skinny frame around the middle and hauled him backward. "Sorry I have to do this!"

As an attack dog, Socks was definitely a failure. His rump slid easily across the polished tiles, and he gazed around in surprise to see who was doing the hauling. When he realized it was Jenny, he wriggled all over with delight and gave her a long, slurpy lick. Then he went back to glaring at the thugs.

"Sit," Jenny said as she wiped a hand over her damp face. "Sit!" She stared helplessly at Michael. "He might let me do anything to him but he won't sit for me."

"He knows who's boss," Michael said smugly, crossing the room to pat Socks and then hold his wife hard against him again. He turned to the officials. "Satisfied?"

"Perfectly, sir," Charles said, and beamed. He turned to his boss. "This lady knows this dog, sir."

"It's not totally conclusive," the older man said, though clearly it was convincing enough for him. "There's a written interview we'd like you both to complete."

"Not now," Michael said. "My wife's been through enough. I do not want my son born prematurely."

My son... The words were like a bombshell.

There was a hiss from Gloria. "Your *son?*"

"Yes, ma'am, my son," Michael said blandly, meeting her look. "We had him checked out so we knew what color to paint his bedroom. We're hoping he'll have red hair, just like his daddy."

"He's not your son." Gloria almost spat the words. "He's my..."

"Yes?" Michael raised his eyebrows.

"He's my grandson. My heir!" It was practically a wail, and despite himself, Michael softened. There was a touch of desperation there.

"Then I suggest you get yourself on decent terms with

my wife," he said softly. "We have no objections to our son meeting you and getting to know you as he gets older— as long as you realize that we're his parents."

"You're not his parents."

"You're saying my wife is not his mother?"

"I—" Gloria was almost speechless with rage.

"Yes?" He smiled at her, waiting for her to go on, and of course she couldn't.

"You'll regret this," she said, and whirled to leave, but Jenny rushed over to her, placing a hand on her beautifully jacketed arm.

"Gloria..."

The woman whirled to face her, and she looked at Jenny's hand as if it was infectious.

"Get your hand off me."

"But—"

"I have nothing to say to you. Unless you agree to return to England like a sensible woman."

"You know I can't do that." Jenny's voice was laced with unhappiness, and Michael heard it and took an instinctive step forward.

"Then I have nothing more to say to you, girl," the woman snapped, and shook her aside and stalked out of the room.

Her hired men followed.

CHAPTER ELEVEN

THE IMMIGRATION officials left soon after.

"We're real sorry to have bothered you again," the older man told them, while Charles made friends with Socks. "You can't believe the pressure we're dealing with over this one. Our report will recommend an end to the thing, and the pressure should stop. She'll be able to insist on one last interview. In the case of a rushed marriage involving a green card, the usual follow-up is an interview to make sure everything's in order, but now that the claim you're living apart has been disproved, we'll put that off until after the birth."

Michael only had part of his mind on the conversation. He was watching Jenny, who was on the floor, Socks sprawled ecstatically over her knees. Lana was down there, too, with baby Greg gurgling on her lap. But Michael's gaze rested solely on Jenny. She looked extraordinary.

In that moment, emotions stirred in Michael that he'd sworn he'd never feel again. And there were new emotions, too—ones he hadn't even known he was capable of feeling. He knew right then and there that he welcomed them. He was falling in love, he thought, dazed. He was falling in love with his wife, and he was loving every minute of it.

"She really is very beautiful," the older official said, watching Michael's face with good-humored understanding.

"I...yes. I'm sorry."

"There's definitely no need to apologize, sir," the man

said, and beamed. "We see all sorts in this business, and it's a pleasure to see a happy marriage. And I sure don't blame you for looking at her. If I may say so, your wife's not the sort of woman you'd want to take your eyes off for a minute."

"No. I..." He forced his mind back to business. Or some of his mind—the part that wasn't taken up with his stunning new discovery. "The interview?"

"It's just a formality, as I said. A check that you know each other as well as most married couples do." His beam widened. "It's my guess that your knowledge might be deeper than most, so there's nothing at all to worry about. We'll contact you in a few weeks. All the very best for the baby's arrival, and if her ladyship causes trouble, please let us know." He shook Michael's hand. "Charles!"

Charles rose reluctantly from the floor, where he'd been petting Socks.

"YOU KNOW," Jenny said casually as Michael accompanied the immigration officials to the door, "I might just slip into something a touch more respectable." She smiled at Megan. "Entertaining in my revolting old pajamas..."

"Hey, I like your pajamas," Lana told her. "They could start a new fashion in comfortable maternity wear." She grinned, but Megan shook her head. She rose from her chair, gave Jenny a hand up from the floor and propelled her toward her bedroom.

"Let's give the girl back some dignity," she told Lana. "Jenny, now's your chance. You make a break for it, and we'll cover your pajama-clad butt."

TWO MINUTES later Michael walked into the kitchen after seeing the immigration officers off the premises, and found Jenny had gone. His sister and Megan wore identical goofy grins as they watched him enter. Michael stopped at the door and stared at the pair of them.

"What?" he demanded.

"What do you mean, what?" Lana asked innocently, and her eyes danced.

"Why are you looking at me like that?"

"Like what?"

"Like I have a huge joke written across my forehead."

"I don't know what you mean," Lana declared. "Do you, Aunt Megan?"

"Who, me? No, dear. I can't imagine. We've sent your Jenny to get dressed, Michael, dear."

"She's not *my* Jenny."

"Oh, I think she is." Megan reached down to fondle Socks's ears. "Deny it all you like. It'll work about as well as convincing me that Socks isn't your dog."

"That's another thing," Lana said carefully. "Where did Socks come from?" She fixed her bother with bright-eyed interest.

"Jenny found him," he muttered.

"And brought him home. I see."

"If you laugh, you'll live to regret it," he warned.

"Behold me terrified." Lana gave little Greg a hug and held him at arm's length. "Greg, honey, your big, bad uncle Michael just threatened me. Did you hear? Were you frightened? Nope?" She chuckled. "Me, neither."

"Lana..."

"Yes?" She smiled sweetly at him, and he practically ground his teeth in frustration.

"Well," Lana said, apparently satisfied with his response. "I hate to be the one to break up this cozy family get-together, but—"

"You're leaving?" Michael asked hopefully.

"Not alone. I hope to have Jenny with me. When you asked me to find her something to wear for the wedding, I realized she had nothing organized at all."

"I don't think she wants more clothes." Michael frowned. "Except pajamas. I'd agree she could use replacements. But she hardly needs more maternity clothes. The baby's almost due.''

"That's what I mean," Lana said patiently. "Jenny looks like she's due to drop her bundle any minute, and how many diapers do you have on hand, brother dearest?"

"Diapers?"

She sighed, as if she was addressing a bear of very little brain. "Yes, diapers, you dope. If you intend to raise a baby without diapers, we'll see the end of this place as a classy neighborhood. Oh, and on the subject of baby gear...you told Gloria that you were painting the baby's bedroom. Which bedroom exactly? And do you have a crib?"

"Crib?"

She sighed again. "Michael..."

"Okay, okay." He held up his hands in defeat. "I'm not entirely nuts. I know what a crib is." Then, as Jenny appeared in the doorway, demurely dressed in her plain secretarial maternity dress, he turned to her in relief. She'd brushed her curls from her face, and he could almost pretend she was back to being his secretary again—a role he could cope with emotionally. "Jen, do you have diapers? Do you have a crib?"

"Not yet." She blinked and stared at the faces watching her. These people were practically too much to take in all at once. Her assorted family.

One husband. One sister-in-law with baby attached. One sort of aunt-in-law. One dumb but gorgeous dog.

She'd gone from rags to riches in the family stakes in one fell swoop, she thought suddenly, and it felt...stunning. There was affection on all their faces, and she felt tears sting her eyes.

But they were waiting for her answer.

"So when are you planning to get them?" Lana asked patiently.

"Sometime soon."

"And this baby?" Lana probed. "He intends arriving sometime soon?"

"In three weeks."

"He has a diary in there with his planned arrival time written in indelible ink?"

"First babies are never early," Jenny said stoutly, and Lana chortled as Michael watched silently from the sidelines. He was doing his own thinking.

"Ha!" Lana scoffed. "I had a lady in my shop on Friday buying a romper suit for her baby, who was due tomorrow. He's now seven weeks old."

"I..."

"Jenny, you need to be organized, and I'm just the person to help you do it," Lana said. "Organization is my specialty. Just ask Dylan. I organized him right into marriage. And Mike. I've been organizing him since he was three years old. So while I'm on a roll, I thought I'd take you back to my shop right now." She smiled at Jenny's bewildered look. "You know I own Oh, Baby!"

"Oh!" Jenny gasped. How many times had she slowed as she'd passed the baby shop, looking longingly in the window at all the delightful things for sale? "Of course. I've been past there. It's lovely. But I can't afford—"

She closed her eyes. Things were getting out of control. How could she tell them she intended to buy discount store clothes, and a crib and stroller secondhand?

"That's irrelevant. I'm paying," Michael announced, and her eyes opened again.

"No."

"Yes!"

"Michael, no," she said, distressed. "I can't—"

"You can," Megan said. She'd been watching Jenny's face, saying nothing, but her intelligent mind had been assessing and coming to conclusions. She moved to take Jenny's faltering hands in hers. "But you needn't accept Michael's help in this area, my dear, because this is what

I'm going to do. You're going to accept your baby needs as a combined gift from me and the staff at Maitland. This is our gift to you.''

Jenny took a step back, but Megan's hands held fast. ''Mrs. Maitland, I can't!''

''You left work on Thursday without being given your farewell gifts,'' Megan said sternly. ''The staff had taken a collection for a baby shower. Ellie's given me a check to add to it. She's grateful for the change you brought to our security offices over the last five months and—'' she gave Michael a sideways smile ''—she's grateful for the changes you brought about in our security chief. I'm equally grateful. Lana will dictate what you need, and—''

''Mrs. Maitland—''

''It's Aunt Megan to you while you're married to Michael,'' she corrected sternly. ''Jennifer, I assume you'd like your job back at Maitland Maternity one day?''

''I... Yes.''

''Then learn to accept gifts gracefully. I never got a chance to give the pair of you a wedding gift—''

''We're not—''

''Married? Don't talk nonsense. You're more married than you think. So take this with my blessings. And, Michael?''

''Yes, ma'am?'' Michael was just plain bemused.

''You were intending to go back to work after lunch?''

''Of course.''

''There's no of course about it,'' she said sternly. ''You're not welcome at work. You haven't had a break for two years. I'm ordering you to take time off, starting today, and help Jenny get herself organized.''

''But—''

''You don't think Jenny needs help?''

''I don't,'' Jenny interrupted, but Megan shook her head. ''There speaks a woman who doesn't own so much as a diaper for a son who's due to appear any minute. Lana, can you take this hopeless pair shopping?''

"I'd love to." Lana was practically choking with laughter. "Dylan's meeting me for lunch. Maybe we could all go out together. Make a day of it. I'll bet we could even persuade Jenny to buy some new pajamas."

"What's wrong with my pajamas?" Jenny protested, and they all laughed. Suddenly Jenny was laughing with them. This was so easy. And the way Michael was looking at her...

She gazed at him, and her breath caught in her throat. There was affection there, and more....

"Maybe you could do with some pajamas with a proper cord," Megan was saying as Jenny's eyes met Michael's and held. They hardly heard her. "But diapers first."

There was nothing more to say.

"Yes, ma'am," said Michael, his eyes still on Jenny's, and it was all he could do to get the words out. "Whatever you say, Aunt Megan."

WHAT FOLLOWED was an amazing few hours. Lana collected Dylan because she figured Michael might need some male support, but to Jenny's astonishment, the men took over.

"Surely we don't need all this stuff," she said helplessly as a miniature baseball league sweater landed on top of a pile of baby gear a mile high.

"You were maybe considering teaching your son cricket?" Michael teased. "You have a green card now, Mrs. Lord. This baby grows up playing American sports."

"Then we need a baseball bat," Dylan said decisively, and swooped off to the other side of the store to find one. "Like Greg has."

"No!"

Michael lifted the bat Dylan found and inspected it with

approval, ignoring Jenny's protest. "This is more like it. Do you have a ball, Lana? Let's try this out for size."

While Jenny watched helplessly, and Lana made piles of diapers and undershirts and sleepers, Dylan and Michael set up an impromptu baseball game in the crowded store. Luckily it was a foam ball. Customers came and went, eyeing the pair with amusement, but Dylan and Michael carried right on.

"It's good advertising, Lana," Michael told his sister. "Bet you sell a ton of these today." And she did. By the time hunger hit, Lana didn't have a miniature bat left in stock.

Then, with the guys still in charge, they carried the sleeping Greg to the car and ended up in Shelby's diner for lunch—where the baseball game started up again. A few stunned residents and nurses from the clinic were promptly organized into teams, and the foam ball flew from booth to booth.

"You're all nuts," Shelby told them. "Get out of here."

Michael gave his sister a hug and turned to watch his wife take the bat. "Sorry, Shelby. We seem to have turned this place on its ear."

"Jenny seems to have turned you on your ear," Shelby said softly, and hugged him back. "I was wrong to be worried. She's special, Mike."

"She... It's only for a bit."

"It can be for as long as you like, as far as I'm concerned," she told him gently. "If she makes my brother look like this."

After lunch, Lana and Dylan headed back to Lana's store with Greg, and Shelby disappeared into the kitchen. Michael and Jen were left with the afternoon in front of them.

"It's only three," Michael said. He frowned. He wasn't used to spare time.

"Socks will need a walk. You must have things to do. If you drop me off at home, then I'll take him."

"Take him by yourself? You should put your feet up."

"I don't want to." Jenny flashed him a shy smile. "To be honest, I've had so much fun, I don't want it to end."

And neither did he.

So they drove home, unpacked their packages, held up each item for Socks's approval—the only thing Socks was interested in was the foam ball—and then rigged up a leash and took their dog to the river.

It was another gorgeous autumn afternoon. Socks greeted it with joy, but Jenny found the warm sun made her sleepy. She was tired. Michael had found an ordinary tennis ball and was throwing it for Socks, and after the tenth throw she sank onto a park bench and watched her husband and her dog wear themselves out.

She felt at peace with the world. Gloria was gone, and she was safe now. Whatever she had to face in the future, Michael would be there with her.

She was where she wanted to be.

And she slept.

"THAT'S IT, you stupid mutt. That's one hundred and twenty-three runs—more than enough for any self-respecting dog. Home!" Michael caught Socks to him, attached the leash to his collar and turned—to find his wife soundly asleep on the park bench.

Jenny.

He stood for a long moment looking at her. She was still wearing that awful secretarial smock, and although this morning he'd found it reassuring, fitting her into the role he knew, suddenly he hated it. She was quite extraordinarily beautiful, and he no longer wanted to think of her as his secretary.

The warm breeze was wisping the curls from her face, and her skin was still pale. She was wearing no makeup. Her lips were soft and full, and her lashes were long and luxurious.

Socks, head on one side, looked questioningly at his mistress. He put one dusty paw onto Jenny's knee, but she didn't stir, and suddenly it was too much for Michael. It would be too much for any man, he thought, and this was his wife. The woman he wanted more than anything in the world.

As if compelled, he bent and kissed her full on the lips, kissed her with a tenderness he didn't know he possessed.

His Jenny. His wife.

As his mouth found hers, Jenny's eyelids slowly opened, and she saw his face before her. Like part of herself.

And somehow, still half asleep, she wasn't surprised. This was an extension of a lovely dream. She'd expected that Michael's mouth would be on hers, and she'd known that this feeling would be so immeasurably sweet she couldn't bear it. She couldn't resist.

"Michael," she murmured, and her hands rose just a fraction. She didn't pull away, but she stirred, and her eyes smiled into his.

It was enough. He needed no other urging. His Jenny.

With a joyous groan he knelt and gathered her to him, and then he kissed her properly, as a man should kiss his wife. He kissed her with a fierceness born of passion. Born of need.

His lips were against hers, and her mouth was softly opening, welcoming, wanting him with an urgency that matched his. Dear heaven, she was so sweet. So lovely. She was so incredibly desirable that it was as much as he could do to breathe. His hands felt the roundness of her belly, and her breasts yielded to his chest, soft, compliant.

Jenny.

And still the kiss held. Her hands were on his face, holding him, deepening the kiss with a possessiveness that told him her hunger and her need were as great as his. The kiss went on and on, while they sat motionless under the cloudless sky.

But at last it came to an end. Two small boys came tearing along the path and skidded to a halt at the sight of them—and then burst into teasing laughter.

"Aw, mushy..."

"Kissy, kissy!"

One of the boys pursed his lips and made a kissing sound. Jenny and Michael broke apart in laughing confusion, while Socks barked his disapproval of this intrusion.

"Clear out of here," Michael ordered the boys, but there was laughter in his eyes. His heart had no room for anger right now. His arms were firmly around Jenny's waist, and there was no way he was letting go. "Can't a man kiss his wife?"

"Kissing makes babies," one small scamp offered, and the other boy hooted with scorn.

"Stupid, they've already made a baby. She's as pregnant as my mom was when she had Sarah. I'll bet she's about to bust at any minute."

"Then what do they want to kiss for?"

Sarah's older brother was unable to find an answer for such a tricky biological question. "Yuck! How would I know?" He giggled, threw Jenny and Michael a scornful glance and raced away with his buddy.

What do they want to kiss for?

Their words lingered, funny, yet profound. What *did* they want to kiss for? Jenny looked deep into Michael's eyes and she knew exactly why.

Peter! No!

The stab of memory caught her by surprise. Why *was* she doing this? What promises was she breaking now? She took a deep breath and pushed away. "Michael, I don't want..."

"Me to kiss you?" He smiled at the distress in her face. "Honest? I very much want to kiss you."

"I can't."

"Jen..." He rose from his kneeling position and sat on

the bench beside her, taking her hands between his. All of a sudden her fingers felt cold, and he frowned. "It's too soon, isn't it? Because of Peter."

"I..." She shook her head. How to make him see the impossible? "He's only been dead seven months," she said miserably.

"I understand."

"No." She pulled her hands away, pushed her curls out of her eyes and stared bleakly at the river. "I don't think you do."

"So tell me," he said softly. Her eyes flew to his.

"You don't—you can't—this has nothing to do with you. I thought you never intended to get near anyone again."

"I'm doing it for the dog," he said promptly, and his answer was so pat she frowned in confusion.

"The dog?"

Lightness was needed here. He was thinking fast. Anything to take the panic from her eyes.

"Every orphan needs two parents," he explained soulfully. "I ought to know that. Your baby needs two parents, so I offered, thinking we could get into the domesticity bit later. But now we have Socks, and the need is urgent. We need to indulge in domesticity right now, or Socks risks a deeply disturbed adolescence."

"And domesticity means kissing?"

"Definitely!"

"You know, Socks might not be the most stable adolescent to work on," Jenny said cautiously, trying for laughter, and Michael shook his head in disbelief and clapped a hand over her mouth.

"Shh. You'll give the dog a complex. Let's just go back to playing doting parents. Do what doting parents do." He smiled at her—that heart-stopping smile that had her insides doing back flips—and tried to draw her into his arms. But she somehow managed to pull away.

"No."

"Then tell me why." His smile died again. Okay. Maybe humor wasn't such a good idea. Maybe honesty was the best bet. "There's all sorts of electricity between us, Jenny, and I don't understand it one bit. It's caught me by surprise, but my instinct here is to go with it. To see where it leads."

"To see if we can fall in love, you mean?" she asked cautiously, and he nodded.

"I guess that's what I do mean." He caught his breath, overwhelmed by what he was about to say. "Maybe... maybe it's already happened."

"You're saying you love me?" Her eyes widened in incredulity. "After four days?"

"Hey, I've known you for over five months. Every weekday for five months."

Her jaw dropped. "Yeah, right. And you spent all that time treating me like I was part of the furniture."

"I didn't."

"Every morning I had the same thing for morning break," she said with asperity. "What was it?"

"Huh?"

"Ha! I told you you didn't notice!"

"How would I know if you had tea or coffee. Does it matter?"

"I had chocolate milk," she said with dignity. "Straight out of the carton."

"Jen..."

"No." Despite her attempt at lightness, the distress was still in her voice. "No way. It's true you've only just noticed me. There's no way I'm letting you commit here, Michael Lord."

Let him commit? *Let him commit?*

"Hell, woman, I want to commit," he roared. "Damn it, I've spent most of my life running scared of commitment. Now I've decided I want to go the whole nine yards, and you say you don't? But I can feel you do!" He made a grab for her again, but she drew back and rose from the bench.

"No!" This time there was no laughter at all. There was fear.

He saw it, and his indignation died at once. He didn't follow, just stayed sitting, watching her.

"Tell me, Jen," he said softly. "What's bothering you? What are you fearful of? Me?"

"No." She hesitated. Maybe he had to know. She had to explain it to herself.

"Peter married me fast," she said.

"How fast?" He didn't make a move. He had the impression that if he did, she would retreat into silence. "Sit, Jen. And tell me."

There was a long, drawn-out silence, and then, slowly, she sat and started speaking. And when she did, her voice sounded as if it came from a long way away.

"We met one fabulous weekend at the home of mutual friends," she said. "Or rather, they weren't really mutual friends. Henry and Kate were friends of mine, and Peter knew Henry from university. Henry had gone home to Peter's for the weekend while they were undergraduates, and Gloria had pink fits because Henry's mother worked as a char, and Henry was a scholarship student."

"Gloria disapproves of the unmoneyed?"

"Absolutely. So Henry became a bone of contention between them. Whenever Peter wanted to infuriate his mother, he'd extend his friendship with Henry. When Peter had a fight with his mother, he took off to visit Henry. He even told her that. He was off to stay with his *unsuitable* friends."

"Oh, great."

"Of course, I never knew that till later," Jenny said, her voice bleak. "All I knew was that Henry's friend was drop-dead gorgeous, and he swept me off my naive nineteen-year-old feet. We were married before I could blink—be-

fore I found out that he was marrying me so he could marry
a totally *unsuitable woman* to get at his mother.''

"He must have been nuts.''

"He was very mixed up,'' Jen said sadly. "I'm not saying he wasn't attracted to me. Like me and you, there was
this…thing.''

"Like me and you?'' He paused, hating the comparison.
"So it's the same?''

"I don't know.'' She flushed and looked at him. "No.
It's not. At least I don't think so. With you I feel—'' She
broke off as he moved fractionally toward her, and her
hands came out as if to fend him off. "No. I don't know
what I feel. But I do know that I'm rushing into no commitment here. You married me as a kindness, and there's
no way I'm taking it further. I've had one man already who
was stuck with me.''

"Is that what Peter was?''

"Oh, yes. Honorably stuck, but stuck all the same,'' she
said bitterly. "He was a mix…half his father, whom I
gather he admired because he had such a stiff upper lip and
was all honor—he died some time ago—and half his
mother, whom you've seen. And a bit of rebellion, which
made him seem vulnerable. He just didn't know where he
fitted in. But he made me promise…'' Her voice died away.

"He made you promise what?''

Her chin tilted, trying to make him see. Trying to make
him understand a little.

"He regretted it, you see,'' she said, faltering as she
fought for the right words. "He tried to break free of his
aristocratic bonds, and it didn't work. So when he was dying, he made me promise to raise our child as he ought to
be raised—as the next earl.''

Michael's brows creased. "And you made that promise?''

"Peter was dying,'' she said miserably. "And I still
loved him—sort of. I'd grown, but he hadn't. By the time

he died it was more a maternal sort of love. I knew why he hurt me—why he acted like he did—but there was nothing he could do to change it. He was desperately injured. I was grief-stricken, in the early stages of pregnancy, alone in a strange country, and I was in shock. I'd have promised him anything if it would ease his distress.''

''But you didn't mean it?''

''At the time, I did,'' she told him bleakly. ''I guess I thought I could do what he wanted—go home to England, live on the estate and become the next earl's mother. There didn't seem any choice. It was only after Peter's death, when Gloria started laying down the rules, that I saw clearly what was involved. Or rather, that I wouldn't be involved at all. I'd be welcome to have access visits as long as I didn't take my son off the estate. I'd have a generous allowance as long as I gave my son none of my commoner ideals.''

''The woman's an autocratic dragon! There's no way you can do things her way.''

''Yeah, but I promised.''

''Jen, it's unreasonable.''

''I know that.'' A hint of defiance returned. ''That's why I'm still here. But it doesn't make it one bit better. It's like I can't bury Peter in my mind. He's hanging over me, like a sad ghost, reminding me that I've betrayed his last wish. And I can't get on with anything.''

''You mean you can't love me?''

She met his eyes. ''Michael, I do love you,'' she said softly. ''You are the kindest, most generous person that I know. But I still feel that I'm married. As if part of me is still tied to Peter and will be forever, and in some stupid way it's tied to that broken promise. Thank you for trying, Michael, but for now...let's just leave it as it is. I need to come to terms with what I've done in my own way. For me, marriage—a proper marriage, with hearts involved, not

the one we've made to keep me in the States—seems like
one last betrayal.''

"When you kissed me then, it was because you
wanted..."

"Because I wanted you," she whispered, the faintest
tremor behind her words betraying her turmoil. "But then,
I've always wanted what I can't have. Love.''

"Let me love you." His voice was urgent—insistent—
but she moved away.

"No. You mustn't. Because betraying Peter again would
drive me to the wall.''

CHAPTER TWELVE

How could you fight a ghost?

There was no hope, and by the end of the following week, Michael decided he was going nuts.

This was some crazy situation, he thought grimly. All his life he'd run from emotional attachment, and now, here he was practically wearing his heart on his sleeve, and Jenny was holding him at arm's length and flinching every time he laid a finger on her.

She was afraid. Afraid of him! Not of what he'd do to her. He knew her well enough to believe she trusted him. She was afraid of what she might feel if she let him close. So he'd walk into the room and she'd hug the dog or curl up on the end of the sofa with Socks between her and the world. Or she'd be out walking when he came home from some errand and she'd read a book after supper—or smile and talk him through his day, keeping the conversation casual, as if she were his best buddy instead of his wife!

And all the time there was this tiny glimmer of fear in the back of her eyes that drove him nuts. He wanted to take her in his arms and kiss the fear away, tell her it was okay, he'd never hurt her and he'd never make her feel she was tying him down.

Damn, why had he ever told her he didn't want emotional commitment? But he had, and that—along with Peter's ghost—was enough to make her run scared.

"So what's up, bro?" Garrett caught up with him the day he came back to work. He only had to look at his little brother's face to know something was wrong. Michael looked strained to breaking point. "I thought you just had a week off."

"I did."

"You look like you've run a marathon."

"Yeah, well, you try sleeping in the same house as Jenny," Michael growled, and Garrett's eyes widened.

"Hey, she's some lady. I wouldn't think you'd mind sleeping in the same *bed* as Jenny."

"That's just it." Michael slammed his fist on his desk with such force that his new secretary gave a startled glance his way. "I wouldn't mind sleeping in the same bed as Jenny."

"Uh-oh." Garrett grinned and rose lazily to close the door on the flapping ears outside. "I see. So sleeping in a different room is the problem. The lady's almost nine months pregnant with another man's child," he said gently. "You need to give her space."

"I love her, Garrett," Michael said, and put his head in his hands and groaned.

Silence.

"You love her," Garrett said at last, in a voice that sounded strange. Obviously he was having trouble taking this in.

"Yeah."

"Well, that's great."

"Not when she doesn't want me."

"Heck, Mike, give her a chance. She must have so many mixed-up hormones pounding around right now. Dead husband, pregnancy, marriage…"

"You recommend patience?"

"Hey, I don't know," Garrett said, exasperated. "You're asking me about women? Short of Lana and Shelby, I know nothing. They're a breed apart. Ask Lana."

"Ask her what?"

"What to do," Garrett said unhelpfully. "Meanwhile,

think of all the hearts you've broken in your time. It won't hurt you to get a taste of your own medicine.''

"Gee, thanks.''

"Don't mention it,'' Garrett said expansively. "Now, why I came to see you…'' He hauled a list out of his pocket and tossed it onto Michael's desk. "Here's a security check for you.''

"What's this?'' Michael picked the paper up and stared listlessly at the row of names.

"Possible parents. Shelby and I are working on it already, but we'd like you to give us a hand.''

He froze. "What the heck… I told you, I don't want to know.''

"The girls do,'' Garrett said. "Lana's changed her mind since she married Dylan. Somewhere out there is our birth mother, Mike, and there's a gut feeling among me and the girls that she's hurting. We need to find her.''

"I don't.''

"Mike, you've held yourself in that icy cocoon for too many years,'' Garrett said gently. "Jenny's chipped away at the ice, and there's warmth under there. While you're waiting for her to come around, use the warmth for someone other than yourself. Maybe Jenny can teach you how.''

"Jenny!''

"Yeah, Jenny,'' Garrett said firmly. "If Jenny hadn't found you—if she'd ended up destitute—maybe she would have given up her baby rather than see it starve. And if she did, would the hurt of losing her child have disappeared after all this time? I don't think so, Mike, and neither do you.''

"Garrett, I…''

"Just look at the list,'' Garrett said firmly. "Talk to Jenny about it. See what she thinks.''

"It's none of her business.''

"If you want her to love you, you have to learn to share.'' He hesitated. There was real pain on Michael's face, and Garrett didn't want to push it, but if the ice was cracking, he wouldn't be the one to withhold the sledge-hammer. "On Saturday night there's a party at Megan's to welcome Camille and Jake home from their honeymoon. It promises to be a real shindig. Fireworks, everything. Now her family's all settled, Megan's feeling like she's on top of the world, and she's showing it every way she can."

"I'm not coming to any family party. You know I won't."

"Megan'll be disappointed if you're not there, little brother," Garrett said, and hauled his lanky frame out of the chair. "And if we're talking of hurting people, there's one lady you'll leave untouched. Hurt Megan and I'll dust you down before breakfast. Or give it my best shot." He shrugged and pushed the list across the desk again from where Michael had thrust it back at him. "Do what you can with that by Saturday. And bring Jenny to supper at my place first."

"Hell, Garrett, I—"

"Treat her like family, Mike," Garrett said kindly. "Maybe the lady'll get used to it. Maybe she'll even like it."

JENNY *WAS* FEELING part of the family, and she did like it. Every day the feeling grew a little bit stronger.

Lana came around and sorted baby clothes with her. She helped Jenny make up the crib, talked baby talk, and taught her how to change and bathe little Greg.

Shelby turned up with offerings of food. "I know that brother of mine can't do more than open a can of beans," she explained, "and you shouldn't be doing any more than cooking toast in your condition."

Garrett kept dropping in—"Just to see how my favorite sister-in-law is doing"—making her feel warm all over. And Megan came, too, just to check. One by one, all the Maitlands, curious at first and then warm and friendly, arrived at her front door and embraced her into their fold.

It was all making her feel so guilty she couldn't bear it.

Every night Michael came home and looked at her with those hungry eyes, and she wanted to drop everything and run into his arms and let him hold her forever and forever.

But she mustn't. Because one day Michael would wake up like Peter had woken up, and he'd be trapped. And like Peter, he'd be too honorable and proud to walk away.

I promise…

How easy it had been to say those words. She held her arms over her pregnancy and hugged her unborn child as she thought things through. She couldn't keep her promise. Even for Peter, she wouldn't hand her baby over. But at what cost to herself?

Oh, Peter…

"YOU WANT TO GO to a party?"

Saturday afternoon. Michael finished writing and looked over to where Jen was brushing Socks. Damn, every time he was in the room she was doing *something*. It was almost a defense.

She looked up, her eyes a question.

"There's a party at Megan's tonight," he told her. "To welcome Camille and Jake home. Supper at Garrett's first."

"How about you go without me?" she asked, turning her attention to a nonexistent knot in Socks's fur. "It's family."

"Yeah, it's family, so everyone expects you."

"I'm hardly family."

"If you can't go because you're feeling too pregnant, then they'll expect me to stay home with you." Hell, they sounded so absurdly formal. It was as if they were strangers.

"Michael…"

"Come with me, Jen," he said urgently. He hesitated, then passed her the sheet of paper he'd been writing on. "We're discussing this. Please. I need your support on this one."

She sat back and read the list, then stared at him.
"Names and addresses. I don't understand."

"They're all the triplets born in this state in the same
year we were born," he told her. "Garrett gave it to me
this week. He's trying to find our birth mother. So far, I've
tried to locate every person who had anything to do with
the triplets on this list. I've been finding their current names
and addresses and whether any of them could possibly be
us. I'm whittling the list down."

She stared at him, then at the list. "You did this?"

"Yeah." He colored. "Like I said, Garrett asked me to."

"But you said you wanted nothing to do with finding your
birth mother. Why now?" She grabbed a chair leg and
hauled herself up from where she'd been kneeling on the
floor. Michael made an involuntary move to help her, then
pulled back. He knew by now what her reaction would be.

"Why?" she asked him again, her eyes not moving from
his face. She knew this was important.

And it was.

"I've been watching you, Jen," he said softly. "I've
been seeing your pain at what's happening. Even before
your baby's born, you're being torn apart by what's best
for him. And maybe I'm seeing..." His voice died away
as he looked at her.

"That what was best for you might have torn your own
mother apart," Jen said gently. "Oh, Michael."

"Yeah, well, I haven't found anyone yet," he said
gruffly. "But maybe I'm giving her the benefit of the doubt
by trying."

She looked at the list. "But..."

"Yeah, but! There's maybes all over the place," he told
her. "Come to Garrett's with me, and we'll talk about it."

How could she refuse an invitation like that?

THEY STOPPED downtown first.

"If you're coming to the party with me, you deserve to
wear something decent," Michael told her.

"Then stop at the camping store," Jenny said, half serious. "A tent's all I'll fit into. Three-man, at least."

"No camping store. Lana told me where to go." He closed his ears to her protests, pulled to a halt in front of an upscale maternity store and then proceeded to take charge, just as he had with the baby clothes. While Jenny muttered protestations about interfering males, he delved through one rack after another and finally found what he wanted.

"This," he said firmly, and she stared.

It was gorgeous—a soft, gold silk maternity dress with a scooped neckline and no sleeves. It was gathered under the breast with white and gold ribbon, then fell away to just below the knee in yards and yards of gorgeous, silken folds.

It would look fabulous on a nonpregnant woman. On Jenny's bulk, she wasn't so sure. But the sales assistant and Michael propelled her into the fitting room and refused to let her out until she'd tried it on. To her surprise, the dress swirled around her in soft folds like a wondrous golden cloud. She looked maternal and serene and very, very lovely.

"You'll be able to wear it after the baby's come," the saleslady assured her, staring into the mirror at Jenny's reflection. "Oh, it's just beautiful, and it'll be perfect even after you get your waistline back."

"I'm never getting my waistline back—I left it in England," Jenny said darkly. "Michael, this is ridiculous. What a waste."

"It's not a waste, Jenny," he told her, turning her by her shoulders to face the mirror again. "Look at yourself and tell me just how ridiculous you are."

"Michael…"

"Just look."

So she did, and what she saw made her stare. Sure, this was a maternity dress, but it was made for someone young

and beautiful. It seemed to light her up from inside. It made
her hair gloss around her face and deepened the blush on
her cheeks. It made her feel...

It made her feel nineteen again. Young, beautiful, desirable. All the things that Peter had knocked out of her with
his disparaging comments and his suggestions that she was
inferior to the women who moved in his social circles.

Her lips twitched involuntarily into the beginnings of
delight, and Michael saw and smiled his satisfaction.

"You like it. That makes the pair of us. We'll buy it."

"Michael, it's way too expensive." But her protest was
feeble.

"All the better to waste my money on. Come on, Cinderella. Let's head for the ball before your pumpkin escapes
from under there!"

"It's a funny thing." The saleslady laughed as she took
Michael's money. "Nearly every time I sell a maternity
dress this close to term, the woman comes back later—and
thinner—and says the baby arrived almost right away. It's
like a lucky charm. I wonder if it'll happen this time?"

"It had better not," Jenny said, startled, and she glared
at her bulge. "You hear that, pumpkin? You stay right
there."

"Come on, then, Cinderella," Michael said, and grabbed
her hand. "Let's go. Midnight's coming up fast."

IT WASN'T quite a ball, but it might as well have been for
the enjoyment she had. Supper at Garrett's was fun. The
whole family made her feel welcome, and although Jenny
felt more and more like she was being drawn in out of her
depth, there was no way she could not enjoy herself. They
were so happy—Lana and her Dylan, big, kindly Garrett
and possessive Shelby, who'd checked Jenny out from
every angle and decided she'd share this precious brother
of hers.

The mood was lighthearted, but there was also the hint

of suspense—a suspense that ended when Garrett said over coffee, "Okay, Michael. What have you got for us?"

Michael hauled out his list and showed it to his three astounded siblings.

"Michael," Shelby breathed, staring at the names on Michael's list. "You agreed to help?" She gazed at him in total astonishment. "Why?"

"Something Garrett said," Michael replied baldly, and Garrett nodded. He smiled at Jenny.

"So it's thanks to you, Jenny," Shelby said.

"I had nothing to do with it," Jenny retorted, flushing under their gazes. "What Michael decides has nothing to do with me."

But it did, and they all knew it. The three siblings took in her flushed appearance and Michael's scowl, and they all came to the same conclusion.

"You might as well look at the list I've made," Michael said finally, breaking the silence, "instead of sitting there and looking so smug."

"They all check out," Lana said, after sifting through the list of names. "I mean, you've traced them all except for these."

Michael had worked on every set of triplets and tried to research the parents' names, as well. He'd also attempted to find an adult contact from each set.

The one family he'd reached so far had splintered. The mother had gone one way with the girls, the father had gone another with the boy. Michael had managed to locate the son—in prison.

"Ugh, I'm glad that's not you, Mike," Shelby breathed. "A mugger. Just what every family needs."

"I may be driven to it yet," Michael said. "Lord knows I've come close enough with you guys for siblings. Or even murder. Justifiable homicide if ever I saw it."

He was hit with a cushion for his pains, but Shelby only had half a mind on what she was doing. Her attention was on the list again.

"What about this last one?"

"None of these might fit," Michael warned. "We could have been brought here from out of state or over the border."

"There's not a lot of Mexicans with our coloring," Shelby retorted. "There's Irish blood in us somewhere. But you're right. Another state's a possibility. Still, our mother had to have known Megan's reputation to have left us where she did, so chances are she was local."

"LeeAnn and Gary Larrimore," Lana read. Michael had duplicates of the list, and she was leaning against Dylan's shoulder as she read. "Two girls, one boy. Triplets born April twenty-sixth."

"The date makes it about right."

"And you can't find any trace of the adults?"

"No." Michael frowned. "Now the out-of-state thing comes in. If it is them, if they're us, then the family must have moved here close to the birth."

"Why?"

"Because there's no trace of a Garrett Larrimore registered as born in Texas in the two years before the triplets were born. I assume our mother wouldn't have registered our births—which explains why there's no trace of us—but Garrett's got to be somewhere. So maybe this LeeAnn and Gary had their triplets here and then took their babies home again. To California. To Canada. To anywhere. The hospital records are useless for that sort of information. I'm doing a national search, but it's not in yet. The only thing is…"

"Yes?" He had the attention of everyone in the room.

"After I found the records of the triplet birth, I did a search for births and deaths of Larrimores for the surrounding few years, looking for Garrett, mostly, but checking anything that came up."

"And?"

"And a Gary Larrimore, aged twenty-eight, was killed two months before this lot of triplets were born."

Silence.

The Lord children were deathly still, and Dylan and Jen sat on the sidelines and watched them absorb this momentous news. Even baby Greg was quiet.

"You mean..." Lana was the first to gather herself. She lifted Michael's piece of paper and read, as if she could see something that wasn't written there. "Our birth father...died?"

"It may not be us. This is all supposition."

"But that would explain it," Lana breathed, horrified. "Oh, that poor woman. To have a little boy two years old and to be told you were expecting triplets! And then to have the man you love be killed. Do we know what happened?"

"I found the local coroner's report," Michael said. "He was thrown off his motorcycle. The coroner said it was raining and his tires were bald."

"So he was poor!"

"We're assuming all sorts of things here," Garrett said hastily. "We're jumping to conclusions." But then he paused and frowned, as if remembering things almost against his will. "You know, that's one thing I remember. There's hardly anything, but occasionally—it's like a shadow, but it's there. A motorcycle."

"You remember a bike?" Mike demanded.

Garrett shook his head. "I think I do. As I said, it's a shadow of a memory, but there was never a motorcycle after we were adopted. I guess... It probably means nothing."

"But it might mean something. And there's no trace of LeeAnn Larrimore after she left the clinic," Michael told them. "She seems to have vanished without trace."

"So we find her." Shelby's eyes filled with tears. "Right?"

Michael put up his hand in warning. "Shelby, we have to eliminate the other names on the list. We can't just focus on one. We still have contacts to make in four sets, including the Larrimores.''

"You know I'll help you, Michael," Shelby said. "I'm due for a vacation and I'd be happy to do some out-of-town legwork.''

Michael nodded. "Just give me a little more time to get as many specifics as I can. But it may take a while, so you'll all have to be patient.''

"But you'll keep trying?" Shelby asked.

Michael's gaze moved to Jenny, and his eyes fell to the gentle swell beneath her gorgeous dress. His mother—whoever she was—had once been like this. So pregnant, and not pregnant with just one babe. Pregnant with three, and with another tiny child dependent on her.

He had no choice.

"Yes. Of course I will.''

"Oh, Michael, you're wonderful," Shelby said, immeasurably moved. "He's wonderful, isn't he, everybody? Isn't he, Jenny?''

"I guess he is," Jenny said in a voice that was none too steady. "Just wonderful.''

AND THEN, individually or in pairs, they made their way to Megan's party. The night was unusually sultry. A storm was coming, Jenny thought as they drove across town. She hoped it would hold off for the evening. She was tired, aching to go home to bed if the truth be known, and her back hurt, but she wouldn't keep Michael from his party.

"You okay?" Michael asked as they arrived, worry in his voice, but she smiled her reassurance.

"Come on, Michael Lord. No chickening out now. Your family tells me you're not the best at socializing. So let's see you do your worst!''

THE PARTY was in full swing when they arrived. There seemed to be couples everywhere, spilling onto the lawns and dancing inside to the tune of a piano player tinkling in the drawing room. The place looked wonderful, lit up like Christmas.

"Megan's daughter Anna will have done this. She's a wedding planner, and parties are her specialty," Michael told Jenny, taking her hand and leading her into the throng. "Megan's family seems to have spent the last twelve months matchmaking. Megan's been through some pretty traumatic times, but now she's feeling like partying. Anyone you haven't met yet you'll be meeting tonight."

"Michael, this isn't... I mean, you don't need to introduce me as if it's forever."

"Treat it as fun," he told her. "Nothing more. Megan's told them what's happening. They all know what's between us is not a real marriage."

Did they? That wasn't the way they greeted her. Jenny was met with warmth and welcome, and she grew quieter and quieter as the evening proceeded. And more worried. So many things were being assumed, even by Michael.

"You're tired," Michael said in concern at about eleven, and she nodded. Her back was hurting, with low stabbing pains, but Michael was more animated than she'd ever seen him. This was obviously an important night for Megan, to have all her family here, and Michael was having fun, too. She wouldn't spoil it.

"I can sleep tomorrow," she said.

"We can go home if you want."

"Soon. Not yet."

"It's raining cats and dogs outside now," Garrett said, coming up to them with Megan on his arm. "I'd wait until it eases before going anywhere. There'll be roads flooded all over. Jenny, can I have this dance?"

"Who me, dance?" She managed a smile. "I need a partner with a pit instead of a stomach, to fit my big bump."

"I'll be your pit," Michael said, elbowing Garrett out of

the way. He smiled into her tired eyes. "One slow dance and then we'll go home. One dance—just for us."

"Michael…" Garrett made to object, but Michael shook his head.

"Sorry, Garrett," Michael drawled, and drew his wife into his arms. "The lady's taken."

"HE LOVES HER," Megan said in satisfaction as Michael led Jenny out to the dance floor. "Finally. After all these years he's fallen for a woman who has a heart."

"I just hope to hell she can learn to love him, too," Garrett said slowly, watching his brother take Jenny and lead into the first few steps. "She's had bad times in the past. There's a sadness in her eyes."

"Yes." Megan's brow creased thoughtfully. "She looks…"

And then she paused.

Because so had Jenny. She stopped dead on the dance floor, and her eyes flew wide in agonized surprise.

"Jenny!"

Michael's exclamation of concern drowned out the sound of the soft piano as Jenny stumbled. His strong hands, already entwined around her waist, caught her as she sagged downward. "Jen?"

"Michael, I…"

"What is it?"

She gasped. Her knees had given way beneath her, and she would have sunk to the floor if he wasn't holding her.

"Take—take me home, Michael," she managed to say. "Or the hospital. Please. Oh, Michael, I think the baby's coming."

CHAPTER THIRTEEN

THE BABY definitely was coming. The pain in her back was a rolling, crippling cramp that enveloped every inch of her being. Michael could feel the spasms run through her body as he held her. She clung to him as if she was drowning, and the couples around them stopped dancing and stared in concern. Michael knelt with her as she doubled over, and his face was tight with panic.

"Jenny, love..."

"Hey, Jenny, what's happening?" Michael glanced up as someone called from across the room, and his shoulders sagged in relief as he saw who it was. Abby. Of course. Abby, Megan's daughter, was Maitland Maternity's chief obstetrician. So many of the hospital staff were family. If Jenny was in labor, she had half the staff of Maitland Maternity right here.

Abby had left her husband and was crossing swiftly to stoop beside the pair on the floor. "Hey, Jenny, let's not panic here," she said, kneeling. "Is this your first contraction?"

"I don't—I don't think so," Jenny whispered. The pain had eased, leaving her room to think. "Maybe not. I mean, I thought contractions were like stomach cramps, but I've been having back pains all afternoon and they've been getting worse. This one...it was the same but different. Much worse, and it sort of slammed around the front."

"That sounds like a contraction to me," Abby said cheerfully. "And a good one. How far apart would these back pains be?" She took Jenny's wrist between her fingers, found the pulse and flicked a glance at her watch.

"Um, two minutes maybe."

"Two minutes! Wow! That's terrific!" Abby's voice oozed confidence and reassurance. "If that's true, then you'll have danced your way through most of the first stage of labor." She grinned. "Okay, everyone, let's clear a path. Michael, we'll carry Jenny to a bedroom to give us a bit of privacy. We seem to be about to have a baby." She glanced at her husband. "Kyle, you want to call for an ambulance, honey? I don't want to risk a back-seat delivery here."

But Kyle was looking through the French windows to the gardens. The unseasonably warm evening had disappeared completely. Rain was lashing against the glass in torrents, and while he watched, lightning flashed. Thunder followed about a millisecond later.

"The storm's right overhead," Kyle said, and looked around the room, assessing. Counting heads. "It's a storm and a half. There'll be flash flooding, and the roads will be unsafe." He nodded as he took stock of who was present. "You know, given the guest list here, staying put might be the wisest option."

"Hey, we're going to the hospital," Michael said, startled. He hadn't taken his eyes from Jenny's white face, and his hands were gripping his wife hard. In turn, she was clinging to him as if fearful of being swept away.

"There are no problems, are there, Abby?" Kyle asked smoothly. He wasn't a CEO for nothing. Sensible decisions were what he was paid for.

"Nope." Abby shook her head. "I'll need to examine Jenny to be sure, but it seems a nice normal labor. A healthy boy being born at term to a healthy mom."

"This baby is not being born at term," Jenny said through gritted teeth. "He's not due till next week."

"You want to tell him that?" Abby grinned again, and

then paused in concern as she saw another contraction hit. She glanced again at her watch. "Remember your breathing, Jenny. Just breathe through it. That's less than a minute apart. Lord, we're moving right along here." She glanced up, searching for Megan in the sea of concerned family faces. "Mom, can we have a bed?"

"And hot water and towels and whatever else you need. Of course, dear. Oh, Jenny." Megan knelt, too—half the world, it seemed, was gathered in Megan's drawing room watching Jenny's contractions. Megan waited until this one passed, then smiled reassuringly into Jenny's fearful face.

"Aunt Megan, I'm so sorry." It was all she could manage.

"Nonsense, child," Megan said firmly. "Anna said we should have a party finale. We were planning fireworks until we were washed out, but a baby...what a magical end to an evening!"

"We haven't got the facilities," Michael snapped. Damn, they were being frivolous, and this was *his* Jenny. He wanted a brightly lit hospital room and every piece of chrome equipment known to man, along with incubators and anesthetics and intravenous drips and...

"Hey, Mike." Kyle's hand was on his shoulder, giving him strength. "We have Abby, who's the best obstetrician in Austin, bar none. Our car is set up like a mobile labor room—what Abby doesn't have in the trunk hasn't been invented. Ford Carrington's right here behind me, and don't tell me you're doubting his pediatric credentials. Katie's with him, and she has midwife qualifications as well as her pediatric training. If there are any problems, we'll call an ambulance and risk the storm. So...pick up your wife and take her where Megan shows you. We're all with you every inch of the way."

And then Kyle smiled at Jenny's white face. "Mrs. Lord, welcome to Maitland Maternity Clinic—the Megan Maitland Annex."

WE'RE ALL WITH YOU...

They certainly were. For Jenny, the next two hours passed in a blur, but what she remembered of her labor was a sea of family. Michael's family? No. For now, they were her family. One by one, they came in and sat with Michael, who didn't leave her side for a minute. They told her she was doing great, that they loved her and she looked terrific, and Michael looked paler than she did.

Lana. Shelby. Megan and Ellie. Garrett. Camille. The piano player started up again, and the party went on in slow mode. Waiting mode. No one was risking driving home in this rain, or maybe they all wanted to stay for Megan's finale.

Or for Jenny and Michael's finale.

"You're doing great, Jenny," Abby told her. "He'll be here soon. Real soon. Push just as hard as you want to, honey. This boy of yours is coming through like a locomotive."

And push she did, though it was like biting down on a sore tooth, or worse, and she really wanted to cry out in pain—maybe she did cry. But the faces around her told her it didn't matter one bit if she hollered the place down, and Michael's hands held her all the while.

Every inch of the way.

And finally...

"He's crowning," Abby said jubilantly. "I can see him, Jenny. The top of his head's coming through. Let's get Ford in here, because soon we'll have a new little person to check over. Okay, ease back, Jenny. Now, once again— Push!"

"I can't. I can't. *Oh...*"

She felt him come. She felt her son move within her, and Michael's arms slipped around her shoulders and lifted her so she could see her tiny, blue-white baby come slithering out into the world into Abby's waiting arms.

"He's...he's..." She could scarcely believe what she was seeing.

"He's just perfect," Abby said, clearing the tiny airway and turning the baby over in her arms. There was a moment of absolute silence, and then Jenny's baby son opened his eyes. He stared up and took one long look, then opened his mouth and hollered!

The piano player stopped as if he'd been struck. There was a hush outside the room. Then the new arrival opened his mouth for his second earthly yell, and was joined by laughter and applause filtering in from the room beyond. The Maitlands and the Lords were welcoming another baby into the family clan.

Ford was running an expert eye over the lusty infant, nodding and smiling his approval. He passed the baby to Katie, who wrapped him in the receiving blanket and placed the tiny baby into his mother's waiting arms.

Jenny's eyes welled with tears as she looked into her son's face.

"Oh, Michael. Oh, look." It was all she could do to speak. She pulled back the edge of the blanket with tenderness and awe, and her eyes flew to Michael.

And back to her son.

"He—he has red hair," she stammered.

"Oh, Lord." Megan had tiptoed into the room, unable to stay outside a moment longer. She crossed to look at the silent infant, cradled in his mother's arms. "That's just the shade of the triplets' hair when they were tiny," she breathed, stunned. "Just that shade. He'll have hair just like his daddy's."

"But..." Abby paused.

"I'm not his daddy," Michael said, but his eyes didn't leave the baby for an instant. "Your husband must have had red hair, Jen."

"My late-husband had blond hair," Jenny whispered. Her eyes flew to Michael and held. "My now-husband has red hair. Michael, you've been so good to me. Maybe this is God's way of saying he's your son, too.''

''No…''

But she wasn't listening. ''Michael, he's as much your son as Peter's. More. You've protected us and cared for us and…'' Her voice broke, and she lay back on her pillows, overcome.

Katie smiled and moved to take the little one from Jenny's arms. ''Let his daddy hold him,'' she suggested, and before Michael could murmur a protest, the baby was lying cocooned in his arms.

He was a tiny, five-minute-old redhead. Wide eyes stared at Michael, filled with awe at this amazing new world. Wondrous eyes. Jenny's eyes. And yet…

These eyes belonged only to this new little person, and Michael, looking at him, felt a protective urge that knocked him sideways. What had Katie said? *Let his daddy hold him.*

''You're calling him Peter, aren't you, Jenny?'' Abby asked, watching Michael with a smile of satisfaction. Jenny shook her head, tears slipping down her cheeks, unchecked.

''Nope. His name is Gary Richard Lord.''

''Gary Richard Lord?''

''Where did that name come from?'' Katie asked.

''Richard was Peter's father,'' Jenny whispered. ''Peter loved his father, and my son should have a part of his birthright. But Gary… I have a sense about Gary. I think a man called Gary Larrimore died a long time ago, and his death is the reason I'm lying in this room right now. With all my new family.''

''JENNY, we don't even know if this Gary Larrimore had anything to do with us.''

''Yes, we do.'' Jenny was almost asleep. She was snuggled into her pillows, her baby son in a makeshift crib by her side, and the world had let them be. There were only Michael and Jenny—and their tiny infant son beside them.

"You don't know Gary Larrimore is my father," Michael said steadily, trying not to turn and look at his—at the baby. "And even if he was..."

"He is. I can feel it." Her eyes smiled at him with a trace of a twinkle. "Call it a mother's intuition." And then the twinkle faded. "And I can't bear it," she whispered. "The thought of your mother being pregnant all those years ago and her Gary being killed before you were born. Leaving her with a toddler, and heartbreak, and all those unfulfilled dreams. I can't get her out of my mind, Michael. Whatever she did, wherever she is, or whatever she's done, this is my way of saying thank-you."

"Thank-you for what?"

"For giving me to you."

And her eyes closed and he was left with nothing to say.

"GARY RICHARD LORD." Garrett stared at his brother in amazement. Michael had left his wife and was in the living room. Megan had made up a bed for him next to Jenny, but he wasn't ready for sleep yet. Garrett had sensed that, and was waiting in the darkened house when Michael emerged. The oldest Lord brother was clearly bewildered. "After...our father?"

"After some person she's imagining was our father."

Garrett's eyebrows lifted. "Real or not, that's quite a compliment."

"It is." Mike's lips thinned, and he looked grim. "She's generous through and through, my lovely Jenny. She just gives and gives."

"So why the grim look?"

"We're not really married."

"Hey, I think you are," Garrett said gently. "The way you look at her..."

"But not the way she looks at me," Michael burst out.

"Oh, she's grateful—incredibly grateful—and I know she's attracted, and she'd never do anything to hurt me, but as for love…" He took a fast pace around the room, then paused and stood staring out at the drenched garden. "Some aristocratic lowlife back in Britain killed that for her."

"You mean he mistreated her?" There was caution in Garrett's question. It was absolutely out of character for his brother to be exposing his pain the way he was now.

"Yes. No! I don't know." Michael was still staring outside, talking almost to himself. The events of the past few hours had shaken him to the core, and it showed. "The way I see it, he married her to frustrate his mother and he never stopped letting Jen know she was trash. As if Jen could ever be thought trash by anyone! But now…" He took a deep breath. "That little baby in there is the next Earl of Epingdale—in fact, I guess he's that already, since his father's dead. And before he died, Peter extracted a promise from Jenny that he'd be brought up to take over his title."

Garrett shook his head at that. "If it means giving him up, then Jenny won't do it. Even I can see that."

"Of course she won't," Michael said grimly. "But it's tearing her heart out. She made that promise on his deathbed, and then when it came to the crunch, she couldn't keep it. She couldn't abandon her baby to Gloria."

"There's no blame in what she's doing."

"She blames herself. And this child is partly Peter's, no matter how much I want him."

"And?" Garrett paused, but the question was already half answered. "You really want him?"

"I want him—and I want his mother—more than anything else on God's earth," Michael said simply. He hesitated, but his heart was exposed for all to see, and there was nothing left to do but explain. "Before Jen, I thought I'd cut myself off from everything. You know more than most that I've tried hard enough. But she needs me, Garrett, and she's so darned proud. She'll take my offer of an identity and she'll spend the rest of her life trying to pay me back, but I don't want payment. I want her! She must see it. She's just filled with love, aching for love.''

"Have you told her how much you want her?'' Garrett's voice was suddenly urgent, and it made Michael blink.

"No,'' he said slowly. "How can I? It'll put more pressure on her. It'd be like insisting that if she lives with me, she has to love me, too. In her position she'll say yes just to please me.''

"It's not possible that she loves you?''

"Of course she loves me,'' Michael exploded. "She's so kindhearted she'd love anyone. Look, until I get rid of the ghost of this Peter, I don't have a snowball's chance in hell of getting anywhere near her, and how can I get rid of a ghost?''

He paused at a sound. "What...'' There was a scrambling at the French windows, and a low voice speaking urgently.

"Shh, you dumb mutt. You want to wake everyone in the house?''

"It's Shelby,'' Garrett said, his eyes creasing with laughter as he crossed to open the door. Shelby came bursting into the room, her auburn hair damp from the rain and her running shoes squelching with water. "What on earth are you doing here?'' he started to ask, and then stopped dead as he saw the dog at her side, and the dog caught sight of Michael.

It was as if Socks were drowning and Michael was the only lifeguard for miles. He launched himself at Michael, leaping right off the ground and catching his shoulders with his huge paws.

Michael was left with nowhere to go. He stood enfolded in soggy dog while Socks licked and whined and wriggled out his loneliness and frustration at being abandoned.

There was a stunned silence from Shelby and Garrett, and there was not a lot Michael could say, either.

"Mmff..." he finally managed to get out, but it didn't make a heap of sense. Shelby grinned. She'd changed into jeans and a T-shirt, which were mud-spattered. She wiped wet hands on her jeans and looked at Michael and Socks with affection.

"What do you think he's trying to say?" she asked Garrett, and Garrett chuckled.

"Thank you very much for bringing me my dog?" he suggested. "Yeah, that must be it."

"Mmff..." said Michael.

"Yeah, that's definitely it." Garrett grinned. "Good thought, bringing him here, Shelby. You wanted to keep the family together."

"Actually," Shelby said carefully, "when I got home there was a message on my answering machine from Michael's neighbors. Several messages, in fact. They'd been looking for him all over. I bet when you get home there'll be messages on your phone, too. Seems Socks was howling the place apart. So what could a girl do..."

"But reunite brother and dog," Garrett finished for her. "Gee, I hope Megan has a decent floor cleaner." And then he frowned at another tap on the window. He turned, and there was Lana, signaling to be let in, her arms piled high with baby clothes and nightwear. "Lana..."

"Hey, it's a family reunion." Lana entered, dumped the clothes on a chair, then looked at Michael. Her face cleared. "So that's where he is."

"Where did you think Mike would be?"

"I meant Socks," Lana said cheerfully. "I might have known he'd get himself here."

"You been looking for him?" Garrett queried, and Lana gave him a grin that matched Shelby's.

"There were five messages on our phone when Dylan and I got home," she said. "Five! All complaining about

Socks and demanding that someone in the family do something. So I left Dylan holding the baby and went to fetch him. Missed him by inches.'' She smiled happily at her sister. ''Guess that was you, huh? Got there before me and rescued Socks. You always were the lucky one.''

''So I get the dog hair and muddy paw prints all over my passenger seat,'' Shelby said morosely. ''As well as dog slobber on my windshield. While you get to carry baby clothes.''

''I figured while I was there I might as well bring them over,'' Lana said virtuously. ''And besides, I wanted to see...'' She turned to look at Michael, and it was very clear what she wanted to see.

''Mmmfff,'' said Michael, and they all burst out laughing. Finally Garrett took pity on his brother and went over to haul the adoring mutt onto the floor. Socks immediately shook his wet self from stem to stern, spraying everyone. He looked adoringly at his master and then flopped down, exhausted, at his feet.

''What a dog!'' Garrett said admiringly. ''Now no one needs a shower.''

''Speak for yourself,'' Shelby said darkly, wiping mud from her nose. ''Ugh. Anyway, enough of mutts. Michael, how's Jenny and the new little one?''

''Asleep.'' Michael cut his reply short, and Shelby stared, laughter fading.

''There's nothing wrong, is there?''

''No, but...''

''But he doesn't know if she loves him,'' Garrett finished for him, and Michael glared.

''Butt out.''

''Of course she loves him.'' Lana ignored Michael entirely. She was talking only to Garrett and Shelby.

''She's called her son Gary,'' Garrett told them.

''Gary?'' Shelby's mouth dropped open, and her voice

was shaky. "Gary," she quavered. "Oh, Michael, that's lovely. She must love you to bits."

"But Jenny promised her husband on his deathbed that she'd allow his son to be brought up as a little earl," Garrett continued, ignoring Michael's dark looks. "So she's going through all sorts of conscience barbs trying to come to terms with bringing him up here in the States. Seems that's getting in the way of her relationship with Mike."

"You mean she can't love Mike because she's broken a promise to her dead husband?" Shelby frowned over this one.

"That's crazy," Lana said, but Shelby shook her head.

"No. I can see that. Too much has happened too fast to Jenny. Widowed, pregnant, remarried, hounded by her mother-in-law, changing countries, worrying about money, giving birth, getting to know Michael... Her head must be spinning off her shoulders."

"So he should just give her time?" Lana demanded.

"Hey, excuse me," Michael said in a voice that boded ill for the fate of his siblings. "This is my love life we're talking about."

"Of course it is," Shelby said kindly. "So shut up, Mike, and let us get on with it." She swiveled to face Garrett. "So Michael definitely loves her?"

"Of course he loves her." Garrett tossed a laughing look at his younger brother. "You ever seen someone so besotted as our Mike?"

"Nope." Shelby grinned. "Can't say I have. You, Lana?"

"Not me." But Lana was thinking fast. "This is tricky, though, Garrett. Jenny can't take Gary back to England. I've met Gloria. She's a horror. But if Jenny's feeling so guilty, she just might."

"No!" Michael said, but he was ignored.

"We have to face it as a possibility," Lana decided. The Lord siblings were nothing if not a team, and they never worked so well as when one of the brood was under threat. Garrett and Shelby and Lana were totally focused, and Michael might as well not have been there. "So what do we do?"

"Keep her promise," Shelby said, and everyone stared at her, even Michael

"What?"

"What exactly did she promise?" Shelby demanded, and Michael shook his head.

"I don't know."

"Hasn't she told you?"

"Yes, but..."

"Then think. Remember. It's important. Come on, Michael, you're trained to remember details. Think!"

"Okay, okay." Michael's brow furrowed. He was way out of his league here, emotionally exhausted, but he knew his siblings too well to think they'd let go.

What had she promised? He thought back, and suddenly the words were right there. "'He made me promise to bring our child up as he ought to be raised—as the next earl,'" he told them. "That's what Jenny said."

"No specifics?" Shelby demanded. "Like promising to live in a castle for nine months a year and keep ten footmen, thirty maidservants and a butler or six?"

"I hardly think so." They thought it was a joke, Michael thought grimly, but he wasn't laughing. "Peter was dying when he made her promise. I can't imagine a dying man would be into specifics. He'd just ask for what he wanted most—that the kid grow up enjoying his inheritance."

Shelby's smile faded, just as his had.

"Then where's your problem?" she asked gently. "Gary Lord can be brought up to be Earl of Epingdale right here. You teach him about his inheritance and his history from day one. You teach him everything he needs to know to take over his father's mantle—when and if he ever wants it. And once a year you use some of that ill-gotten cash you have floating around to take him over to visit his family seat.''

This was crazy. ''But...''

''But what?''

Michael stared, his mind racing a mile a minute, discarding one thought after another. One thing stood out above all. ''Gloria will never agree.''

''I don't see Gloria as having a choice,'' Shelby said bluntly. ''As far as Gloria is concerned, it's that or nothing.''

''She'll give Jenny hell if she goes to England.''

''Not if you're beside her,'' Shelby said triumphantly. ''And all the other little Lord kids you intend having. They'll play baseball in the ancestral halls. You can raise the Stars and Stripes from the ancestral flagpole. Hey, you could even invite us! Garrett, Lana—how do you feel about visiting a real live English castle?''

''We could do it,'' Lana breathed. ''For Jenny.''

''Of course we could do it—for Jenny,'' Shelby said soundly. She took Michael's hands and reeled him in to give him a hug. ''And for Mike, too. So what do you say, brother mine? Give it a go? Or not?''

CHAPTER FOURTEEN

JENNY WOKE to flowers. Flowers as far as the eye could see. There were flowers by her bed and there were flowers on the blanket box at her feet. Vases and vases of them. By the window there were stands—maybe a dozen stands—and every one had a vase with maybe thirty blooms in it. Their smell was all around her.

The window was open. There were more flowers in the gardens beyond the terrace, and the smell of rain-drenched flowers was everywhere.

There was the faintest murmur beside her, and Jenny looked down to see her son stirring in his sleep. His tiny fist was just touching his rosebud mouth, and his bottom lip was trembling. Her son! Gary. With one wondering finger she touched his cheek. His eyelids fluttered open, his face turned momentarily toward her, and he stared at his mother with a look that would stay with her for the rest of her life.

And then Gary Richard Lord decided it wasn't time to stir yet. He had more important things to do. Like sleep.

"He's a real sweetheart," a voice whispered, and Jenny's eyes flew to the door. Katie was standing there. Katie, the nurse who'd been with her every moment of her labor.

It was true, then. It had all happened.

"I thought it must have been a dream," Jenny said wonderingly, and she winced when she moved. "Well, maybe not. Maybe it really is real."

"You feeling sore?"

"Like I've been steamrollered."

"He makes a great little steamroller." Katie looked at her small charge. "He has the best set of lungs in the state. Ford and I have decided it's just as well he was born here. Maitland Maternity would have given him his marching orders for disturbing the peace."

"I think I did my own bit of yelling last night," Jenny said ruefully. "I sure messed up the party."

"Well, that's a heap of nonsense," Katie told her, smiling. "Megan hasn't had such an exciting party for years." She eyed Jenny closely. "You really hurting?"

"Only when I laugh." Jenny's eyes drifted to the couch at the side of the room. Katie saw where she was looking and she shook her head.

"Abandoned," she said mournfully. "That's what happens to the women of the tribe after they've produced the son and heir. You've been deserted by the man you love. He'll be off handing out cigars and practicing his chest puffing."

"But I don't—"

"Hey, he'll be back," Katie reassured her. "I bet he's gone to get more flowers. As if these aren't enough. He's been gathering them for hours. Where he's gotten them all from, I don't know."

"Michael brought all these?" she asked in amazement.

"I sure did, and you deserve every one of them." Michael's gruff voice came from across the room, and she turned her head on her pillows. Her husband was coming in through the French windows—and yes, he was carrying more flowers.

"Holy cow, you'd think it was a wedding." Katie grinned.

Michael dumped the flowers on an armchair and crossed the room to take Jenny into his arms and kiss her senseless before she could remember a single reason he shouldn't.

Jenny didn't have the energy to fight him. Well, maybe she did, but she didn't even try. She lay back and let herself be soundly kissed, and just for a moment she let herself believe this was how it should be. Her wonderful, beloved husband kissing her after the birth of their child. What could be more perfect than this? One baby plus one husband.

Plus a ghost.

Peter was still there, and as Michael finally released her, he saw the echoes of her past lingering in her eyes.

"Jen?"

"Michael, your flowers are wonderful," she said softly but quickly, as if to make things more formal. "I... Thank you. But how did you get them? You haven't stripped Megan's garden?"

"Your son snores," he said, smiling into her eyes with a look that made her heart do back flips. "There was no way I could sleep. Katie stayed in calling distance, so I went rose hunting." He grinned. "There's not a garden on the street left untouched."

"You stole them!" That shook her. She sat up and fixed him with the same look she'd used when he was trying to impose his will on her as a secretary. "Michael Lord, are you nuts? You'll be arrested."

"I left twenty bucks and a thank-you note in every mailbox," he told her virtuously. "There was no way I was waiting for the florists to open."

"You're still nuts."

"But nice nuts?" he asked hopefully, and she chuckled, then withdrew imperceptibly. He saw it, and didn't take things further. He had a plan, and it involved a bit of careful persuasion. Plus a lie or two. Pushing things wouldn't work.

"Jenny, I'm here to take your Gary Richard away for a bit," he told her. Then, at her startled look, he turned to Katie. "Tell her, Katie."

"Jenny, Megan wants you to stay right where you are for a few days," she told her. "We think it's best. If you're happy to do that."

"Of course. But Megan—"

"Megan thinks it's just wonderful," Megan said, coming into the room as if on cue. It was still before nine in the morning. It had been three before Megan had slept the night before, but she looked as immaculately dressed and as fresh as if she'd had a full night's sleep. "As CEO, I should be telling you to get yourself into Maitland Maternity, but we're big enough now to cope with losing the business of one mother and babe."

"So you'll stay here?" Michael said to Jenny as he eyed his aunt doubtfully. They'd clued Katie in on what was going on, but Megan didn't know.

"Of course, I'd love to stay here. If it's okay." But there was a furrow between Jenny's eyes. "But why do you need to take Gary away?"

"Ford wants to check him," Michael said promptly—a bit too promptly, and Jenny's frown grew. She knew this man.

"But last night Ford said he was okay." Her eyes flew to her son, and panic flared. "There's nothing wrong?"

"Of course there's nothing wrong," Katie said reassuringly, but Jenny was still suspicious.

"Then why?"

"I imagine Ford wants his bilirubin levels taken for jaundice, and a heel prick for thyroid function," Megan volunteered, and all eyes veered toward her. Good grief, Michael thought. What was she going to say? Had she guessed?

"I don't understand," Jenny said.

"I don't suppose you do, child," Megan told her graciously. "But all newborns are required to have their bilirubin levels taken, though your little Gary doesn't look jaundiced to me, and their heel test needs to be done for thyroid malfunction. They're simple tests that take only a few seconds, but they need to be done in a hospital with the right equipment. I imagine Ford would be unhappy about delaying it."

Michael held his breath. He looked at Katie—and saw she was holding hers. Was Megan really saying this?

"Will you be long?" Jenny asked, still looking at her tiny son. "Can I come with him?"

"There's no way you're going anywhere," Megan told her sternly. "And it takes all of ten minutes to get to the hospital. An hour at most for the test—that's if there's a wait—and back here by a little after ten. You'll have the little one back by then, right, Michael?"

Michael, stunned, could only nod.

"Of course. And I'll take the best care of him."

"I know you will," Jenny whispered. "It's only…" She looked at her tiny son, and her eyes welled. "I don't like to be away from him for a minute."

"An hour only," Michael said softly, and bent and kissed her on the lips.

"MEGAN…"

"I don't know what you're doing and I don't want to know," Megan told him as Michael carried Gary out of the room after Jenny had fed him. "What I don't know I can't tell. You just get him back in an hour. You promise?"

"I promise."

"And Michael…" Megan's eyes creased into a smile.

"Megan?"

"Good luck."

THE HOTEL was the grandest in Austin. Michael had guessed she'd be here, but he'd phoned first to make sure. "Certainly," they'd said at seven this morning. "Her ladyship is booked to the end of the week."

He'd half expected—feared—that she'd gone back to England, which would have made it so much harder. Now, though, everything that should be said could be said. Right now.

But not alone. He wasn't a fool. Michael remembered

the thugs, and he remembered Gloria's threat of a private
jet. Gary was too precious to risk.

So he waited in the foyer as planned, and two minutes
after he arrived, Garrett and Lana and Shelby came through
the revolving doors to meet him.

"She let him go! Well done." Lana was first to reach
him, and her eyes devoured the newborn Gary. He was so
swaddled in his blankets, all she could see was one pink
nose. Michael was taking no risks at all. "And Ford said
it was okay to bring him?"

"Ford met me at Megan's. He's given me the all clear,
and he'll cover us if Jen starts asking questions. But we
only have an hour."

"So let's do it," Garrett said. He looked at his three
siblings and grinned. "Four Lords and one baby Lord
against one old lady. Poor old lady."

THERE WAS NOTHING poor about Gloria. Garrett hadn't met
her. He did the knocking while Michael stayed in the background.

Michael had paved the way with a call.

"Gloria, it's Michael Lord, and I'd like to talk to you.
There are things you and I need to discuss."

He almost saw the curve of satisfaction play on Gloria's
mouth as she'd taken in what he said. She'd be expecting
some sort of proposition. A request for money.

Every man had his price. That was the way she worked,
Michael knew, and she wasn't to know the Lords had a
different set of values entirely. Like absolute loyalty.

So she'd given him her room number, and Michael stood
back while Garrett faced her, Shelby and Lana flanking
him.

"What on earth..." Gloria's breath whistled in as she
saw the group by the door. "I don't know you."

"I'm Garrett Lord," Garrett said smoothly. "I'm Michael's big brother. Gary's uncle, in fact. And these are
Michael's sisters, Lana and Shelby. Gary's aunts."

Gloria stared at them, contempt mixing with confusion on her face. Behind her, in her luxury hotel suite, Michael caught sight of her two lackeys solidly behind her. They weren't thugs for hire by the hour, then. She had them at her beck and call—and she must have summoned them fast at Michael's phone call.

He was right, he thought. He'd have been a fool to bring Gary here alone. How would she react now, with Gary surrounded?

She was confused. "I don't know any Gary, and I have nothing to discuss with Michael's—" Then she caught sight of Michael. Her voice stopped with a sharp intake of breath as she saw what he was holding. She took an involuntary step backward, and her jaw dropped about a foot.

"We're here to introduce you to your grandson, Gloria," Michael said gently, taking a step forward to stand beside Garrett. "Gary Richard Lord was born last night, and we'd like to know what you intend to do about it."

SHE INTENDED NOTHING. Not yet. For a long, long moment Gloria couldn't speak at all. She stood, totally flummoxed, while her hirelings came up behind her, looking almost as confused as she was.

"Aren't you going to invite us in?" Garrett said at last. He was sizing up the group before him and acknowledging Michael's wisdom in setting this up. Last night he'd thought it was stupid, bringing four people to face this woman. But one look at the thugs behind Gloria and he knew that Michael had done the right thing.

If he had come here on his own, they could simply have relieved him of the baby and disappeared.

Not now. Not with four of them. Lana and Shelby had power dressed for the occasion, and the Lord siblings looked every bit as formidable as the thugs behind her ladyship. The only way they could reach Gary was to draw guns, but then they'd be involved in a shoot-out with four

U.S. citizens. No matter how desperate Gloria was, she wouldn't be that stupid.

So the thugs had nothing to do but stand aside. Gloria did the same, and the four Lords—and baby—entered the suite without a protest.

It was like something out of a bad play, Garrett thought grimly, but by the look on Michael's face, he knew this was deadly serious.

But there was no threat. Not now. There was just one old lady's reaction to watch, and so much depended on this.

"Jenny gave birth to your grandson this morning," Michael said softly, and Lana walked forward and lifted the covers from Gary's tiny face. "Would you like to see?"

"I..." Gloria looked as if every ounce of air had been sucked out of her. Suddenly she seemed old—defeated. "Why should I?"

"Because he's your grandson," Michael said. "Because he's Peter's son, and I assume you loved Peter. Jenny's called him Gary Richard. Richard is for your husband."

"Richard." There was a sharp intake of breath. "I don't believe it."

"What don't you believe?" Michael's voice was quietly insistent, and his eyes didn't leave her face. Everyone else had faded into insignificance now. For Michael there was only this woman in the room. Everything depended on the next few minutes. His future. His love for Jenny.

No way could Gloria realize that!

"I can't—"

"Look at him," Michael said, and he took two steps forward so Gary was almost touching Gloria's black cashmere cardigan. She took a step backward, then another. She did look just like Wallis Simpson, Michael thought suddenly, and wondered whether that was the image she aimed for. A woman who swayed men's emotions.

"Look at your grandson," Michael said again, and pressed Gary forward, as if he would entrust her to hold him.

Gloria didn't take him, but she did look down.

Gary's hair was so red, Michael thought ruefully, and wondered for the sixtieth time whether it had been crazy to bring him here. But...

"Dear God," Gloria said, and her face crumpled as she saw the tiny child. Her hands flew to her cheeks, and she stared, while the icy mask of self-control and vicious intent faded to nothing.

There was only awe.

"Richard had red hair," she whispered finally. "My Richard."

"Peter's father?" Michael frowned. Jenny hadn't said that. It hit him with a pang. Last night, Jenny's words had been like a gift to him. If she'd known the red hair came from her dead husband's family...

But Gloria was shaking her head. "My Richard," she said again. "Not Peter's father. Peter's brother."

Another silence. The air was thick with it, and suddenly Shelby couldn't bear it.

"Hey, I need a cup of tea here," she told everyone loudly. "There's a kitchenette through here, right? You don't mind if I make one, do you, Gloria? I'll make one for you, too. You English always want tea. You two—I need help." And before Gloria's hired men could say a word, she'd taken an arm apiece and marched them to the other room.

"I know when I'm not wanted," she told them as she propelled them forward. "I'll bet you do, too. You look like the sort of guys that can take hints real well. Speaking of which.... Garrett! Lana! Come!"

And Michael was left alone with his son and Gloria.

And with the silence.

"You want to hold him?" he asked, and he proffered the baby as if he was the most precious thing in all the world.

"You mean it?" She looked at him in disbelief.

"I mean it. If you want."

"I do...oh, I do." And Gloria gathered Gary into her arms and burst into tears.

"How come..." Michael asked, when he figured Gloria could speak again. He'd pushed her into an armchair and found a tissue or two to mop the flood. "How come I never got to hear about this Richard? About Peter's brother?"

Gloria looked at him, then at Gary. She could scarcely keep her eyes from him.

"Peter didn't know about his brother," she said. "No one did."

Michael frowned. "I don't understand. You want to run that past me again?"

"I had a baby before Peter," she whispered, almost as if she was talking to herself. "In those days...well, a baby that hardly made it through the delivery was hushed up. Not spoken off. Especially in a family like ours. He... Richard lived for a day, and he was just perfect, but then he died while I was asleep. It was my first sleep after having him. I went to sleep thinking I had the most beautiful little boy in the world, and when I woke up they'd simply taken him away."

"Why?"

"Because he was dead," she said flatly, and the bitterness was still there after all these long years. "So they took him. I don't even know where they buried him. 'Never mind, dear,' they said, 'there'll be another.' And I was expected to get on with it. My mother burned everything. Every single baby thing. Start again, she said. She told me I shouldn't even think about him."

Michael stared at her, then looked at Gary. No! His heart simply balked at the thought. How would he feel now if that happened to Gary? How would Jen bear it?

How must Gloria have felt?

Maybe the lady wasn't quite as bad as she was painted, he thought, a sick feeling churning his gut. Maybe there were reasons she acted the way she did.

"So then you had Peter?"

"He was my replacement baby," she said bitterly. "Everyone said that. Have another one to replace it. *It!* Like replacing a broken cup. So I did, but he didn't—replace him, I mean. The pain…it never went away."

No. It wouldn't. Unaired and unacknowledged, it had simply festered, like a canker. Michael saw that as clearly as any psychologist would, and he saw why Peter could never have been satisfactory. Poor Peter!

"And now I have a grandson who looks like him." Gloria's voice was choked. "I can't bear it."

"What can't you bear?"

She lifted her tear-drenched face to his. Her mascara had run, causing two black rivulets to stream down her wrinkled cheeks. She was looking older by the minute. "I can't bear that I can't have him," she whispered.

"You can."

She stared. "You're saying you'll give him to me?" An incredulous hope flared in the woman's eyes, extinguished almost as soon as it was lit.

"Of course I won't," Michael said flatly. "You're his grandma, not his mother. Jenny's his mother, and to all intents and purposes, I'm his father. You'll have to accept that as fact, and we can go from there."

"I don't know what you mean."

"I mean you're giving no middle ground," Michael told her, his voice gentle again. "You want him all or not at all. But Jenny doesn't want him to grow up without knowing you."

The woman looked at the sleeping baby, and her face twisted in pain. "I can't believe that."

"After the way you've treated Jenny, neither can I," Michael said frankly. "But this little boy has an English heritage. He needs to learn about it."

"You only want my money!"

"There is no way Jenny or I will touch any money that has any connection with you," Michael told her flatly.

There was no joy to be gained in letting her think she had any control. "But if you want access…"

"You'd let me have him part-time?"

"You could visit him here," Michael told her, "while Jenny and I are present. And if we were invited, then maybe we'd bring Gary over—stay awhile, so Gary could get to know what he's in for. Maybe a month or so every year."

"What, all of you?" The thought was clearly repulsive.

"It's all or nothing," Michael told her, and he stooped and lifted the white-wrapped bundle from her arms and held him close. "Jenny and Gary and I…we're a family. You accept us all or you don't accept any of us. That's the deal. Take it or leave it, but that's the way it has to be."

"I don't—"

"Think about it before answering," he said urgently. "Think of what you're losing if you refuse. Jen wants to do this—for Peter's sake." There was no point in saying he hadn't mentioned this to Jenny. "Jenny's staying here." He handed her a card with Megan's address on it. "If you want, go and see her and see if you can rebuild a few bridges before you lose everything. I'm sorry, but that's all I have to say to you. Think about it. Garrett! Lana! Shelby! Let's go."

And he whistled up his siblings and marched them out of the hotel room before she could say a word.

"How'd it go?" Garrett asked curiously as the elevator doors closed behind them.

"Who knows?" Michael's face was grim.

"We heard what you said." Garrett grinned and shrugged. "There wasn't a lot of tea-making going on in the kitchenette. There were five pairs of ears flapping so hard they'd almost have powered the kettle on their own. It's true. She loses everything if she doesn't agree."

"The only catch to that," Michael said grimly, "is so do I."

"YOU HAVE A VISITOR."

Jenny laid down her correspondence. Half the world seemed to have sent her cards and baby gifts. She looked up as Megan peeped into the room.

"You're not asleep!" Megan exclaimed. "Heavens, child, you know those were doctor's orders. Sleep, sleep and more sleep for the next few days."

"I'm fit as a flea," Jenny said soundly. "If I didn't think Michael would fuss more than you, I'd be out of here in a minute." She smiled to take any offence from her words, and Megan smiled back. But Megan knew enough to sense why Jenny had agreed to stay. This gave her a few more days of time out, away from Michael.

"So are you up to visitors? I said I thought you were asleep, so you have a ready-made excuse."

"No, it's fine. But who…"

"I think you might have to see for yourself," Megan told her, and whisked herself out of question range.

Two minutes later, she ushered Gloria in and closed the door behind her.

THE LAST FEW TIMES Jenny had seen Gloria, all she'd felt was fear. As it was, her hands went down to clasp Gary, who was sleeping tucked into the bedclothes at her side. She lifted him and held him against her breast in the age-old gesture of a mother protecting her young. Gloria saw— and she winced.

"My dear…"

That was a change. Gloria had only ever addressed her with silky-smooth disdain or vindictive dislike. Jenny's eyes widened, and she suspected a trap.

Gloria sighed. She didn't attempt to approach the bed, just regally took a seat on the chair, carefully smoothing her tailored black skirt over her silk stockings.

"There's no threat to you from me," she said softly. "Your husband brought me here. He's waiting outside to drive me back to my hotel, and tonight I'm returning to England.''

"Michael brought you here?''

"He did.'' The older woman's face creased into a tired smile. "He came to see me a few days back, to introduce my grandson. His son. He's quite a young man, your husband.''

"I...yes.'' There was no answer to that one. Jenny was poleaxed.

"I came to agree to his proposal and to ask that you accept mine,'' she said.

"I don't understand.'' How on earth had she gotten her voice to work? It was beyond her.

"Michael told me you wouldn't,'' Gloria went on, and then paused. "I can see I need to explain.'' For the first time her voice faltered. She took a long look at the baby in Jenny's arms, then she closed her eyes and took a deep breath. "I intend to start at the beginning, if you'll listen....''

So, while Jenny lay back in stunned silence, Gloria told her what she'd told Michael. She told her story calmly and rationally, without any of the pain Michael had heard, but there was no way Jenny could miss the suffering behind the words. And when she fell silent, there was a much different feeling in Jenny's heart from the fear that had been her first reaction to this visit.

"Oh, ma'am.''

"No,'' Gloria said strongly. "Not ma'am. I should never have made you use that. My name is Gloria. I know I've never let you use it, but I wish it now. If you will. What I'm saying...what I'm telling you is not an excuse for what I've done. I don't have one. I was hurt, so I hurt everyone around me for such a long time. I've done much damage, and I can't undo it. It wasn't until I saw your baby that I realized. I've poisoned most things. All I'd like to do now is try to salvage something from the mess. For Peter's memory. And for Richard's.''

She paused, but then held out her hand to stop Jenny from interrupting. The gesture was imperious. Gloria might be sincerely sorry, but the noble blood in her family background had bred a haughtiness she probably wasn't even aware of herself.

"I would very much like to keep in contact with you all," she said firmly. "Not just with my grandson, but with you and with your husband, too, and with any children who might follow. With that in mind, I'd like to write. I'll write once a week, and there's no need for you to write back. Photographs will suffice. I'll pay for any postage and processing. I'd also like very much to be present at Gary's christening, but if that's not acceptable, then I'll understand." She paused, and she finally took her eyes from the baby and looked at Jenny. The haughtiness faded.

"Your husband says he'll pay for an extended holiday in Britain each year, but I'll fight him on that one. I'll do the paying." She almost sounded humble. "It would be my honor—my absolute privilege—to have you all stay in my home. As you know, the estate is huge. It's my sorrow and shame you were never invited there while you were married to Peter, but we have guest apartments to spare. Come, and bring as many friends as you want. Make it your home. Your…your home away from home."

"And at the end of our stay?" Jenny asked, her voice hushed in shock at what she was hearing. "You'd let us go again?"

"If I can't bear to let go, then I'll lose you completely," Gloria whispered, and it was as much as Jenny could do to hear her. "I don't think I could bear that. I've been so stupid. I've lost so much already."

CHAPTER FIFTEEN

MICHAEL didn't come near her after that. He must have waited outside, taken Gloria to her hotel and then returned to Maitland Maternity. For the next couple of hours Jenny lay in baffled bewilderment, going over the events of the last few hours in her mind.

Michael had gone to see Gloria. Michael had taken Gary to see her.

Why?

And she knew. She knew!

Where was he? Why didn't he come? As the afternoon wore on, so did Jenny's patience. Finally at five o'clock, Shelby bounced in to see her, having given Socks his daily constitutional. Socks led the way, towing Shelby, and both dog and woman stopped in astonishment at the sight of Jenny dressed—in her gorgeous golden dress—and packing her bags.

"Where," Shelby said carefully. "are you thinking of going?"

"Home," Jenny told her. "It's time."

"Does Megan know?"

"Megan's right behind her." Megan came into the bedroom carrying a pile of clean diapers. "Of course I know. Like Jenny says, it's time."

An hour later, Michael came home from work to dump the paperwork he had to do that evening, before heading around to Megan's to see Jenny. When he arrived he found his wife and his son and his dog sitting before the living room fire, waiting for him.

"Jen?"

"Michael." To any onlooker it would appear to be a normal evening after work. Gary was fast asleep in his infant seat by the fire. Jenny looked placidly at her husband as Socks bounded over to greet him. "Welcome home."

But Michael didn't feel normal. He put Socks aside with a halfhearted pat and focused on his wife. "Why are you here?"

"Waiting for my husband to return." She smiled at him. "Like a good and dutiful wife. Socks, go fetch your master's slippers."

Socks gave a goofy grin and just sat there. Jenny sighed. "Rats. Some things will never change. Sorry, Michael, you don't seem to have a docile dog. Will a docile wife do?"

Michael had stopped at the door. Now he felt as if he'd stopped breathing. The world seemed to stand still, waiting.

"I don't think I'd know what a docile wife was," he said carefully, and she smiled that gorgeous, blindingly brilliant smile of hers, and rose and came over to him. She was wearing her wonderful dress, he thought, dazed. She was looking just...

Just too desirable for words.

"Michael, thank you," she said softly, and she caught his hands. The faint scent of her perfume drifted into his orbit.

"Thank you?"

"For seeing Gloria," she said simply. And then she took a deep breath. "And by doing so...making it possible for me to move forward. To bury Peter."

"It means you can go home," he said, and his voice sounded harsh even to him. "The way Gloria is, given some cast-iron guarantees, I'd imagine you could go back to England. She won't threaten you now."

"Why would I go back to England?"

"It's your home."

"Home is where the heart is," she said softly, and her hands held his. They were smooth against the roughness of his male skin, and it was all he could do not to pull her forward and gather her into his arms. It was more than a body could stand.

But he must. Still he held himself rigid. Waiting.

"You've grown attached," he said, trying to keep the sudden burgeoning of hope from surging into something he couldn't control. "I guess."

She tilted her chin and met his look with the clear-eyed gaze he loved so much. "You guess right. I have."

"To Socks. To Lana and Shelby and Megan."

"Yep."

"And to this place, maybe." He looked at the fire. "It's a good place to live."

"The white furniture has to go."

"The white furniture can go." Hell, he sounded like a zombie. "You just say the word."

"Michael?"

"Mmm."

"We're talking around the point here." She hesitated. All the courage she had deserted her.

But he needed to know. She had to say it. "And the point is?"

There was a long, long silence. He didn't take his eyes from hers, and their gazes linked and held.

Then, suddenly, Jenny had all the courage she needed right there in her heart. All the courage she needed was written plain on his face. She only had to reach out and take it from him. Use it herself. He'd done so much for her. He'd committed himself so far. It wouldn't hurt her to take this one last step of trust.

"I couldn't bear to go back to England, Michael Lord," she whispered, "and you want to know why not?"

"I... Yes." It came out a gravelly croak and brought a smile to her lovely eyes. She stood on tiptoes, and she kissed him ever so lightly on the mouth. And still he stood motionless.

"Because I love you, you great ninny," she scolded. "I think I have for months but I couldn't admit it, even to myself. But now... Now you've unlocked the chains, and you are my own darling husband and I have fallen so in love with you that I can't bear to think of leaving your side for a moment. Ever. And I'm sorry if you can't bear to be hemmed in and domesticated, but you did say you were in love with me and that's what you get when you— *Michael!*"

The last word was a squeak as she was swept off the floor and spun around the room with a great shout of joyous laughter. "Michael!"

"What?" She stared into his laughing, triumphant eyes as he spun her still. "What, my love?"

"Put me down this instant," she demanded. "I have more to say."

"I'm not putting you down."

"I'll sic the dog onto you."

"Yeah, right." He spun her again. "Really, Jenny? You really love me?"

"How can I know what I feel when I'm so dizzy?" she asked, her gorgeous dress flaring as he spun her around and around. "Michael, put me down!"

And he did.

But it was no help at all. When he whirled her around she was dizzy, but when he set her down, he began to kiss her, and her world tilted so crazily she knew she'd never be in control of it again.

A KNOCK drove them apart.

In fact, it was the fourth knock that did it. Or maybe even the fifth. It was hard to be sure when one set of ears was asleep, two sets heard nothing, and even Socks was too interested in the proceedings to worry about a small thing like visitors. But finally Socks noticed, barked his dire warnings and drew their reluctant attention to the intrusion.

"We're not home," Michael said, but Jenny chuckled and pushed herself away to go open the door.

"It'll be your family—and I love your family almost as much as I love you," she said serenely. "So learn to share."

"Yes, ma'am."

It wasn't his family. It was the Suits.

Michael groaned.

"Is anything wrong, sir?" Once again, these were different officials, and Michael recognized neither of them. The older one was a woman in neat black, the younger a string bean of a male with a large protruding Adam's apple. They walked in as Jenny stood aside, and they looked around the living room as if they were inspecting for termites.

"Don't tell me," Michael said. "You're from immigration and are here to kick Jenny out of the country. Gloria changed her mind?"

"I'm sorry?" The woman—Delia, according to her name tag—set her briefcase down with a definite thump. "I don't know any Gloria. But yes, we're here to do a check on your wife's immigration. There was an order that said as soon as the baby's birth was registered, we needed to make a follow-up visit."

"That figures." Gloria had insisted on as much, and she wouldn't have been able to rescind a request like that. Oh, well. The officials had driven Jenny to him in the first place. He could afford to be civil.

He could afford to be nice to anyone right at this minute, he decided, because Jenny was still looking at him with hungry eyes, and he had a whole lifetime to get to know how to appease that look.

"Okay, let's do it," he said firmly, and reached for Jenny's hand.

"We really just need to check that your wife and child are home now, and we'll make an interview time later," the woman said, startled. "I gather the baby's not very old."

"Five days. Do it now."

"Do it…"

"Let's get this over with." Michael's arm came around his wife and held her close. "We have better things to do than answer questions. Like consolidate our marriage. And consolidate and consolidate and consolidate for the next fifty years."

IN THE END it was a weirdly intimate affirmation of their marriage.

"When did you meet?" Delia asked, while her associate tried to look efficient. As an immigration officer, he made a very good onlooker.

"At work," Jenny said, but she was hushed by her husband. He held her tight and grinned.

"Nope, Jen. They don't want to hear that. They want the real story."

"Real story?"

"There was this slipper," he said promptly, turning confidentially to the astonished Delia. "Made of glass. Gorgeous, it was. Who could resist a slipper like that—or the girl who was wearing it? It's taken me ages to find her." He turned to look at Jenny, and the smile in his eyes lit her from the toes up. "Excuse me, but I just have," he said softly. "If you two will turn the other way…"

"This is serious," Delia snapped, while the string bean goggled.

"So are we." Michael didn't even bother looking at her. He had eyes only for Jenny. "This is the first evening we've been together as a family," he explained. "I have

everyone right where I want them to be. My wife. My son.
My dog. If you knew the trouble I've had with that darned
slipper..."

"The dog won't fetch it like he's supposed to," Jenny
explained, joining in with a giggle. "The bother of slippers!
To say nothing about pumpkins! Whew. Pumpkins were
nearly the end of our marriage. Do you know, my husband
expects me to make pumpkin pies! I won't, of course.
That's my best carriage he's expecting me to cook." Then
she faltered, turning laughing eyes to Michael. "Whoops.
Maybe that was the wrong thing to say? If I refuse to make
pumpkin pies, does that mean I can't be a U.S. citizen?"

"Just answer the questions, please," Delia said, a trifle
desperately, and Michael gave dates and times and places
with such aplomb that Jenny could only stare. It was as if
he really had been planning to marry her from the very
start.

"Are you married?" Michael demanded as Delia paused
for breath on page six of her prepared questionnaire.

"Yes, I—"

"What does your husband drink for morning break when
he's at work?"

"I—" The woman stared. "That's hardly relevant."

"Yes, it's relevant. What does he drink?"

"Coffee, I guess," she said doubtfully, and her partner
coughed.

"Actually, Mrs. Lavorn, Stewart always has soda water
and a mud cake," he said apologetically, and cast an em-
barrassed glance at Michael. "Mr. Lavorn works in my
department."

"Ha!" Michael shook his head. "He'll have to be de-
ported."

"What?" Delia cried.

"If you really loved him, you'd notice," Michael said
solemnly. "I watched Jen drink chocolate milk every day
for six months. I loved her then and I love her now." He

smiled and took both her hands. "I love the way that curl just twists a little bit across her forehead and bounces. And the fact that she sleeps with her hand curled under her cheek like a child. And she sneezes three times every morning."

"And he eats his cereal straight from the box when he thinks I'm not watching," Jenny said with loving severity.

"I do not!"

"You do, too. I caught you," she said triumphantly. "Just because Socks cleaned up the dropped evidence, you figured I'd never know."

"And yet you love me!" There was real wonder in his voice.

The laughter died.

"And yet I love you," she whispered. "Of course I do. Oh, Michael, my love, how could I not?"

"Harrumph," said Delia, and her partner cleared his throat.

They didn't notice.

"I love you, too," Michael murmured into her hair. He'd pulled her close to him, against his heart, right where he intended to hold her for all time. "Jenny, my love, I love you now and I love you forever and forever and forever."

"I think we might go." Delia managed to interrupt, and there was a glimmer of a tear in her authoritarian eyes. "I think we have enough to satisfy our needs."

"If you'll excuse us," her partner muttered apologetically.

But there was no need for any excuse. They left, and Michael and Jenny and Gary and Socks didn't even notice their departure.

EPILOGUE

THE MAITLAND NEWSLETTER lay open on the hospice coverlet. Stunned, LeeAnn Larrimore let it fall as she turned to gaze out the window at the city of Austin.

Somewhere out there were her children. Her loved ones. Garrett and Lana and Michael and Shelby.

Would they ever come to see her? Did they want to make contact?

She couldn't presume. She'd never interfere in their lives, she told herself bleakly. She'd forfeited that right all those years ago. But on the page she'd been reading was a small black and white photograph that made her heart turn over.

The picture was of a man and a woman. The woman was holding a child, newly born. She was looking serene, her face radiating happiness. And the man… The pride and the love in the man's eyes were there for all to see. *Michael Lord, head of security at Maitland Maternity, and his wife, Jenny, proudly announce the birth of their son, Gary Richard Lord.*

Gary!

Did they know? What weird stroke of fate had made them choose Gary as their son's name?

''Gary,'' LeeAnn whispered, and the echo of a long-lost love filtered into the room, bringing with it the first vestige of comfort she'd had for a very long time. ''My Gary.''

It mustn't be coincidence. They must know—and in spite of everything, they'd forgiven her.

"Please."

She lay back on her pillows and felt the first faint stirrings of strength. Maybe she could live a little longer. Maybe she could wait.

Because her children were coming.

Please...

Harlequin Romance ®

Delightful
Affectionate
Romantic
Emotional

Tender
Original

Daring
Riveting
Enchanting
Adventurous
Moving

Harlequin Romance ®—
capturing the world you dream of...

HARLEQUIN ®
Makes any time special ®

Visit us at www.eHarlequin.com

HROMDIR1

HARLEQUIN®
INTRIGUE

WE'LL LEAVE YOU BREATHLESS!

If you've been looking for thrilling tales of
contemporary passion and sensuous love stories
with taut, edge-of-the-seat suspense—then
you'll love Harlequin Intrigue!

Every month, you'll meet four new heroes
who are guaranteed to make your spine tingle
and your pulse pound. With them you'll enter
into the exciting world of Harlequin Intrigue—
where your life is on the line
and so is your heart!

THAT'S INTRIGUE—
ROMANTIC SUSPENSE
AT ITS BEST!

HARLEQUIN®
Makes any time special ®

Visit us at www.eHarlequin.com

INTDIR1

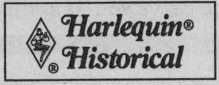

Harlequin® Historical

From rugged lawmen and valiant knights to defiant heiresses and spirited frontierswomen, Harlequin Historicals will capture your imagination with their dramatic scope, passion and adventure.

*Harlequin Historicals...
they're too good to miss!*

Medical Romance™

LOVE IS JUST A HEARTBEAT AWAY!

New in North America, **MEDICAL ROMANCE** brings you four passionate stories every month... each set in the action and excitement of big-city hospitals and small-town medical practices. Devoted doctors, sophisticated surgeons, compassionate nurses—you'll meet this group of dedicated medical professionals in this thrilling series. Their fast-paced world and intense emotions are guaranteed to provide you with hours and hours of reading pleasure.

To find out more about this exciting new series, contact our toll free customer service number: 1-800-873-8635 and reference #4542 when calling. You won't find it in bookstores!

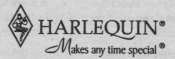

HARLEQUIN®
Makes any time special®

Visit us at www.eHarlequin.com   MEDDIRA

HARLEQUIN®
makes any time special—online...

eHARLEQUIN.com

your romantic books

- ❤ Shop online! Visit Shop eHarlequin and discover a wide selection of new releases and classic favorites at great discounted prices.

- ❤ Read our daily and weekly Internet exclusive serials, and participate in our interactive novel in the reading room.

- ❤ Ever dreamed of being a writer? Enter your chapter for a chance to become a featured author in our Writing Round Robin novel.

• • • • • •

your romantic life

- ❤ Check out our feature articles on dating, flirting and other important romance topics and get your daily love dose with tips on how to keep the romance alive every day.

• • • • • •

your community

- ❤ Have a Heart-to-Heart with other members about the latest books and meet your favorite authors.

- ❤ Discuss your romantic dilemma in the Tales from the Heart message board.

your romantic escapes

- ❤ Learn what the stars have in store for you with our daily Passionscopes and weekly Erotiscopes.

- ❤ Get the latest scoop on your favorite royals in Royal Romance.

HINTA1